DIAMOND JUBILEE

Kevan Jones

With special thanks to Erika Izawa, for initial read, feedback and encouragement:
Jane Moss, creative writing tutor 2011 — 2013, and
The classes of Roomfortynine 2011-2013.

With love to Yasmin and John.

ACKNOWLEDGMENTS

I would like to thank the following:-

The Sandwich Community Events Association for entertaining me over many years and in particular for inspiring me to write about the Sandwich Celebration, Le Weekend Festival and the Folk and Ale Festival of 2012, albeit in a work of fiction.

Royal Liberty Morris of Havering for confirming that the "Molly" on the front-cover of this book was definitely "their Pete."

The Playhouse Theatre, Whitstable, for entertaining me over the past decade.

Lt Col N J Grace OBE RM, Principal Director of Music Royal Marines, Headquarters Band Service Royal Marines, Portsmouth, for his perusal and feedback in relation to a copyright and accuracy enquiry.

Peter Rothschild for sharing his knowledge of the organization and people of the Romney Hythe & Dymchurch Railway with me and for showing me a couple of "Grand Days Out."

Lydia Tickner, Events Manager, English Heritage, Dover Castle, for her liaison with the WWII re-enactors in relation to a copyright enquiry and for putting-on a splendid annual event.

The BBC in relation to the "Diamond Jubilee Concert" and a copyright enquiry.

Imagem, Boosey & Hawkes, R&H, The Music Sales Group, Eaton Music, Warner Chappell, MDS London, and PRS for Music for their advice and assistance in relation to my copyright enquiries following "Infopaq v Danske." *That was a long and tortuous journey.*

Dominic Canty, writer of "Dead Men Should Know Better," for his encouragement at this stage of the books' production.

Those celebrities who were kind enough to grant me permission to use their names and finally The Kings Head, The Chequers, The Red Lion and The Sportsman for their hospitality.

Kevan M. Jones

CHAPTER 1

Marlene really liked her flat. She'd rented it from the estate agents on the ground floor, a couple of years ago. Market Street was right in the centre of Sandwich and everything she needed was there; a minimarket, cafes, restaurants, banks, a second hand clothing shop, and a hairdresser.

She could do a circular walk of the pretty medieval town in an hour or two; ice cream on the Quay, opposite the Salutation Gardens, a short walk along the Stour Estuary, then up onto the Bulwarks and along Millwall to St Bart's. She'd often enjoyed watching the bowling from the Rope Walk and the young boys fishing in the stream by The Butts.

Her favourite pub was the King's Arms, opposite St Mary's Church. When the weather was nice she loved to sit in their private little garden and have lunch. The other thing she liked about the town was all the events taking place. This weekend it was the Sandwich Celebration; a two day event to mark the two hundred and fiftieth anniversary of the invention of The Sandwich; first prepared for the Fourth Earl of Sandwich, John Montagu, in 1762.

As she took to a plastic chair, outside her flat, The Betteshanger Welfare Band waited for their last number. The conductor waved his magic wand and the band played "There's No Business Like Show Business." Marlene liked this tune and sang along. She admired the musicians dressed in their green jackets with gold braid and their brass instruments, expertly balanced in their hands. Toddlers danced energetically on the sidewalk; onlookers picnicked on tea and pasties, purchased from a red and white van. Blue and yellow bunting fluttered in the cool early summer breeze. As the song came to its end the audience stopped singing and applauded. The band stood and bowed; then stowed their instruments in cases.

Marlene's attention was then drawn to The Sandwich Concert Band who were seated behind her; realizing they were about to take over from the Betteshanger, she reversed her chair and settled down. Their first number was "Oxford Street: March," a very different sound, which included woodwind, drums, triangle and a xylophone. She spotted a young man with obvious learning difficulties and smiled as he waved his forefinger in the air mimicking the band's conductor. "The Magnificent Seven," and other film scores followed in quick succession.

Two gargoyles, carved into the red brickwork, stared into the diminishing crowds as Marlene returned to her flat. She lived on the second floor of a Victorian Gothic building; decorated with wooden figures. There was a man with a ship's anchor, a maid holding an iron, a stone mason equipped with hammer and chisel and a horned devil with big ears. Black oak framed the yellow rendered walls. Her bedroom windows were large and divided into eight segments, leaded with a combination of squares around the borders and circles in the middle.

Marlene was tired after climbing the stairs. She opened two of her bedroom windows for ventilation then settled onto the comfortable mattress of the heavy oak four poster bed. She dreamed of her late husband Tommy and the happy times they'd had in their Victorian terraced house in Dover with their best pals Derek and Patraicc. She started to whimper when she re-called Tommy's desecrated headstone; the gossip within the local community; fingers being pointed and children being taken to the other side of the road as she passed. She woke with a start when she remembered his unmarked grave and realized how lonely she was.

CHAPTER 2

Marlene had taken the train to Deal earlier in the day. She'd enjoyed a warm welcome and nice lunch in The King's Head. She'd chatted casually to the other customers, seated around small tables and a central bar in the gloomy interior. She'd passed treats to their dogs from her handbag. A couple of pints of Guinness and a steak and ale pie had set her up nicely for a promenade along the seafront to Walmer Green, where the Medway Concert Brass Band were due to play.

When she'd stepped out into the high winds and spittle she'd doubted they would be there but was still determined to check. As she walked along Beach Road she noticed the colourful fishing boats sitting on the pebbles amongst diesel winches, railway sleepers, patches of oil, jerry cans and lobster pots. "They look pretty from a distance," she thought, "but not so nice close up."

When Deal Castle appeared on her right she admired the white cupola above the round crenellations and the deep verdant moat. She was surprised they weren't flying the Union Jack from the flag pole and wondered which buffoon had failed to hoist it, on this The Queen's Diamond Jubilee weekend.

As she passed a bungalow, sitting on the beach beside the footpath, she noticed it was named Clan William House and took a peek into the interior. The walls of the study were lined with book cases and mounted on a large tripod facing out to sea was a neat telescope.

By the time she reached the paddling pool, she knew that the band wouldn't be playing. It was such a shame; the weather had been so nice last week and normally the pool would be teeming with young families picnicking on the green and splashing in the water.

3

When the Bandstand finally appeared she could see that it was deserted. It looked sad and lonely, as did the bearded old man sitting in the storm shelter.

"Do you mind if I sit with you for a while?" she said.

"Don't mind if you do." He sipped from a can of Tennent's Super. "Would you like a drink?" He proffered her a can.

"I mustn't," she said, "I've already had two pints of Guinness and I've got a long journey home." They chatted for a while and she learnt that he was a retired veteran. Then she decided it was time to go.

As she walked back towards the town she noticed a familiar figure walking towards her. She hadn't seen him for years but she would know him anywhere. She lifted herself up, pushed her shoulders back and stuck her chest out. She didn't want *him* to see that she was getting old.

"Hello Derek," she said. "What are you doing here?"

"Hello Marlene," he said in surprise... "I've just been visiting Deal Castle."

"I haven't seen you for years," she said.

"About ten, I should think."

"You haven't changed a bit."

"You neither."

She smiled gratefully. "That's very kind of you, Derek."

Long black hair, a grey stripe in her parting betrayed the true colour: a slight nodding of the head as she spoke; a round jolly face that had previously been lean; plump cheeks and a guppy's mouth with teeth like white pegs. What had she done to her body? Breasts where there'd only been chest but the big brown eyes and set of the nose were just as he remembered them.

"Have you discovered the fountain of youth?" she said.

"I've been staying off the booze and keeping fit."

"Well, it's obviously working. What are you doing now?"

"I'm on my way to Walmer Castle."

"Do you fancy a quick drink, for old times' sake?"

"Not now, I want to finish my tour, but if you give me your telephone number I'll ring you later and I'm sure we'll be able to sort something out... Where are you living now?"

"In Sandwich; moved there a couple of years ago." He removed his

4

mobile from his pocket and noted the number. It was a landline so there was no way of checking it there and then.

"I'll give you a tinkle later, say after seven, and we can make a date."

"Okay Derek, that would be nice...It is good to see you after all these years." He noticed that she was gushing; kissed her on the cheek and patted her bottom.

"Derek, you are naughty. I was right when I said you hadn't changed."

"Well I must be off now or I won't have enough time to look around Walmer."

"Have a nice time and ring me later," she whispered hoarsely.

CHAPTER 3

It was a pleasant evening for a walk. The sky was a pale blue with puffs of white smoke rising amongst thin streaks of low grey cloud. A light breeze was blowing but it was quite warm. He was dressed in a flat cap, tweed jacket, green trousers and brown shoes. He carried a Natural Green hessian bag from Tesco which contained a bottle of Champagne for Marlene, over a thin raincoat. His hat was pulled down at the front and the collar of his jacket turned up. He didn't look up as he made his way to Regal Estates and pressed the button marked Top Floor.

Marlene was watching the opening scenes of The Diamond Jubilee Concert. She was singing along to "Let Me Entertain You" and enjoying the spectacle of the Bearskins outside Buckingham Palace. The doorbell rang and she pressed a button inside her flat to release the street door. Then she checked her appearance in the mirror; not bad for seventy. She'd dyed her hair and the grey was now invisible. She'd worked on her make-up, including the dark rings under her eyes and was wearing her favourite red lipstick. Her black dress was crossed over her ample bosom and was tied at the sides.

Home-made prawn cocktails sat on her kitchen table which was dressed with a white tablecloth, candelabra and Union Jack napkins. Scented candles burnt in her bedroom. She turned the kitchen radio on to listen to the concert and switched the TV off in the lounge. There was a rat-a-tat-tat on the door. Derek's familiar knock; now that he'd arrived she felt flustered. Had she got carried away in her loneliness and excitement?

As she opened the door she was struck a sharp blow which instantly crushed her windpipe. She wanted to scream, "What are you doing Derek?" She tried to struggle but she couldn't breathe. She drifted off into a state of oblivion as her brain was starved of oxygen; death didn't seem so bad.

She had no idea what time it was when she surfaced but she found herself in familiar surroundings, lying on her four poster bed. The radio was still on and she could hear someone singing along to, "Need You Now." As her senses sharpened she realized that her throat was very sore; there was a hard obstruction there and she was making hollow rasping sounds with each breath. She tried to touch her neck and discovered that her right hand was tethered. She tried with her left and realized all of her limbs were tied to the bed.

He heard her stir while consuming a second prawn cocktail. He'd hardly eaten all day but now he was ravenous and determined to enjoy the supper she'd prepared for him. After swallowing the final mouthful he looked in on her, while wiping his mouth with a napkin.

She looked up at him with wide questioning eyes and noticed that he was wearing white overalls and latex gloves. "We Don't Talk Anymore" played in the background. He left her; terrified eyes stared at the space that he'd so recently occupied. She heard the familiar creak of springs from her wing chair. 'He's watching the TV,' she thought in astonishment as she tried to wriggle free.

She didn't know how long she'd been alone but the late evening sunshine was streaking through her leaded windows, making strange patterns on the walls and illuminating the dust suspended in the air. 'That's funny,' she thought, 'I've never noticed that before.'

He removed the quilt covering her body when he returned and she realized that she was naked. "You know, I used to love you Marlene." She remembered their first kiss; he was very drunk and tasted of vomit. His voice trailed off. "Of course, that was before you betrayed me." Tears pricked the corners of her eyes, ran over here plump cheeks and filled her ears. He gently stroked her left breast. Tom Jones belted out "Mama Told Me Not To Come."

Marlene heard the cork pop as he opened the Champagne. The fizzy wine went down nicely with the seafood risotto from Marks and Spencer. He was enjoying himself and sang along with Toms' next number.

When he returned, he stood at the foot of Marlene's bed with his favourite twelve inch slicing knife and oval sharpening steel; tap and scratch, tap and scratch went the metal surfaces. Marlene was fixated; tap and scrape, tap and scrape went the metal again. Was it all over? Was this how it was going to end? If it was she hoped it would be over quickly; she didn't want to die a slow painful death.

He stopped and inclined his ear. She could hear the Queen being welcomed to the concert; the crowd applaud and "Mack The Knife." He sang along, as he moved to her side and gripped her left breast.

As the life blood gently pumped out of her body Marlene could hear the Military Wives Choir and the African Children's Choir performing "Sing" in honour of Her Majesty's Diamond Jubilee. She thought how beautiful the children's voices were. She was very moved by their music and wondered how precious life was, now that she was so close to death.

He watched her departure with mixed emotions and felt her presence in the room for a few minutes after she'd passed away. Her spirit seemed contented, as if she'd gone to a better place. He didn't know how long he'd been sitting there but when he came out of his trance-like state he recognized "Mystery Tour."

He went into the living room and reclined on the sofa. He was exhausted and decided to watch the rest of the Jubilee Celebrations. The nation welcomed The Queen and the Duke and Duchess of Cornwall to the podium. He listened carefully to the speech made by Charles. He saw the Queen light the National Beacon, watched the firework display and felt proud of his British heritage when they played "Land of Hope and Glory."

When the show was over he returned to Marlene's bedroom. He removed the bonds from her limbs and the short length of garden hose, which he'd used as a tracheotomy tube. These were transferred to the kitchen sink; washed with his knives in plenty of soapy water and returned to the hessian bag. He then made a systematic but tidy search of the flat, looking at the walls in the bedroom, checking the bedside cabinets, dressing table, wardrobe and floor coverings for anything linking him to the corpse. He'd checked the bed before putting Marlene in it.

He found a small address book containing a few names and addresses and two diaries; one for 2011 and one for 2012. There weren't many entries in the diaries but he took them anyway; he didn't want to leave the police any information about Marlene's lifestyle. He repeated this process in the lounge. In the kitchen he saw that the calendar on the wall had the words *Dinner with Derek* noted in the space for 4 June. He picked up the calendar and removed the first six pages. When satisfied, he washed up the dinner plates, glasses and cutlery used for his meal. He checked the waste bin for any clues. He couldn't do anything about the dustbin outside and just hoped that it would be emptied before Marlene's body was discovered.

He released the bluebottle flies and maggots, collected from the decomposing body of a road-kill pheasant. He noted how quickly they settled down for dinner. He turned the central heating up to twenty one; not too high to arouse suspicion but high enough to keep the insects busy. He removed his overalls, shoe covers and latex gloves; sealed them in a plastic bag then dressed in his flat cap, tweed jacket and leather driving gloves. They would go into the incinerator with the other items later.

It was three thirty when he stepped out into the street. The full moon was on the wane with the approaching day. It would be light in just over an hour. He didn't expect to see anyone on his way home. It was another bank holiday; most people would be having another lie-in; more importantly the police would be stripped to their bare bones.

The journey was uneventful. He parked his van on the edge of town, in an area where it wouldn't arouse suspicion and after changing into his running kit gently jogged home. He was happy to see that the lights in his house had been extinguished and that his TV was off. The timers had worked. His private car was where he'd left it. His neighbours would believe he'd had a night-in, watching the Jubilee Concert, just as he'd intended.

CHAPTER 4

It was Sunday. Matt Sanderson was at home enjoying the unexpected early morning sunshine. He was an early riser; liked to start his day with a cup of tea and a cigarette in his back garden, where he would patrol his borders to inspect the plants in his care. The recent high winds and heavy rain had played havoc with his foxgloves, which were leaning like drunken church spires, and his comfrey was only standing due to the support of its shorter neighbours.

He was "Gold", the on-call senior officer, for East Kent covering the weekend. His tour of duty had started at 2pm on Friday and wouldn't finish until 2pm on Sunday or later if he was called out and until then he wouldn't be able to have a drink. He'd been dying for a gin and tonic during the Saturday afternoon sunshine, after cutting the grass, trimming the caenothus at the front of the house and having a general tidy up, but one needed to maintain a clear head; you never knew when the telephone would ring or what sort of advice you would be expected to give. Of course his twenty nine years of policing experience, including five in his present rank, would normally provide the answer.

He crept upstairs to look at his wife Rose. He could hear her softly snoring. Mutley, his black and tan Jack Russell, heard him and gently slipped off the bed for a head rub. He followed Matt into the kitchen and watched him prepare his breakfast cereal. They both retired to the back garden where Mutley was rewarded with a treat for being quiet, before going off for a rummage in the flower beds. He quickly found a fresh scent and started running around the garden in a demented fashion until he was exhausted; then he leapt onto his master's lap and rolled onto his back for a good chest rub.

Matt liked the 'Allo' Allo! series and after some leg pulling, from both his senior and junior colleagues, he'd finally accepted that he did look a little like Arthur Bostrom. He woke Rose, just after nine, with a cup of coffee and a "Good moaning."

"Thanks for letting me lie-in." She pulled him towards her and gave him a wet kiss on the cheek.

"I thought I'd take the dog out while you're getting up," he suggested.

"Okay, darling, I'll make breakfast when you get back." He would be gone for just over an hour. A nice long walk, along the sea defences between the Sandwich Bay Estate and Sandown Castle, followed by a hearty breakfast should set him up for the day. He made sure that he had his mobile phone and pager before setting off; he couldn't leave Rose to fend off his colleagues with excuses if he'd forgotten them.

The wind was blowing from the southwest, when he left; not too strongly but it was always windy here; that was one of the few disadvantages of living right on the beach. Even in fine still weather there was always a breeze; it came from the land in the morning, when the sea was warm; a brief pause when it would be too hot; then from the sea, as the land warmed up; then another brief pause in the evening. You only had to go two miles inland to Sandwich and it could be stifling on a hot day.

As he walked along the embankment he watched Mutley hunting for rabbits on a scrubby bit of land. Matt remembered when he'd first got him; he'd found the way in but couldn't find the way out and had to re-trace his steps to the hole in the fence to escape his confinement.

The sea was calm. It nearly always was unless it was high tide and there was a strong north easterly. This area between the land and the Goodwin Sands was known as The Downs. Navies used to take shelter there in inclement weather. It was also a gathering place for merchant vessels, awaiting escort overseas during the wars with our continental neighbours, but today it was completely empty.

The scrub opened up onto The Royal Cinque Ports Golf Club, a links course not as famous as Royal St George's nearby. The bunkers were being raked and the greens trimmed, by keepers riding motor mowers. He could see the building line of The Chequers Restaurant in the distance and thought of the many enjoyable evenings he'd spent there with Rose.

When he reached Sandown Castle he was ready to turn back. He smiled as Mutley leaped and disappeared into the long grasses and rooted about on the pebbly beach. The sky to the west had filled with dark clouds by the time they reached the Sandwich Bay Sailing and Water Skiing Club and he reckoned it wouldn't be sunny for long.

Rose was pleased to see him as he let himself in through the stable door. "Did you have a nice walk, darling?"

"Wonderful."

"Meet anyone we know?"

"No, just a few dog walkers along the edge of the golf course."

"Did Mutley find anyone to play with?"

"He was far too busy chasing rabbits and licking fish scraps on the beach; he'll probably have an upset tummy later...Talking of tummies, mine thinks my throats been cut."

"Cooked breakfast?"

"Yes, please... I'll just ring the office to see what's brewing." He picked up the telephone and tapped in the number for the CID at Dover. "Hello. Detective Chief Inspector Sanderson here. Can I speak to Detective Sergeant St John Stevens?"

"Just a moment," a female voice responded. "Sarge', it's the boss on the phone."

"Hello, guvnor, what can I do for you?"

"Anything I should know about?"

"Well, we've got a couple in for ABH from a pub fight. We're about to charge them and they should be on their way. Two from a burglary on a trading estate; they've admitted it and we'll be bailing them soon and apart from that it's been unusually quiet."

"Any prisoners requiring extensions?"

"None that would concern you, Sir."

"Any interesting crimes?"

"No, nothing. As I said, it's been unusually quiet."

"Thanks, Singe, don't hesitate to call me if you need anything."

"Will do, guvnor; try and enjoy the rest of the day."

When Matt returned to the kitchen Rose was dressed in a pink Keep Calm and Carry On apron. He noticed that she'd been busy with her blonde curly hair and her make-up. "She was a proper English Rose," he thought.

"Everything okay?"

"All quiet on the eastern front. Now where's my breakfast?"

"If you put the kettle on and sit down it'll arrive a lot quicker." Matt settled down with the newspaper. He'd not had a chance to look at it before. He'd been too busy in the garden on Saturday and after dinner he'd watched a whodunit until, just before the ending, he'd fallen asleep.

"Here you go darling," Rose said cheerfully, as she placed a lavish breakfast in front of him; eggs, bacon, sausage, mushrooms, baked beans, toast and fresh coffee. "Anything interesting in the paper?"

"David Cameron and George Osbourne are to appear at the Leveson enquiry next week."

"Oh, we'll have to watch that. It'll be far more interesting than PMQ's," she said sarcastically.

CHAPTER 5

"DCI Matt Sanderson."

"Hello sir, this is Sergeant Smythe from Control. We've had a report of a suspicious death in Market Street, Sandwich. One of our officers was called to a collapse behind locked doors at Regal Estates. He contacted the agents to gain access and when he went inside he found that the elderly female occupier had been mutilated in her bed."

"Who's the officer?"

"Terence McGinty." Matt knew him well; he was a steady officer with about fifteen years' service; they often bumped into each other when Matt was enjoying his downtime in Sandwich.

"Anyone with him?"

"A PCSO, but she's in a terrible state. We've dispatched several other officers to the scene but McGinty will be on his own for the next fifteen minutes or so."

"Okay, Chris, open an incident log. Show that I've been informed at thirteen-twenty-five, tell McGinty that no one is to go into the premises and no one's to leave. I'll be there in ten minutes. Inform Press Bureau. I'll ring in with more details once I'm there." Matt fetched his tie; he didn't want to look scruffy if he had to deal with a murder in front of the press. "Rose, I've got to go into Sandwich," he shouted. "It sounds like there's been a murder above Regal Estates."

"In Sandwich! No, nothing like that ever happens in Sandwich."

"Have you already forgotten about the murder of Mary Bax in 1782?"

14

As Matt drove into Sandwich he noticed that the town was very busy; he'd forgotten that it was Le Weekend Festival, when the residents of Sandwich got together with their twins from Honfleur. He wasn't making good progress so decided to dump the car in Knightrider Street before cutting through the ancient alleyways to Market Street. When he emerged by St Peter's Church he could see that the area immediately in front of Regal Estates was packed with revelers; elderly couples sat on plastic chairs and families with young children stood on the pavement as they waited for the girls from Les Troubadours de Paris, to give their next performance. "Just what I need; loads of people stomping over my crime scene," Matt thought.

PC McGinty spotted him straight away. "Hello Matt."

"How you doing, Terry?"

"A bit shaken up; to be honest I've never seen anything like this before."

"Where's your PCSO?"

"I've sent her into the estate agents with the gentleman who called us. She was in a terrible state but I think she's pulled herself together now."

"Is there anyone else in the premises?"

"Mrs Dixon, she lives in the first floor flat. She's decided to watch the festivities from her bedroom window. She knows that a Detective will want to speak to her later."

Matt noticed two uniformed officers weaving their way through the crowds. After brief introductions he said, "Okay lads, I want you to create an outer cordon here," indicating the street door, "no one comes in and no one leaves. One of you can start an incident log, beginning with a note that Terry and I are going to visit the scene. Have you got overalls, shoe covers and evidence bags in your car?" One of the officers indicated a substantial briefcase.

"We've brought a major incident kit with us. That should contain everything we need to start off with."

Five minutes later Matt and Terry emerged from the recess in front of the estate agents dressed in pale blue overalls, matching caps and latex gloves. They carried covers to put over their shoes. Matt noticed that the Parisian Dancers, wearing feather boas and colourful dresses over white petticoats with black trims, were assembled at the top of the street. The men in the audience were giving them admiring looks. Matt had to admit there were some crackers amongst them and in other circumstances he would have stepped back to watch their performance. Few of the onlookers paid him and Terry any attention but he did spot a local newspaper journalist, Dylan Barry, within the crowd.

"Be very careful," he said, to the officer manning the cordon. "The local press is here. I may speak to them when I come out but in the meantime just tell them we're dealing with a suspicious death."

"Right you are, Sir."

"Okay, Terry, now that we can't be overheard you'd better describe the layout of the premises and tell me what to expect. There's no need to come back into the flat; just stay by the door. I don't want to contaminate the scene any more than I have to." Terry described the flat and the route he'd taken into the bedroom; it was like an indelible image printed onto his brain. Matt left him at the front door, crossed the kitchen to the bedroom and took the route that Terry had described.

He wasn't prepared for the scene that greeted him. It all seemed so surreal. CanCan music played in the street outside. He could hear the girls whooping as he pictured them kicking and twirling their legs erotically for the audience. Bright sunlight streamed through the leaded glass windows and illuminated beams of dust suspended in the air. The victim was lying there in front of him with her limbs pointing to the corners of her four poster bed. He could see that she had a hole in her throat and both of her breasts had been removed.

Then he thought that his imagination had got the better of him. She appeared to be moving. He looked closer and realized that her body was swarming with maggots and flies. He could hear the audience outside clapping and singing, "Dah Dah, Da Da Da Da Dah, Da Da Da Da Dah, Da Da Da Da Dah." The stench of rotting flesh was suddenly overpowering and he wanted to vomit. It was time to leave. She'd definitely been murdered but there'd still be a post mortem to confirm she hadn't died of natural causes.

He carefully retraced his steps back to Terry. He heard the cancan music come to an end. The audience whistled and clapped. His head swam at the top of the steep stairs. He sat down abruptly and recalled his first mutilated body; they never left you; not completely.

"You don't look so good," Terry said.

"I'm okay, Terry… The flies and maggots were a nasty shock though… What sort of sick bastard does that to an elderly woman?" He reached into his pocket for his mobile and telephoned control, "DCI Sanderson. Can I speak to Sergeant Smythe please?"

"Hello Sir. How did you get on?"

"We've definitely got a murder on our hands. It looks like she's been here for a while. Contact scenes of crime and instigate a major incident call-out. There are hundreds of people in Sandwich and I would like to know who they are before they leave."

"I've got a map up on the screen and can instigate road blocks but that'll leave the eastern area without a fast response car."

"Just do it as quickly as possible. This is a really nasty murder and the killer might be among the revelers."

"Leave it with me, Sir. I'll ring you with an update and won't go home until you're ready to release me." Matt had forgotten that it was change-over time up until that point.

"Perhaps the late turn can collect the fast response vehicles from the early turn and leave the early turn with the run-arounds."

"Good idea, Sir."

"And one final thing; PC McGinty is going to open the police office in Sandwich as a rendezvous point for any officers attending the scene."

"All received. Speak with you later." Matt could feel perspiration pricking his hair follicles and ran his right hand through his jet black hair to remove some of the moisture.

"Okay, Terry; I think you got the gist of that conversation; let's go downstairs and speak with the neighbour; you can take her to the police office when I've finished with her; take her statement and find somewhere else for her to stay. She'll need to take some clothing, enough for twenty four hours at least. Don't forget to bag up your protective clothing and hand it to the exhibits officer downstairs. When other officers arrive you can delegate one of them to take Mrs Dixon wherever she wants to go. When you've done all that I want you to make your statement and if that's not enough," he took a deep breath, "you could always sweep the yard with a broom up your arse."

Terry smiled, "Feeling better?"

"Much. Let's get on shall we?"

Matt followed Terry down one flight of stairs and watched as he knocked on Mrs Dixon's door.

"This is DCI Sanderson," he said, "may we come in?"

"She's dead, isn't she?" Mrs Dixon said.

"Were you close?" Matt said gently.

"No not really. Dorothy and I were just neighbours. We used to pass pleasantries with each other, but no we weren't close. I'm sorry that she's dead though; wouldn't wish that on anyone."

"Can you tell me when you last saw her?"

"The day of the Queen's Diamond Jubilee Concert; didn't see her as such but I heard her. She had the radio or the TV on for the whole performance. It was a little bit loud but I didn't mind because I was watching it as well."

"So that would have been on Monday?"

"That's right. She must have watched it right to the end. I turned my hearing aid off once it was over and didn't hear another thing. Then I noticed that dreadful smell on Thursday or Friday. I was going to ask her if she could smell it as well but I didn't see her."

"And then what happened?"

"I was telling my daughter about it this morning and she said I should call the estate agent or the police. I couldn't get hold of the agents so I called the police."

"Where does your daughter live?"

"Sittingbourne."

"Would she be able to put you up for the night?"

"I should think so… How did she die?"

"I can't discuss that with you but I'd be grateful if you'd go to the Police Office with Terry so that he can take your statement."

"Oh how exciting. I've never been to a police station."

"I'll leave you to it, Terry."

Matt slipped out of his protective clothing when he reached the cordon at the bottom of the stairs and packaged the items in exhibits bags. He handed those to one of the uniformed officers and said, "Can you deal with the exhibits until the major incident team arrive?"

"I'd be delighted to, sir." Matt looked at his watch. It was 2:35. Was it really only an hour since he'd received the call-out? He sent Rose a text to say that he wouldn't be home for the foreseeable and asked her to lock up properly. She was normally very lax about leaving doors unlocked. He didn't want to go home and find her in a similar condition to Dorothy. He expertly avoided Dylan Barry, the newspaper journalist, and went into the Estate Agent's office.

The agent was taking tea with Marion, the PCSO, a horse faced girl with exceptionally long eyelashes. She'd clearly been crying as her large eyes were rimmed red. She brightened a little when she saw Matt, who she knew from her frequent patrols around the town. The agent stood up and offered his hand in greeting.

"Tony Spencer," he said, "I called Terry, when I noticed that dreadful smell outside the flat."

"Matt Sanderson, Detective Chief Inspector; I'm in charge, at least for the present."

"Pleased to meet you; I wish it could have been in different circumstances."

Matt looked at his PCSO. "How are you doing Marion?"

"A lot better now. Tony's been taking care of me." She coloured a little and then said, "I hope I haven't let you down, sir."

"Not at all; now what have you found out about our victim?"

"Tony's printed a copy of the lady's rental agreement. It's all here. The lady's name is Dorothy Skinner. She's seventy years old or I should say that she was seventy years old. She used to live in Spain but moved here a couple of years ago." Marion handed the documents to Matt. It was indeed all there; full name, address, phone number, copy of her passport, credit reference checks and so on.

"Do you mind if I sit down?"

"Please do." Tony proffered a chair. "Would you like a cup of tea?"

"I could murder one… Sorry, white no sugar."

"Now Marion, I know this is hard, but just how much did you see?"

"Not much, Terry told me to get out when I started to get upset."

"I'll need a statement from you later but I don't want you to discuss the victim's injuries with anyone, even her family; we need to keep those details to ourselves so only the perpetrator and the investigation team know of their nature. Is that clear?"

"Yes Sir."

"Have you discussed them with Tony?"

"No, I don't think so." Tony returned with tea in a blue china cup and saucer.

"Here you go," he said, as he placed it on the table.

"I was just asking Marion if she'd disclosed the victim's injuries to you but she's not sure. Can you help her out?"

"No she hasn't. We've been discussing other things to take her mind off it." Matt studied the tenancy application form and noticed there was no next of kin listed.

"We shall need to take a detailed statement from you in due course and I might need you to identify the body, if we can't find any relatives."

"I'll do whatever I can to help."

CHAPTER 6

Matt's mobile rang. It was the Press Officer Joan Armstrong, an old hack who used to work for one of the nationals. He could picture her now; a small wiry woman with dyed curly red hair, bright red lipstick, matching fingernails and a deeply creased mouth, from years of puffing on at least forty a day. She was drawing her state pension; should have been putting her feet up and writing her memoirs but wasn't ready to retire. She still got a buzz from breaking news stories.

"Hello Matt. We need to talk."

"Go ahead," Matt said, as he made his way into the small kitchen at the back of the police office.

"The press has identified your victim, via local sources, as Dorothy Skinner." Matt noted that it was nearly 8pm. It had been an intense six and a half hours and suddenly he felt very weary.

"The bastards… How dare they release the victim's details without my consent! We haven't even had time to identify the next of kin let alone have the body formally identified; she's still in situ in her flat and won't be going anywhere until the crime scene examiners have finished."

"Precisely, but we do need to get ahead of the game. I've seen the media frenzy on the main news channels and I'm on my way to meet you. I've been in touch with Detective Chief Superintendent Baxter and he has agreed to an impromptu press conference, not far from the scene."

"I bet it was that bastard Dylan Barry. I've seen him lapping it up in the square outside the Guildhall. The news channels have had satellite vans outside since about five thirty and he's been making a nuisance of himself all afternoon. We've even had to put in a cordon to the police office so that my staff can have unfettered access."

"I doubt if it was him. He's been very professional and has been describing the festival prior to the discovery of the victim's body and the visible police operation that you've instigated. He's mentioned several times that he's spoken to the officer in charge of the case but police haven't formally identified the body."

"So how did her identity get out?"

"She was identified via social media."

"I suppose it was inevitable in this age of instant messaging. Have you identified the source?"

"Not yet. That can wait until later. The important thing is that we have a press conference a.s.a.p. Can you suggest a venue?"

"I could ask the local authority to open the Guildhall but that might take some time."

"Perhaps we could do it in the street, outside the police office."

"Whatever you say Joan; you know I'm not keen on the press."

"It's a double-edged sword; we need them on our side. We don't want to give the impression that they're leading the investigation."

"How long are you going to be?"

"I'll be there in about thirty minutes. I suggest that you briefly speak with the reporters outside and schedule the press conference for 9pm. Let them set up a temporary studio for you; they've got the resources."

When Matt left the police office he was immediately recognized by the press pack as the officer in charge of the case. A reporter he didn't know shoved a microphone in his face and he was blinded by the white light produced by a camera.

"Any updates for us Chief Inspector?" A chorus of voices made the same request. The lights went out on Dylan Barry and the remaining camera crew jostled for a good position.

"In a short while I shall be making a formal announcement regarding the progress of this enquiry." He noted with satisfaction that they were all listening intently. "As you know this investigation is in its very early stages and we still have a lot of work to do. I am therefore asking you to be patient and not speculate on the manner of the victim's death or her identity."

"Is it right that she's known locally as Dorothy Skinner?"

Matt raised his voice. "At 9pm I intend to make a formal statement."

"Where?

"If you'll just stop interrupting me I'll give you the details," he snapped. Silence except for the buzz of the nearby generators. "At 9pm I intend to make a formal statement," Matt began again. "I propose to make that statement here, outside the police office. In the meantime, I'd be grateful if you'd assemble yourselves into some sort of order so that there's no scrum when I emerge. I would also ask that there are no interruptions when I'm speaking. Thank you ladies and gentlemen; that's all for now."

"Hi Matt, how are you doing?" Joan said when she arrived.

"Stressed… I've got a murder enquiry to run; staff asking for my advice; a fucking media circus on my doorstep and now some bastard has released the victim's details without my permission."

"So, you could say that you're having one of your good days?"

"A good day would be - being at home with my feet up in front of the TV watching some other poor sod struggling with this enquiry while sipping a large gin and tonic and knowing that I don't need to go to work for three days."

"Now Matt, you know as well as I do that you love it really."

"Ready," Joan said. Matt nodded. "Come on then." A hushed silence fell upon the street outside.

"Ladies and gentlemen… At about 1pm today police were called to a flat in Market Street Sandwich where they discovered the body of a woman in her seventies. Her death is being treated as murder. The victim has yet to be formally identified. Police have been unable to trace her family and her flat is still being examined by forensic examiners. I am aware that the victim has been identified locally as Dorothy Skinner. I would ask that anyone who knows her, especially any relatives, contact the Operation Carnegie incident room on 01622… Thank you for your time; that's all for now. "

"Well?" Matt said.

"That was okay; a bit brusque maybe."

"Accuracy, brevity and speed - that's what they taught us at training school."

"Well you scored one hundred per cent on those," Joan said, "but I think we'll have to do some work on your manner."

23

"What's wrong with my manner?"

"Put the kettle on and I'll explain."

CHAPTER 7

Patricia felt out of place. Her new home was in Sarre Court, a Manor House Hotel that had been converted into flats. Her property faced extensive grounds; ancient trees swayed above well-kept lawns enclosed by thick high brick walls. The trees were protected; there weren't many in this part of Kent. It was mostly farms; the Garden of England they called it. The tennis courts were surplus to requirements but she had a nice little garden and there was no maintenance; the two female gardeners tidied it up for her whenever they were doing their rounds. The flat itself was immaculate, not like the scruffy old house that she used to occupy with all her junk. She had been forced to discard most of that during the move but managed to keep hold of the small Gideon Bible, given to her son, Michael, when he left school. She kept that in her bedside cabinet.

She was a little woman, only five feet tall. Her grey hair was curly and had a mind of its own; it looked like a head full of snakes this morning. Medusa: only not Greek and not a Goddess. She used to be voluptuous, like Marilyn Munroe her husband Derek used to say but now loose flesh hung from her small frame. Black eyes sunk into wrinkled sockets stared back at her together with a thinning nose, scarred by the removal of a cancerous mole. She didn't notice that her cardigan was holey or that the wool on her dress was bobbled.

"I'm not sure that I should have bought that flat," she said, to herself, as she boarded the Bus for Canterbury and showed her Freedom Pass. "It's in the middle of nowhere."

"No shops in the village; I should've thought of that before buying… Nice windmill at the top of the hill though. They do a good breakfast, if you like that sort of thing, and the staff are very nice," she muttered, as she settled onto the front seat on the top deck.

"The village pub is a bit expensive, there's nothing for under a fiver, still it is a Cherry Brandy House and I like cherry brandy," she said, as she travelled along the road in open countryside. "My next door neighbour, Bobby, seems very nice. I'm not sure about Simon on the other side. He looks like he could do with a good wash and a haircut… Well I'm there now so I'll just have to make the best of it."

She was looking forward to seeing Michael. He'd promised her a picnic on the River Stour and she loved eating out at lunch time. She thought that he was very handsome and a bit like his father, in looks at least but not in temperament. He always treated her like a princess and was never selfish, not like that bastard who used to force himself on her whenever he'd had a skin full. She's surprised that Michael has turned out so well after being brought up in a house full of shouting, screaming, violence and unwanted sex. He must've been able to hear her sobs whenever his father misbehaved.

As she alighted from the bus she could see Michael waving to her. His bald pate glistened in the early afternoon sunshine above black rimmed spectacles. A fat face framed his broad nose and a childish grin. He'd dressed down in an open necked white shirt, a charcoal grey linen suit and black leather shoes. Normally he'd wear a tie but that would probably be too much for a picnic on the river.

As he embraced her she noticed that he smelt good. Chanel for men, he remembered. She felt ecstatic as he held her hand and led her through a labyrinth of streets to the punt's jetty. The Punter was waiting for them, smartly dressed in white with a straw boater and navy blue waistcoat.

"Good afternoon Michael. And you must be?"

"Patricia. Michael's mother."

"Well, good afternoon to you to Patricia. My name's Francis and I'm your guide." Michael held his mother's hand as she stepped on board.

"There's plenty of room for two," she said, as she sat down. Michael joined her and lifted a white linen tablecloth to reveal the picnic; handmade pork pies, fresh crunchy apple slices, pickles in tiny little pots, cheese straws and a fresh salad. "That looks delicious," Patricia said, as he handed her a napkin and Francis pushed off.

"Champagne or cherry brandy?"

"Ooh, champagne for now. Can I have the cherry brandy later?"

"Of course you can." The champagne cork popped and the wine fizzed in the neck of the bottle. Michael expertly filled two glasses, "Anything for you Francis?"

"Not while I'm on duty," he said, as he poled the depths of the river. "Now, Patricia, this isn't just a punt along the river; this is a journey through history," he paused to make sure that she was listening and when she smiled he continued. "The building that we are approaching is called Greyfriars."

She sipped her champagne and coughed as the bubbles went up her nose.

"I'm so sorry."

"The Greyfriars Chapel is all that remains of the first English Franciscan Friary. It was built in 1267 and then abandoned by the brothers in 1538 following the dissolution of the Roman Catholic Church." Patricia admired the flint built church which straddled the river and the greenery that hugged the river banks.

"It's very beautiful," she said. "These apples are wonderful, Michael, especially with the pork pie." Michael smiled as they disappeared into a tunnel. He'd known all along that his mother would be more interested in the picnic. A little further on, they approached another fine building crossing the river.

"This is the Eastbridge Hospital; founded in the twelfth century for pilgrims who were coming to Canterbury to visit the site of Saint Thomas the Martyr. As the name suggests it is built on a bridge over the river." Patricia regarded the scenery with pleasure and noted the buildings' reflection on the water. Francis saw that she was smiling and grinned at her as she drained her champagne flute for the second time.

"More champagne, mum?"

"Oh no, better not. I won't be able to walk." She spied the cheery brandy bottle, "I wouldn't mind a brandy though," she giggled.

"That was wonderful Michael, can we go around again?" Patricia said when the tour ended a little later.

"Not today, mum, I've got another surprise for you," he said, grinning.

*

When they arrived at her flat she admired herself in the same mirror that had betrayed her loose flesh earlier.

"I really like this new outfit, Michael, but I hope the charity shop can get something for the old one."

"I'm sure they will," Michael lied, knowing it would be ground down into industrial rag.

"I want to show you something, Michael." He followed her into the lounge where she produced a black and white photo. "Who's that?"

He studied the photograph carefully, "It looks like me, but I don't remember it being taken."

"That's because it isn't you. It's your father, at your age." Michael looked at the photograph again. It really did look like him. He could easily be mistaken for Derek.

"Can I keep this photo?"

"You can borrow it; make a copy, if you like, but please bring it back. I don't have many pictures of your father... I sometimes wonder what happened to him."

*

The breaking news on the evening broadcasts was the same. It was all about the murder of an elderly woman in Market Street Sandwich. A local news reporter named Dylan Barry was being interviewed live on air. It was obvious that he knew very little about the victim but he knew a great deal about the location and the weekend festival that had been taking place when her body was found.

CHAPTER 8

The sun was like a bright disc slowly falling to earth in the western sky; dark clouds formed into a horseshoe overland but the sky overhead was a clear washed-out blue. Tall grasses, their heads heavy with seed whispered in the stiff offshore breeze. Mutley was in his element, hunting rodents and leaping out of the grass like a springbok in his excitement. The white bridge of a fishing trawler glowed above navy topsides reflecting the late evening sunshine. She revealed a red oxide hull as she rode at anchor. Matt noticed that the tide was very low revealing the original sandy beach, at the foot of the clay and shingle embankment. He remembered walking barefoot on the sand just after he and Rose had purchased their house. White horses broke over the Goodwin Sands while inshore a lazy swell slid onto the beach in a curling white and brown froth.

Matt was tired; it had been a tough couple of weeks since Dorothy's corpse had been discovered and this was his first opportunity to be, *thankfully*, alone with his thoughts. His long shadow stalked him with every pace, as did the images of her mutilated and decomposing body.

What did they know about Dorothy Skinner? Not a lot. He'd consulted the Border Agency who, on visual inspection believed her passport was genuine. However a search of their database and enquiries of the Passport Agency revealed that it had never been issued. The document had subsequently been examined forensically. The outcome had been shocking. It had been produced by their printers and the agency had started a covert operation.

The Border Agency had been unable to find any record of Dorothy Skinner travelling overseas using that name. They'd cautioned that she may have travelled in another's car and in that case there might be no record.

Two officers had been sent to Spain to liaise with their counterparts but to date they'd found no records relating to her. His officers had been to the address she'd supplied in Marbella. It was occupied by a Spanish couple who occasionally let rooms but they had no recollection of her.

They'd made appeals in the media for anyone who knew Dorothy to contact the incident room. This had provided some successes but they'd been unable to establish exactly where she'd come from prior to moving into her flat on 30 June 2010. A financial investigation hadn't revealed anything illuminating. The credit referencing agencies only had data on her going back to the middle of June 2010; that was when she'd applied for the tenancy on her flat and told the agent that she'd previously been resident in Spain.

The Missing Persons Bureau had been consulted. Nationally they dealt with around 350,000 missing persons incidents per year; of those approximately 2000 remained outstanding a year after going missing and roughly 20 per week were found dead. They'd supplied details of those outstanding who matched Dorothy's profile; each had been checked carefully; their dental and medical records examined with negative results.

She'd left no diaries or address book. There were few entries on her calendar. Chemical treatment had revealed entries for The Sandwich Celebration on 11 and 12 May. The Medway Concert Band in Walmer was noted against 3 June; enquiries had revealed that the concert had been cancelled due to bad weather. They'd found several witnesses to show that she was in the area on that day as she'd had lunch in the Kings Head Deal. She'd left the pub at about 13:00 but hadn't made the return trip to Sandwich until 14:20. They'd found CCTV images of her using the railway to travel between Sandwich, Deal and Sandwich. A team of officers had been tasked with tracing all of the passengers on both trains, taking their statements and eliminating them from further inquiry.

She'd been captured on CCTV in Marks and Spencer in Deal buying prawn cocktails, a seafood risotto and cheesecake at 13:55. Another team of officers had interviewed all of their employees and were similarly engaged in tracing and eliminating the shoppers who'd been to the store. There was nearly an hour that couldn't be accounted for between 13:00 and 13:55. At most it was a ten minute walk from the Kings Head to M & S so where had she been? Had she met someone during that hour? Exhaustive enquiries had revealed no witnesses to suggest a promenade along the seafront or mooch around any of the other shops in Deal.

The most significant entry on her calendar was a dinner date with someone named Derek on Monday 4 June. Had she been buying the food for him on Sunday 3 June? Had they met in Sandwich between Market Street and the station, on the train, in the street in Deal, in the King's Head, along the seafront, in Marks & Spencer, somewhere else? These were important questions that needed answering. So far they'd interviewed twelve Dereks including one from the sex offenders' register. Only one had been eliminated from further inquiry; he'd been on holiday between Friday 1 and Friday 8 June.

They'd been unable to establish Dorothy's time of death. The Forensic Scientists hadn't been much help. The bluebottle larvae, maggots and pupae they'd retrieved from her body and flat suggested that she'd been dead for at least ten to fourteen days. Matt had considered that revelation on several occasions and believed that the killer may have introduced them into the crime scene. That suggested an element of premeditation.

He agreed with the Criminal Psychologist who believed that the murder was an act of revenge and the killer had told them something through the removal of her breast implants. What was it that was hidden in her past? If he could only answer that question he might have a motive. He knew only too well how she'd died. The pathologist's report and the black and white photographs on the wall of his office were a testament to how she'd suffered physically; he could only imagine how she'd been tortured mentally.

He was still worried about doggedly pursuing anyone named Derek. He'd managed to keep that name out of the press much to his number two's annoyance. Detective Inspector Brian Kelly was trying to pursue his own agenda but how could he be sure that Derek had murdered Dorothy? How could he be sure that Derek was his real name? That might be the name that Dorothy had on her calendar but how did she know that was his true identity? The only person who could answer that was Dorothy and she wasn't available for interview. He'd insisted that this name wasn't revealed to the press but wondered how much longer that could be sustained. He'd been involved in a high profile murder investigation when he was a constable and seen a middle-ranking officer hijack the inquiry before taking it off in the wrong direction. He was determined that wasn't going to happen to him. The important thing was to keep an open mind and eliminate any Dereks who cropped up during the investigation.

Dark clouds swallowed the sunlight, plunging the salt marsh to his left and Sandwich Town into temporary darkness; then the sun pierced holes in the cloud and drenched the land in a radiating pale yellow light. This event lifted Matt's sombre mood. Like all Englishmen in a storm, he believed that the weather would improve eventually. He applied this belief equally to this case. At the moment they were in the dark but through dogged determination and meticulous attention to detail, *his job*, all would be revealed. The wind was loud in his ears as it increased in intensity. A small aircraft buzzed overhead but like the killer could not be seen. The skies darkened with rainclouds. A sparrow-hawk twittered as she looked for her prey in the long grasses, in much the same way as Matt sought his quarry. Then the sun turned a deep pink as it set overland, turning the trees on the distant horizon into a dark silhouette. Matt realized that he was almost home. "Home, Rose, Sanctuary," he thought. No more demands until Monday, unless there was an unexpected breakthrough.

*

Matt woke to bright sunshine and an empty bed on Saturday morning. Rose had decided to let her man sleep. This enquiry was taking its toll on their marriage; she'd hardly seen him since Dorothy had been found, fourteen days ago. He'd been up early every day with Mutley, showered and gone to work. Most days he hadn't returned until the late evening news and then he'd been tired, pale and moody. They hadn't talked very much; he was just too tired to communicate. She'd never seen him look so burnt out but she hoped he'd open up once he'd had a break. She knew a little about the murder, what she'd garnered from the TV and the newspapers. She'd seen Matt on the south east news, looking very smart and bristling with energy, as he appealed to anyone who knew Dorothy to come forward. He was quite different to the listless man who came home to her every night. She was looking forward to seeing him after her early morning walk.

"Hello darling," she said, "how are you?"

"Looking forward to a couple of days off," he said, as he embraced and kissed her on the forehead. "I'm starving. What's for breakfast?"

"You're obviously feeling better. I can always tell because the first thing you think about is your stomach."

"Have I been that bad?"

"Worse than ever."

"Well, you know, things always look better after a few days away from the coalface." She smiled sympathetically; he always said that when things weren't going well.

I've got a lovely day planned," she brightened, "we're going to relax and stay at home. I've made you a nice lunch; you can have a few drinks and then I'm taking you to the Whitstable Playhouse."

"What are we going to see?"

"A Day at the Races by Navek Senoj." He rolled his eyes at her. "You'll enjoy it, I promise, as long as you don't go to sleep and start snoring." He laughed at that remembering the time she couldn't wake him up; his ribs were sore for days afterwards.

Matt felt a lot better. He'd had a wonderful day. He'd spent some time in the garden; his comfrey was now staked with willow and the borders had been tidied. The mower had made short work of the grass cutting and the lawn looked splendid, the best for years, due to all the recent rain. He'd had a lovely walk with Rose along the Saxon Shore Way to the Prince's Golf Club. They'd even had time to lie on the pebbles in the afternoon sunshine, while Mutley went exploring.

"For dessert, you'll have to have ice cream at the theatre," Rose said, as he washed down steak, hand cut chips, and salad with a second glass of Rioja, "Now go and have a siesta while I clear up. I'd like you to stay awake and keep me company this evening."

Matt's mind was clicking like a clockwork timepiece; he'd been re-examining the case and problem solving subconsciously while he'd slept. Rose woke him at 5:45 with a strong cup of coffee and his favourite biscuit.

"Thank you darling... Can you hand me my note book; I need to write down a few things before I forget them."

She returned a few minutes later. "How are you?"

"I'm wide awake and looking forward to our night out."

"Good, into the shower then; I've laid your clothes out on the bed; sports jacket, shirt and trousers. No tie, you're not on duty tonight."

"Yes, boss!" He stood up and saluted.

Seagulls screamed beneath a quilted sky as Matt and Rose arrived at The Playhouse Theatre, a converted church in Whitstable High Street. They were early but the bar was very busy and buzzed with chatter. Rose found some seats next to a couple of elderly ladies while Matt went off to the bar for a G&T and a white wine spritzer. When he returned with the drinks she said, "I think I'll go and buy a programme."

A few minutes later she returned with a booklet and studied it with glasses perched on her nose, while Matt sipped his gin and soaked up the atmosphere. It was good to be back in the real world. The last time he'd been with this many people it had been quite different; a sombre meeting in the incident room on Friday... Chatter and laughter rang in his ears. It promised to be an entertaining evening.

He regarded the black and white photographs of The Lindley Players adorning the walls opposite. His mind suddenly replaced them with the images of Dorothy's corpse on the walls of his office and tears momentarily pricked his eyes. Rose looked up from the programme.

"How's your G&T?"

"Very good," Matt said, as he recovered. "Now what's this play about?"

"It's about two boys who visit Weston-Super-Mare during the long hot summer of seventy-six. The story starts off in the morning at their home in Bristol then moves to the pier in the afternoon."

"Is that it?"

"No that's act one."

Three bells rang. They made their way up two flights of stairs to the auditorium and presented their tickets to a white haired gentleman dressed in a dinner jacket and bow tie.

"It looks like a full house," Matt observed as they sat down. The lights dimmed. Carousel music played over the sound system and the curtain lifted to reveal Brian, June, Marvin and Kris discussing their plans for the day over the breakfast table.

"That was wonderful," Matt said, at the end of Act One.

"The dialogue was brilliant. I really feel that I know each of the characters."

"I liked the way Brian was encouraging the boys to be adventurous."

"In complete contrast to June, who was anxious about them going out on their own."

"I loved the way the boys transformed themselves into cyclists by ripping their jeans and sweaters off as soon as they were out of sight."

"When they were supposed to be taking the train."

"Cycling was a very clever way to take you to the pier amusement arcade," Matt said.

"Victoria, the horse racing machine was very amusing."

"Complaining about a lack of punters with the most exciting part of her sequence to come."

"I just knew the boys were going to win on Crucifix when they started their commentary."

"I bet they're going to win the Grand Draw in act two; now how about that ice cream?"

Carousel music played and the lights dimmed. Kris keenly studied Victoria's sequence. Marvin kept look-out.

"We've seen these two before," Dr Syntax breathed to the other horses, Little Wonder, St. Patrick, Jack Spigot and Gypsy.

"Our owners won't be pleased," muttered St Patrick. "It's Jack's turn to win the next race and they know it. Please bet on another horse!"

A shilling fell into Jack's slot at 4-1. The other horses urged him to hold back but the clockwork mechanism propelled him forward to the finishing line. Four shillings dropped into the winners' slot. The boys congratulated themselves; not too enthusiastically. They didn't want to attract the attention of the child catcher.

A shilling on St Patrick at 3-1 and they were off again. St Patrick was right at the back of the field. He trailed behind until the final furlong; then shot forward at an unbelievable pace to win. Another three shillings fell into the winner's slot.

Bill, the Bookie, was worried. He couldn't cover the next bet on Gypsy. "It's time to break down Victoria," he screamed.

"But there's nothing wrong with me. I've just been serviced and oiled."

"I can't cover the bet. It will be debtor's prison for me."

A shilling slipped into Gypsy's slot at 6-1 and they were off.

The boys chuckled.

"Win the Grand Draw and we'll have plenty of money for Ice Cream, Swimming-"

"Fish and Chips and a ride on the Ghost Train."

Bill was hysterical. "Hold back everyone!" He tried to get onto the track but was soldered to the spot. He willed Gypsy to fall and then he prayed. The last five shillings fell into the winner's slot. Bill held his head in his hands.

The boys collected their winnings, shrugged their shoulders at the missing 5p and wandered off laughing.

"Time for ice creams," said one.

"On the house," said the other.

"That was a wonderful play; thank you for dragging me out to see it," Matt said, taking Rose's hand as they made their way along the High Street.

to the Harbour Car Park.

"I'm glad you enjoyed it and stayed awake. It's your turn to pamper me tomorrow; I fancy a lie in with a good book and the papers."

*

Rain pelted against the kitchen windows on Sunday morning as Matt dried Mutley and removed his dripping hat and raincoat. He felt refreshed but wasn't quite ready to return to the office; another day off and he would be ready for anything. He put the kettle on before going into the utility room and hanging his wet clothes on the airer. Then he made his way upstairs.

"Good moaning. Tea or coffee?"

"Coffee and a cooked breakfast would be nice," Rose said, looking up from her book, "and you'd better put an apron on. I don't want singed chest hair with my sausages."

"I'll give you singed hair and sausages if you're not careful."

"Ooh, yes please." Matt climbed into bed. "You're a bit cold; come here and let me warm you up." Mutley jumped off the bed, scurried over to his mattress and pulled the quilt over his head. He peeped out a few minutes later and covered his eyes with his paws. Breakfast would have to wait.

CHAPTER 9

Michael had been attracted to Denise, his assistant manager, for a very long time and was sure she felt the same way about him. They'd had several dances with each other at the many Christmas parties he'd organized for the staff; quite a few of them had been slow dances and many the last of the night. Then there'd be the awkward goodbyes and another year would pass. Denise was thirty nine and still lived at home with her mother in St Nicholas-at-Wade. She'd never been married. She seemed destined to be her mother's carer and a spinster for the rest of her life, so she was rather surprised when Michael asked her out for Sunday lunch.

The Red Lion in Stodmarsh was buzzing like a hive when they arrived for the twelve thirty sitting. Robert, the landlord, greeted them like old friends and they immediately felt at ease. He showed them to a table for two within a private booth created by wooden trellises.

"Can I get you something to drink while you look at the menu?" Robert said.

Michael looked at Denise. "A glass of white wine, thank you."

"Pinot Grigio?"

"That would be lovely."

"And for you Sir?"

"A large glass of Rioja."

"So two large glasses of wine?" Denise laughed and nodded.

"He's a real charmer," Michael said, as Robert walked away.

"The whole place is charming," Denise said, as she took in her surroundings. Dried hops decorated the wooden frames of their booth and the oak beams above their heads. A Welsh dresser against the opposite wall displayed an assortment of crockery, old cooking utensils, books, miner's lamps and other paraphernalia. Interesting prints adorned the walls.

"How did you find this place?"

"By chance, when I was out cycling. I was doing a circuit along the sea wall from my house to Herne Bay then down the two-nine-one into Fordwich and along the back roads towards home. I'd just struggled up a steep hill and decided to stop for refreshments. It was a beautiful sunny day and I had a drink in the garden, with the ducks and chickens. I think I was their only customer."

"You must teach me how to cycle." Denise said... Michael was delighted. It sounded like this might be the first of many dates.

"Have you got a bike?"

"No. I haven't cycled since I was a schoolgirl but I'd like to learn." The drinks arrived. "I think we'd better look at the menu." Michael realized that he'd been staring again.

"What are you going to have?" He said.

"I fancy the roast chicken."

"Can I take your order?" Robert said.

"One roast chicken and one beef, thank you."

Michael couldn't believe that his life had changed so much in the past week. He'd asked Denise out on Wednesday and ever since she'd accepted he'd found himself staring at her absent-mindedly. She really was a beautiful woman; straight chestnut coloured hair cascaded over her shoulders and down to the middle of her back. Dark brown eyebrows, like the brush strokes of a competent artist, complemented her fan-like eyelashes. Her face was round and lightly made up, her nose straight and dainty, her lipstick a deep sophisticated red, her smile radiant. The staff had noticed that they were infatuated with each other straight away.

"Has something suddenly happened between you two?" Adam had said.

"I'm taking her out on Sunday."

"About bloody time too. She's been in love with you for years. Treat her well, though, or you'll have me to answer to."

Michael laughed as he looked down at Adam. "You gonna punch me on the knee?"

Adam grinned. "No, my height's much better suited to a nut in the bollocks."

Now here she was beautifully dressed in a white silk blouse, black cropped jacket and matching pencil skirt. A riding crop brooch was pinned to her left lapel.

"Do you ride?" Michael said.

"Most Sundays, if I haven't anything better to do. Of course, I had to cancel today's lesson. " She beamed. He reached across the table and held her hand.

"It seems a shame to hurry the love birds," Robert said, as he collected their meals from the kitchen. "Has anyone else placed the same order?"

"Table ten; they've only just arrived but I'm sure they won't mind."

"Where do you ride?" Michael said.

"Limes Farm near Hawkinge."

"Do you own a horse?"

"I used to when I was young and could ride all the time but now I just use the centres' horses."

"Chicken for you madam and roast beef for you Sir," Robert said as he laid the plates on the table. "Can I get you anything else? Mustard? Horseradish?" Denise shook her head.

"Some English mustard for me," Michael said. Denise picked up her knife and fork and cut the first slice of meat into a small mouthful.

"The chicken's wonderful."

"So is the roast beef, it's more like a slice of fillet. Would you like to try some?" Denise nodded and loaded her fork with another piece of chicken. When Michael proffered his fork she smiled and gently took it from him between thumb and forefinger.

"It's delicious, cooked to perfection. Now why don't you try the chicken?" He did. "Well?"

"It's very nice, not as good as the beef though… Would you like to swap?"

"Don't be silly, I can have the beef next time." She coloured when she realized what she'd said. Michael just smiled. There it was again. A future… He'd not had one of those in a very long time and he'd never had a relationship to consider. This was new territory; exciting and scary. He couldn't understand why Denise wasn't settled with a clutch of children and then it just popped out.

"Why aren't you married Denise?" She looked thoughtful for a moment and then her eyes sparkled mischievously.

"I've been waiting for the right man to ask me out for years and he's only just got round to it." Michael was uncomfortable under Denise's unflinching gaze; he was no longer in complete control of his emotions and felt that his face was as red as a raw side of beef. All he could manage in response was a weak,

"Sorry."

"Who said that I was referring to you?" A look of dejection crossed his face and then she laughed. "I'm only teasing."

"How was the food?" Robert said.

Michael looked down at the empty plates. "I feel like Oliver Twist," he said.

"Oh, you'd like some more... Would you like to try the beef this time madam?"

"Yes, please."

"One slice, a few potatoes and some veg?" She nodded, "And the same for you Sir?"

Michael smiled. "The chicken was very nice but the beef was excellent."

"Two beef then."

They couldn't believe their eyes when Robert returned a few minutes later with two small plates of food. "I don't do this for everyone you know... Two large glasses of Rioja?" They both nodded and grinned at each other.

"We'll have to go for a walk around the village after this," Michael said.

"Is there anything here?"

"No, not really, just a small church, a couple of farmhouses and an excellent pub. I think we'll have to become regulars." There it was again, only this time Michael had said it. Denise's smile was radiant.

The walk through the village could have lasted less than ten minutes but was more than an hour as the happy couple stopped and discussed every property. In the end they decided that the double fronted Georgian farmhouse backing onto descending farmland with traditional low-rise tarred barns was the property for them. All they had to do now was win the lottery but you couldn't do that without a ticket. Michael bought one from the local store on the way home.

"You keep it," he said. "If you don't come in on Thursday I'll assume we've won and you've legged it."

"You don't think I'm going to let you off that lightly, do you?" She put

40

her right hand on his chest and kissed him on the lips. He let the kiss linger. "See you tomorrow," she said, as she slipped through his arms and disappeared through the front door into her house.

Michael was overwhelmed with love. He re-lived every moment of their date on the short drive home. Had he done anything untoward? He didn't think so. He remembered her saying, "I've been waiting for the right man to ask me out for years and he's only just got round to it." Perhaps he should have suggested another outing before dropping her off. A stroll along the seafront from his house to Plumpudding Island, then they could follow The Wantsum to St Nicholas and drop in on her mother. He was ready to be introduced to her and wondered what Denise would say. "Hello mum, this is my boss." No that wasn't the way that he wanted to be introduced. "Hello mum, this is Michael, my boyfriend." That sounded much better.

CHAPTER 10

The sea was like crinkled tin foil reflecting the blue sky when Matt and Rose emerged from their garden onto the shore road. It was warm, after the recent rains, with a light breeze. The ridge of the embankment was colourful with crimson, pale pink, white and purple wild flowers. As they meandered hand in hand along the stony track local residents and dog walkers recognized Matt from his regular appearances on the TV and in the local newspapers. They acknowledged his presence with cursory nods but respected his down-time. He was a man under tremendous pressure from the media to solve the most sensational murder in Sandwich for over 230 years.

The meadow opposite The Chequers Restaurant was busy with miniature cream, white and toffee coloured calves, prancing among their sedate mothers, when Matt and Rose arrived for dinner. This was the first fine evening of the week; it had been the wettest July on record. Matt barely acknowledged the greetings of their hosts, Pieter and Gary, as they shook his hand warmly and kissed Rose on both cheeks. He was seething with rage. He could still see DI Kelly's pugnacious face, red as a hot poker before this morning's briefing.

"We should be concentrating all of our efforts in Deal this weekend," his voice had boomed, "and we should be looking for Derek."

'Well it was Friday the thirteenth Matt,' thought dejectedly, 'so what more could be expected from his junior.'

Over the past five weeks this had become a recurring theme. Kelly was his second in command. He had joined the force from the Met after a meteoric rise through the ranks in a little over nine years. He was thirty one, dark haired and bovine-looking with a stern gaze and a simmering temperament. He was used to getting his own way and at six foot five towered over Matt. From the outset he'd constantly tried to bully him into taking the enquiry in one direction and one direction only.

"Derek is the key to solving this murder," he'd growled in a haughty manner, as he looked down on his superior during one of their first meetings.

Matt had realized then that theirs wasn't going to be a happy marriage. "For the time being I'm the officer in charge of this case," he'd said, with brutal directness. "I acknowledge that someone named Derek appears to be a key suspect but I'm not willing to follow that line of enquiry to the exclusion of everything else. We must correctly identify our victim and look into her past. I'm sure that's where we'll find Derek, if that's his name, and it's also where we'll find a motive for her murder."

"A complete waste of time," Kelly had retorted with disdain, "I'm not going to ask my troops to go off and interview anyone not named Derek."

Matt wasn't easily worked on by outward show and stood his ground. "They're not your troops and you'll do as you're told. I forbid you to go off interviewing all the Dereks in the county without good reason. I don't want the press getting hold of that name, without my permission, as the killer might not be Derek."

"Well who else do you think it is?" Kelly said; his face set in a mask of determination.

"Someone that the victim knows, someone that she invited to her flat for dinner, someone she trusted, someone who has knowledge of human anatomy and knows how to perform a tracheotomy; a surgeon or a paramedic perhaps. Now find me a Derek that ticks those boxes and I'll gladly let your dogs loose. In the meantime you'll do as you're told."

Matt was poor company for Rose during their meal. He hardly said a word, obsessed as he was by Operation Carnegie. He'd cancelled the leave of most of his detectives over the coming weekend and drafted in a lot of uniformed support for his gamble in Sandwich. He was a worried man with limited police resources; perhaps he should've sent some of them to Deal, as Kelly had insisted, but in his opinion it was better to do a job properly in one location rather than compromise in two. Sandwich was where Dorothy found her demise and the public would expect a heightened police presence there, at the first music festival following the discovery of her body.

"Can I offer you a liqueur?" Gary asked solicitously, after giving Rose a quizzical and worried look. He knew Matt well but he'd never seen him looking so withdrawn. When they'd last seen him he'd been very cheerful, looking forward to his retirement and taking some gardening leave. He'd hardly touched his food and appeared to have shrivelled with age.

"A whisky would go down nicely, a large one."

That was new; he usually asked for a Baileys. "Scotch or Irish?"

"Anything," Matt replied with a wan smile.

*

It was Saturday; a day for rest, friends and family. Uniformed officers and murder squad detectives manned check-points at all routes into the medieval town of Sandwich, creating an island with the River Stour to the north. It was the first full day of the annual Folk and Ale Festival. Major Incident boards reminded participants that there'd been a murder in Market Street at the beginning of June and displayed images of the victim, above the words:

CAN YOU IDENTIFY THIS WOMAN

(Known locally as Dorothy Skinner)

Due to the inclement weather white awnings had been erected as interview rooms. Questionnaires had been printed and distributed. Those interviewed were asked: if they knew the victim; how they knew the victim; how long they'd known her; what name she used; where did she live; where did she go; what did she do and who were her friends. Their personal details, including occupation and contact telephone numbers, were taken even if their responses were negative. This information would be fed into the HOLMES computer for future reference.

By eleven o'clock the trades-people and some of the musicians had passed through the check-points en-route to their venues. The first groups of revellers were queuing patiently to be interviewed and were eager to help in any way they could. They were still reeling from the shocking murder of an elderly woman within their community.

The atmosphere deteriorated as the skies darkened with rain clouds and the first showers arrived. The queues quickly diminished to a trickle and the detectives were able to take more care with their interviewees. Eventually the sky became an even stony grey and by one o'clock the rain was falling in sheets. The streets were empty, apart from the musicians on the stage and the stallholders contracted to work between the Guildhall and the Police Office. The nine pub venues were buzzing.

Matt cut a lonely figure, sheltering under his golfing umbrella, as made his way around the medieval battlements to the various check-points. 'It was a dreadful shame,' he thought, ' that the painstaking work of the crime scene examiners and forensic scientists had produced no leads.' He had returned to Dorothy's flat when they'd finished; pink chemicals had stained the walls; black powder highlighted the grouting and lime-scale in the bathroom and covered the woodwork but the only fingerprints found had belonged to Dorothy, the previous tenants Brian and Sheila, the estate agents and their cleaner. Smudged marks had suggested the use of latex gloves but none had been found; neither had they found the murder weapon, the bindings or the tracheotomy tube. The victim's breast implants had been located in her refrigerator but no DNA, other than the victim's, had been traced.

Matt was greeted with outward deference by most of his colleagues but the responses from Kelly's team were less enthusiastic. Even the publicans seemed unhappy with his presence and by six he'd retired to the police office with his thoughts. At least Marion, the PCSO who'd found Dorothy, was pleased to see him.

"Hello Sir, can I get you a cup of coffee or something?"

"That would be wonderful," he said, noticing, not for the first time her large brown eyes as her lashes fluttered in her horse-shaped face.

"How's it going?"

"Not very well, I think the weather's scuppered our chances."

"Well, it's supposed to be much better tomorrow," she said. She turned her back on him, swished her mane of golden hair, adjusted her rump and filled the coffee cups. "Here you go… Sugar?"

It stopped raining at six and by nine some of the rainclouds had dispersed revealing patches of blue and white sky. The officers who'd been manning the check-points were packed into the police office dressed in their wet apparel; several polished their glasses while condensation dribbled down the windows. Matt rose to address them.

"Thank you for your efforts today. I know it hasn't been a pleasant task with the terrible weather we've had and I'm sure you're not looking forward to doing it all again tomorrow. However, I must stress that it is completely necessary as we still know very little about our victim... Now before you leave, do you have any questions for me?"

"Did we gain anything from today's exercise?"

"Yes, we've traced a few more people who were captured on CCTV in the minimarket over the weekend of the second to fourth of June but we haven't had a breakthrough if that's what you mean... Anyone else? No, well, thank you ladies and gentlemen. I'll see you again tomorrow."

*

Bright sunshine filled the streets under a milky blue sky; the ground was still wet in the shade but in the places touched by the sun smoky vapours rose from the tarmac. Matt was up early and walked into town. He felt positive; he hadn't seen that bastard Brian Kelly since Friday and a he'd had a pleasant walk with Rose and Mutley in the morning. As he let himself into the Police Office and settled into the interview room to study Saturdays questionnaires he felt very focused; today would be better than yesterday he told himself.

He sorted the handwritten documents into two different piles; females and children and male adults. He was sure that his quarry was a man. Then he looked at their occupations. There were a few paramedics, a couple of doctors, some services personnel and several men named Derek. He didn't recognize their full names but put them to the top of the pile for priority research, interview and elimination.

At ten he was joined by Marion and distracted by her broad shoulders, deep chest above a narrow girth and pointed hips over her rather generous rump.

"Good moaning," he said, in his best French accent, "would you like some coffee?"

"I'll get it; you've far more important things to do." He watched as she busied herself with the makings. She was a welcome distraction.

As he sipped his coffee a little later he noticed the first of the stallholders arriving in the cobbled street outside.

"I felt really sorry for those poor sods yesterday; standing in the rain all day without a customer in sight. I doubt if they even got their rents back."

"It was dreadful, wasn't it, but it looks a lot better today."

"And how are you coping with the post-traumatic stress disorder?"

"Oh, I'm doing okay. I still have the occasional flash-back and sometimes I have nightmares. I'm very lucky though because I can always talk to Terry; he knows exactly what I saw and we have similar problems... You are going to catch the bastard that did this, aren't you Sir?"

"Of course we are Marion; it's just a question of time and resources."

Sunlight flooded into the cobbled square illuminating The Guildhall, a large Tudor style building with black timbers between white render and herring bone brickwork. The clock struck twelve and right on cue Rough Musicke struck their first chords beneath the red and blue bandstand awning. Matt ventured out into the square at one when Crisis began playing and joined the picnickers, who were munching on Portuguese snacks and cider purchased from the stalls nearby. He would've loved a drink but he was on duty; still there was no reason why he couldn't enjoy the music for a few minutes. He admired the bandsmen; he was hopeless at playing music but appreciated a good knees-up. The guitarist, a man in his late fifties with unruly grizzled grey hair, caressed his instrument as another dressed in a leather cowboy hat squeezed his accordion affectionately. The street buzzed with people in conversation and colourful stalls sold an eclectic mix of guitars, banjos, clothing, handbags, wallets, sunglasses and pet foods.

A rotund lady wearing a zebra printed blouse over a plain black skirt with green Croc wellingtons introduced the band; a middle aged woman took to the stage in cobbled shoes. She danced when the music played; her shoes clattered loudly on the metal stage and Matt thought of the lovely weekend he and Rose had enjoyed the previous year. He reckoned there were only a hundred people in the audience; not a very good turnout but it was still early.

A mouth organ sawed through the notes of their next number accompanied by guitar and singer; couples danced in front of the stage and Matt wondered how the peace of such a wonderful community could be so easily shattered. Tears pricked his eyes; somehow he felt responsible not only for the terrible crime but for failing to solve it. As the song came to an end the audience applauded; the red, white and blue bunting above them strained in the increasing breeze and the first few drops of rain splattered the cobbles.

Matt collected his umbrella and moved on into No Name Street as a funnel of black cloud slowly filled the western sky. Morris Men assembled before him; an elderly gentleman, dressed as a Molly, with long grey hair tied in pig tails and wearing a pink dress over a rather generous beer belly grinned as he strode into the street with his minions. He rattled the bells on the anklets above his working boots. Drinkers sat at tables outside The Fleur de Lis chatting and eating while picnickers adorned the tables opposite the No Name Shop. An accordion, accompanied by drums, squeezed out the tune of "The British Grenadiers." The Molly danced with his companions, most of whom were smaller than the metal staffs they carried.

In Market Street the atmosphere was baleful; the market stalls were there but there were no customers to keep them busy. The area immediately outside Dorothy's flat was deserted; the only signs of life being a small group of subdued musicians sitting outside the Commissioners for Oaths. Shoppers emerged from the minimarket opposite and quickly hurried by. Matt's eyes were drawn up to the gargoyles set into the brickwork where a scene from hell had been played out... A roaring in his ears drew his attention further skyward and he watched as a Spitfire and Hurricane flew overhead. 'They'll be on their way to the Deal Memorial Bandstand,' he thought.

CHAPTER 11

Thousands of people converged on Walmer Green to mark the twenty third anniversary of the bombing of The Royal Marines School of Music; barely a metre of ground was uncovered between the paddling pool and the lifeboat station, save for the terraced area in front of the local dignitaries, facing the bandstand.

As Michael looked for somewhere to sit he saw a couple of boys, overwhelmed by white pith helmets above dark blue parade dress, selling programmes and made his way over to them.

"Are you hoping to join the Marines?" he said.

"We are," replied one, flashing heavy braces over his white teeth.

"We have to wait until we weigh sixty five kilograms," added the other. "They won't let us join before then as we'll lose so much weight during training."

"So you're planning to join the commandos rather than the band then?"

"That's right."

"Would you like a programme?"

"Yes please. How much are they?"

"We're asking for a contribution of two pounds towards the cost of printing and putting on the concert but a pound will do, if you don't have change." Michael slid a five pound note through the slot into the collection bucket.

"Will that do?"

"Yes, thanks very much." The boy with braces handed him a booklet and they both sauntered off towards a group of indecisive onlookers.

Michael flicked through the brochure and found the programme of music in the centre pages; he meandered off, found a space in the crowd to the south of the bandstand and sat on the slightly damp grass. As he settled down the overture "Orpheus in the Underworld" came to an end and the conductor Lieutenant Colonel Nick Grace stepped up to the microphone.

"I would now like to introduce you to Major Tony Smallwood, the director of music of the Royal Marines Band, Portsmouth." There was a ripple of applause from the audience. "Tony is not only our director of music but recently led a fifteen piece band to Afghanistan delivering fantastic musical support to our troops at the various bases in the region including Bastion, Kabul, Lashagar, Kandahar and some smaller forward operating and patrol bases ... This was bringing operational military music directly to the front-line demonstrating the quality, flexibility and adaptability of the band service." More hand-clapping followed and when it died down, "This will be Tony's final appearance at this bandstand as he retires later in the year after thirty years of service to the band... He will be conducting a couple of his own arrangements and will front our Royal Marines with some favourites from the Big Band era... Ladies and Gentlemen I give you Tony Smallwood." The Major stepped up to the microphone and bowed to the appreciation shown by the audience.

"Thank you for those warm words Nick; I am allowed to call you Nick?" Lt Col Grace nodded his head. "Now Ladies and Gentlemen I would like to introduce you to a well-known local soprano, Margaret Threadgold, who will sing 'The Armed Man; A Mass for Peace.' A very elegant lady wearing evening dress stepped forward and bowed to polite applause from the audience. " 'The Armed Man' charts the growing menace of a descent into war, interspersed with moments of reflection, shows the horrors war brings and ends with the hope for peace in the new millennium, when sorrow, pain and death can be overcome."

Tony turned away from the audience to face the band. He raised his left hand and the baton in his right came to life; the haunting voice of the soprano overlaid the music. The audience was deathly silent and only applauded when they were quite sure that the piece was over... "The Buglers Dream" and "Olympic Fanfare" followed.

At two the drone of petrol engines filled the air from the north. Michael looked skyward and saw a Spitfire and Hurricane dip their wings, in salute to the Royal Marines Band and their fallen comrades, as they flew overhead. Then he stood, with much of the audience to show his appreciation. After the fly-past his gaze was drawn to the mass of people assembled in front of a long row of colourful terraces; the Bandstand Bakery; The Admiral Owen which had been decorated with The Union

Jack and Olympic rings; the bow-fronted windows of a derelict house painted with images of the Royal Marines Band on the march and The Royal Marines Association HQ. He felt proud to be amongst these patriotic people who would never forget the murders of their bandsmen by the IRA.

After an arrangement of big band music Michael was ready for the interval and he joined a queue of people waiting to buy Diamond Jubilee CD's and DVD's.

"Can you come here more often?" he quipped with the bandsmen. "This is the first time we've seen the sun for ages."

"It's been just as bad in Portsmouth."

"Probably makes a change from Afghanistan though."

"Yes, we were there last summer. It was hot as hell but it was good to do something different."

"What were you doing there?"

"We were working the ambulances ... Some of our guys were pretty smashed up."

"It was nice talking to you," Michael said, taking his leave, as the queue swelled behind him.

Michael walked onto the pebbly beach with a large mug of tea and sat down among beached leisure craft and white painted sheds. The sea was flat, except for a few ripples dulling its surface and he watched a helicopter buzz overhead. This was his first outing without Denise in three weeks and he was missing her company. They'd been together every day after that first date; going out after work. They'd walked the historic city walls of Canterbury, the sea fronts of Whitstable, Herne Bay and Westgate.

He'd bought her a bicycle on the second weekend. She'd practiced all day on Saturday. On Sunday they'd cycled along the sea defences to Plumpudding Island and followed The Wantsum into St Nicholas. There he'd been introduced to Yvonne, Denise's mother. He'd enjoyed afternoon tea in their back garden and discovered that she was jolly good fun.

She'd pulled his leg several times about being young and in love and he sensed that she approved of the match. Denise had told him that her mother liked him on their way back to his house. They'd feasted on take-away prawn and chicken curries and watched a DVD in the evening before she'd said goodnight. It all seemed so dreamy now and Michael realized for the first time that he was truly love-sick.

The band started to play "Against All Odds" as Michael returned to the green. A short time later the audience was introduced to "The Andrews Sisters"; three young women dressed in green military lovat suits who sang "Don't Sit Under The Apple Tree." He chuckled to this number and then enjoyed their rendition of "The Candyman." He noticed the white cupola of the Royal Marine Barracks reflecting the sunlight in the background as this song came to its end. Then Band Corporal Georgia returned to the front of the stage without her hat and he realized how tiny she was; not much taller than the seated musicians but boy could she sing.

Families with children picnicked on jam doughnuts, hotdogs, ice-creams and fizzy wine nearby. Michael suddenly realized that he wanted a family and children of his own. He wondered if he and Denise were too old and thought he should broach this subject with her later; perhaps he should ask if she'd like to get married. As if to re-enforce this thought Tony Smallwood stepped up to the microphone and said, "We've now got another solo for you by a local lad. He's the son of retired Colour Sergeant Alan Upton and his baby boy Eli is in the audience. It's called 'The Children of Sanchez' played on the trumpet by Band Corporal Mark Upton."

The light hearted entertainment was over and it was time for the rededication service. After introductory prayers the band and audience stood to sing the first three verses of " Praise to the Lord"; then the buglers played the Last Post and Reveille and Michael thought of his fallen comrades. He was surprised to find tears pricking his eyes. "Nimrod" by Elgar followed then there were more prayers; "The Naval Hymn" and the final prayers and blessing.

The audience was very vocal when they played "Rule, Britannia" and "Land of Hope and Glory." The sound bounced off the walls of the terraced houses nearby and startled the seagulls into flight. The afternoon finished with the Royal Navy march "Heart of Oak" and the Royal Marines regimental march "A Life on the Ocean Wave."

"Hello Denise, it's me," Michael said into his mobile. "I can hardly hear you... Yes, the concert's just finished... I should be home in an hour... How did your riding lesson go? Excellent, I'll pick you up at about seven thirty... I love you too... Bye."

CHAPTER 12

"DCI Matt Sanderson."

"Hello Sir."

"Hello, Terry. How are you?"

"Very well, I'm ringing to let you know that I've just been approached by an old boy who says that Dorothy Skinner is actually Marlene Johnson."

"Really?"

"Yes, he says that he went to school with her in Dover."

"Why has he waited until now to come forward?"

"He's been in Thailand for the past two months with his Thai wife and only found out about the murder on his way to the Folk and Ale Festival this afternoon."

"Why didn't he speak to one of the detectives on the check-points?"

"They were busy and he recognized me. We go back a long way. I've nicked him a few times; mostly petty stuff; drinking and driving, shoplifting, drunk and disorderly; pissing in the street with no regard for passers-by. He likes his football and his drink."

"Sounds like a colourful character but how reliable is he?"

"He says that he's fairly sure it's Marlene on our posters; something about the eyes and nose but he hasn't seen her for about ten years."

"Where are you now?"

"By the Woodnesborough Road check-point."

"Is he willing to come into the Police Office to talk to me?"

"Yes, I'll bring him over and he says can you put the kettle on?"

"This is DCI Matt Sanderson," Terry said, "and this is Trevor Hazelwood."

"Thanks for coming in to see me," Matt said, as he shook Trevor's hand, "I apologize for the surroundings. This is supposed to be a part-time police office. It's really a shop that the organization rents and is usually manned by volunteers. If you'd like to follow me. Tea or Coffee?"

"Tea with two sugars."

"And for you Terry?"

"I'll have a coffee without." As Matt filled three mugs with the makings he sized up the man before him. He was probably about seventy years old; his hair was dark with a little salt in it and he was clean shaven. His eyes appeared sharp and there were none of those tell-tale signs of old age, in fact he appeared to be quite fit. Matt decided to start the interview informally.

"So I understand that you've been in Thailand for the past two months?"

"That's right. I always go at the end of the football season and again in January to escape the awful winters we have. My wife's Thai but immigration won't let her emigrate to the UK."

"That must be very hard for you both?"

"No, not really; it just makes it more special when we are together."

"What does she do when you're away?"

"She runs a small hotel just south of Hua Hin."

"How long have you been married?"

"About five years. I found her through a Thai agency. I didn't want one of those escorts that everyone had been through. I wanted a respectable girl and they did all the referencing for me." Matt noticed that Trevor was fingering what appeared to be a medallion around his neck.

"That's an interesting item you're wearing."

"It's a talisman to show that we're married, a bit like a wedding ring."

"Shall we take our drinks into the office so that we're not disturbed?"

"If you like."

"Terry, I think you'd better come with us."

"Is this okay, Trevor?" Matt said.

"This will do nicely," Trevor said, as he sat down on the most comfortable chair.

"Do you mind if I make notes?"

"Not at all. Where'd you like me to start?"

"Well, I understand that you've identified the lady on our poster as Marlene Johnson?"

"That's right."

"How do you know her?"

"We went to school together in Dover."

"That must've been a long time ago?"

"It was but we grew up in the same neighbourhood after that."

"Where was that?"

"Well I was living in Paul's Place, Dover and she was living with her husband Tommy in Matthew's Place."

"When was the last time you saw her?"

"Oh, it must be at least ten years ago. She took up with Paddy or Patraicc after Tommy died and then they both disappeared. Did a midnight flit, probably to Gretna Green." Matt was beginning to think that Trevor was a bit romantic.

"Did they have any children?"

"Who?"

"Marlene and Tommy?"

"No, but Marlene got pregnant when she was nearly eighteen and Tommy married her to prevent a scandal; you know unmarried mothers were scorned in those days. Anyway she must have had a miscarriage as there were no babies."

"I see."

"There were a couple of young boys around there though, much later on after Tommy was made redundant."

"And who were they?"

"Well the dark haired one belonged to Paddy and the other one belonged to Derek." Matt did his best to hide his surprise and didn't look up at Terry who continued to lean nonchalantly against the opposite wall.

"Do you know Patraicc's surname?"

"No, I'm afraid not, just Patraicc. That's all I know but I do know that

Derek's was Stevens. He used to live in Tower Hamlets Street with Patricia and I think their son was Michael or Mitchell, something like that."

"Are they still living in Tower Hamlets Street?"

"No, Derek disappeared. I heard that he had another family in Calais. Mitchell, he grew up and joined the Army. Patricia, she moved away. I don't know where."

"Do you know the number in Tower Hamlets Street?"

"No, but it's on the same side of the road as The Dewdrop. I can show you, if you like. Derek and I used to sit on the pull down seats outside the pub and have a pint of Guinness, on the occasional sunny day; not that there were many of those… Is all this helping?"

"If Dorothy is Marlene Johnson as you say then this is very helpful."

"Have you got any more photos of her?"

"As a matter-of-fact we have a small photo album."

"Well, if you want to show me those I'll be able to confirm one way or the other."

"I'll need to make a phone call to get them brought over. It might take about an hour. Is that alright?"

"It's alright by me as long as I'm outta here before the party's over. I've got some drinking to make up for and some friends to catch up with."

"Terry, take my phone and ring Caroline Hughes. Ask her to retrieve Dorothy's photograph album from the exhibits store and bring it here a.s.a.p. Tell her to use the two-tones if necessary; I want them here within the hour."

"Right-o guv," Terry said, as he left the room.

"Okay Trevor, I need to take a formal statement from you based on what you've told me so far but before we get going shall we have a tea break?"

"Good idea. I could do with a fag as well, don't suppose you've got any?"

When Matt and Trevor returned from the yard several detectives were taking sandwich breaks. Matt acknowledged their questioning looks but said nothing; he didn't want to reveal his excitement and wanted to correctly identify Marlene before breaking the news to his team. Then his most loyal detectives would be getting a much longer day than they'd bargained for. Brian Kelly's bunch would miss out; they needed to know who was in charge before he would reward them with massive overtime payments. Two could play divide and rule.

"Hello Rose… I don't think I'll be coming home tonight… Put the dinner in the dog… Yes, I think we've finally had a breakthrough… I'll tell you all about it when I get a chance; probably just before your bedtime… Love you lots… Bye."

CHAPTER 13

The Operation Carnegie Incident Room was on the first floor of a modern red brick building. Access was gained via a keypad to the left of the fire door. The room itself wasn't enormous but felt large due to glazing fitted on two of the outer walls. Some of the staff had remarked that it was like sitting in an airport terminal; others complained that it was more like a gold fish bowl. The windows were impenetrable from the outside to prevent prying eyes from photographing the intelligence pinned to the walls. Six teams of seven officers shared thirty workstations arranged in groups of six. A wooden framed room with mirrored glass sat like a Police Box in the left hand corner; an aluminium bar on the door declared that this was the office of DCI Matt Sanderson. Two men in grey suits waited within the office.

Four of Matt's best officers had volunteered for overtime following the breakthrough the previous day. It had been a tough night and most of them had been up for twenty four hours when the weekly briefing started at 7am. It had been extremely productive though. Trevor Hazelwood had identified their victim as Marlene Johnson and the others in her photograph album as Tommy Johnson, Derek Stevens and Patraicc Delaney. Their photographs had been reproduced above their names and now adorned one of the pin boards.

"Good morning ladies and gentlemen," Matt said. The last few voices within the office faded away. "Thank you for coming in early this morning. As some of you know we had a breakthrough in this enquiry yesterday and we now believe that Dorothy Skinner is actually Marlene Johnson." Matt turned to the pin board and tapped her photograph with a garden cane.

"From enquiries made during the night we have been able to establish that Marlene was born in 1942 which made her about seventy years old

57

when she died. She used to live in Matthews Place Dover with her husband Tommy Johnson," Matt tapped his photograph. "We believe that Tommy died of cancer in the late nineties… Dean, I understand that you used to pound the beat in Dover and I'd like you and your team to focus on that part of the enquiry. I want a fully researched package on Marlene Johnson. Most importantly I want you to identify her GP and obtain her old medical records; according to our witness she used to attend The Peter Street Surgery prior to her disappearance in 2001. Find out if she'd had any operations or organs removed so that we can compare them with the pathologist's report; also find out who her dentist was so that we can compare her teeth against her dental records."

"I'll do that myself."

"Good, I want the rest of your team on house-to-house enquiries and I want the results on my desk by 2pm today."

"Okay Sir."

"The next subject is Derek Stevens; like all of the others he was featured within Marlene's photograph album but unlike the others we know quite a lot about him, thanks to a Missing Persons enquiry conducted by a retired police officer, named Paul Adams… Derek was born on 13 March 1937 and he used to live with his wife Patricia Stevens and son Michael Stevens in Tower Hamlets Street Dover." Matt looked up to make sure that he still had their attention and noted Kelly's loyalists were looking impressed.

"On Monday 23 July 2001 Derek was reported missing by his wife Patricia. Enquiries made revealed that he was drinking in The Admiral Harvey in Bridge Street Dover with his best mate Paddy or Patraicc on Friday 20 July until closing time and subsequently with the Landlady Bernice Roberts until about 1am on Saturday 21 July. He hasn't been seen since. Patricia had also reported him missing in 1991 and 1995; on both occasions he'd returned when he was ready and hinted to the investigating officer that he had another woman in Calais… For these reasons he was treated as a low risk missing person." Matt looked around the room to make sure that no one was waning.

"According to the witness that we traced yesterday Derek used to frequent Marlene and Tommy's house with his son Michael… Charlie I want a full profile on this subject." Charlie nodded. "I'm sure you realize that we need to know as much about him as possible, especially as it's his first name that appears on our victim's calendar at about the time of her death. I would like your team to trace and interview Patricia Stevens, Michael Stevens and Paul Adams. I'd also like you to pull the Missing Persons Enquiry form from the archives just in case the officer abbreviated the text when copying it onto the computer."

"Anything else, Sir?"

"Once you've located Patricia and Michael and interviewed them I want you to search their addresses for the clothing that Derek was wearing when he disappeared. Obtain search warrants, if necessary."

"Okay Sir."

"We also know that Derek used to visit Marlene and Tommy with his best friend Patraicc Delaney." Matt tapped his photograph on the notice board. "After Derek's disappearance Delaney apparently moved in with Marlene and then they both disappeared, sometime between Christmas and New Year 2001. We don't know much about Delaney other than he had a son, a dark haired youth, who used to frequent Matthews Place... Ed."

"Yes Sir."

"I want you to go to The Admiral Harvey on Bridge Street and speak to the landlady Bernice Roberts, if she's still there. Apparently Derek, Patraicc and Tommy used to be regulars. If she's moved on interview the punters and try and track her down. We really need a lot more information to identify Delaney."

"Okay Sir."

"Roger, I want you to re-examine the CCTV footage for Derek Stevens. When he went missing he was wearing a tweed flat cap, tweed jacket, green trousers and brown shoes. I know it's been nearly twelve years since he disappeared and he's unlikely to be wearing the same clothing but we've got to start somewhere."

"Yes boss."

"Kate, I'd like you to continue running the office. I appreciate that I didn't have time to brief you before this meeting but I can see that you've been making notes. If you raise those as actions and liaise with Dean, Charlie and Ed they'll make sure there are no omissions and allocate them to their teams."

"Okay sir."

"And, finally," Matt said, "it has come to my attention that someone has been briefing the press against my express wishes." All eyes looked in Brian Kelly's direction as he opened the door to the incident room. Matt smiled, "Please do come in Brian... That's better... Now, as I was saying; should anyone feel that I'm not capable of leading this investigation I'd be glad to discuss their concerns privately in my office. In the meantime, everything we've discussed must be kept out of the public domain *until I have decided* what should be released... Okay Ladies and Gentlemen I think we've got enough to be getting on with. Brian, if you'd like to join me in my office."

"This is Detective Inspector Brian Kelly," Matt said, to the men from internal affairs. "I'll leave him in your capable hands. Good day gentlemen. Good day Brian." Matt smiled inwardly as he left Kelly to his fate; he needed a cooked breakfast, some time with Rose and a little rest. His next meeting wasn't until 2pm when he expected to be updated with the results obtained by Charlie, Dean and Ed.

At 5pm he would meet, Tony Baraclough, the Press Reporter who'd contacted Joan Armstrong to establish the veracity of Kelly's allegations against him. He was looking forward to that; hopefully he would have something concrete for him; the correct identity of their victim and a probable suspect in Derek Stevens. Baraclough would be the only reporter to get exclusive access. He would give him thirty to forty-five minutes prior to the press conference that Joan had scheduled for 6.30pm; more than enough time to dispel any suggestions of incompetence.

CHAPTER 14

"Hello darling," Rose said, as Matt let himself in through the barn door. "You must be exhausted."

"I'm buzzing at the moment; we're finally getting somewhere and I've managed to get rid of that pain in the wotsit Brian Kelly."

"How did you manage that?"

"He's been talking to the press; must've thought I was stupid. The reporter rang Joan to try and verify what he'd been told; turns out they know each other from prehistoric times. She assured him that I was no fool and persuaded him not to publish anything until we'd met... Well it didn't take a rocket scientist to work out who'd been blabbing so I asked the boys from complaints to interview Brian when he arrived. That didn't take long; apparently he realized he was sunk as soon as they asked for his force mobile. The silly bugger still had the reporter in his contacts list and his call logs showed they'd been talking."

"What's happened to him?"

"He's been suspended pending a full investigation. It'll be the end of his career I expect." She reached up and kissed him. "What's that for?"

"Being so clever."

"I was lucky."

*

"Patricia Stevens?"

"Yes."

"This is Charlie Speck from Kent Police."

"Has something happened to Michael?"

"I'm ringing about your husband Derek?"

"Have you found him?"

"No, but I'd like to come over and talk to you about him."

"Okay dear."

"Can you give me your new address?"

"Cleven Lodge in Sarre Village. Do you know where that is, dear?"

"On the road to Canterbury?"

"That's right... How did you get this telephone number?"

"From the nice couple living in your old house."

"Are they happy there?"

"I think so."

"I used to love living in that old house. All of my happiest memories are there. That was before Michael grew up and Derek disappeared... When would you like to come and see me, dear?"

"This morning."

"You'll have to give me a couple of hours. I've only just got up and I need to make myself presentable." Charlie noted that it was 9:30 already.

"Ten-thirty?"

"Can we make it eleven o'clock?"

"Eleven it is."

"How will I know it's you when you call?"

"I'll be wearing a black suit and I'll show my warrant card."

"Okay dear. See you at eleven."

"One more thing before I go. Do you have Michael's telephone number and address to hand?"

"He'll be at work now, dear."

"Can you tell me where he works?"

"At Brooks the butchers in Canterbury... What do you want him for?"

"We need to talk to him about Derek as well."

"Oh, I see... Can I give you his telephone number and address when you get here. I'd like to make sure that you are a policeman."

"Yes, that'll be fine."

"Good bye then." Charlie heard the handset being replaced on the receiver. He was glad the call was over. Patricia was obviously going to be hard work.

"Ron, Charlie here. I've just spoken with Patricia Stevens… She's a bit dotty but says that her son Michael works at Brooks, the butchers, in Canterbury… I'd like you to interview him as soon as you can; take Audrey with you… Yes, we need the full works; all the background family history and everything he can remember about Derek's disappearance… If you can't drag him away from the shop then straight after work… Make sure you've digested the details in the original missing persons report and cover all of the relevant points in the statement... I'll ring you later to see how you're getting on."

Sunlight flooded through the ancient oaks as Charlie turned onto the sweeping driveway of Sarre Court and absorbed the picturesque gardens fronting the Old Manor House and Cleven Lodge. He was a little early but very conscious of time restraints. He'd have to catch up with the rest of his team and be back at the incident room by 2pm, so that he could update the DCI.

He took a great deal of pride in his work and usually he'd like to devote more than a couple of hours to this type of enquiry. As such, he knew that it would be an exhausting session for him and Patricia. He'd no doubt make some omissions and have to return at a later date to fill in the gaps but it couldn't be helped.

As he let himself into the communal entrance lobby he noticed that it had been re-decorated in a modern style with burgundy walls, white woodwork and new chrome fittings. That was in stark contrast to the passageway leading to Patricia's flat, which reminded him of an asylum; pale green walls decorated with an odd assortment of pictures. He pressed the intercom and heard the electronic catch on the security door buzz. He pushed the door open and a few moments later saw the smiling face of a little woman appear.

"You must be Charlie Speck?"

"That's right," he said, proffering his warrant card. She hardly looked at it.

"You'd better come in." He followed her and soon found her living room. "Cup of tea, dear?"

"That would be lovely; no sugar… Do you mind if we sit at your dining table?"

"Go ahead, dear, make yourself comfortable." Charlie noticed that the flat was very clean, furnished with a large leather sofa, oak dining table and leather backed chairs. The kitchen was towards the back of the living room behind a glazed partition and appeared to be much better equipped than the one he had at home.

"Nice flat you've got here."

"My son found it for me. It was a complete wreck but he did it up and then asked me to move in. I helped with the deposit but he pays the mortgage and I give him a modest rent in return… Now how can I help you Charlie?"

"We're re-investigating the disappearance of your husband."

"Why?"

"Well, it's been two years since the last review and these cases are supposed to be reviewed annually."

"I see."

"I'd like to go over the case again and make some notes."

"Okay."

"Can you tell me what you remember about Derek's disappearance?"

"Well, he was supposed to come home for his supper on the Friday night. I'd cooked his favourite; liver and bacon with chips, mushy peas and onion gravy. Well he was often late on Fridays so I decided to leave it until Saturday but he still didn't come home. He didn't come home on Sunday either and by Monday it was beginning to smell."

"What was?"

"His dinner."

"His dinner?" Charlie repeated.

"That's right dear. I left it in the oven so that I could warm it up for him."

"Then what happened?"

"Well, I was so worried about him that I rang Michael, on his mobile of course. I wouldn't want to use the butcher's number; that might affect their business. Anyway, I think I must have been gabbling because he told me to calm down and put Derek's dinner in the dustbin."

"And then what happened?"

"He said that I should call the police; perhaps Derek had been arrested or involved in an accident. Then I had visions of him lying dead under the wheels of a car and I started crying. Michael volunteered to call the police for me. He's such a good boy you know."

"Do you know where Derek went on Friday?"

"Yes dear. He went drinking in The Admiral Harvey with his best mate Patraicc. They'd been friends ever since they were in the merchant navy. They used to go out with Tommy as well but he died of cancer, a long time ago."

"What was Tommy's last name?"

"Johnson. He was such a nice man."

"And where did he live?"

"Matthews Place, not far from The Admiral."

"Did you speak to Patraicc after Derek went missing?"

"Oh, yes. I rang him on Saturday and he said the last time he saw Derek was on Friday night. I'm not sure that I should tell you this but the landlady, Bernice, had a lock-in after hours. Would you like another cup of tea Charlie?"

"Please."

"What can you tell me about Patraicc?"

"What do you want to know?"

"Where did he live?"

"Before he moved in with Marlene, he used to live in Dickson Road; just around the corner from us."

"Who did he live with?"

"His wife Margaret and his son Robin; that was before they split up."

"What made them split up?"

"I wouldn't like to say. You'll have to ask Margaret and Robin about that."

"Do you know where they're living now?"

"Maidstone, that's all I know. I haven't heard from them in… It must be nearly thirty years."

"Where did Patraicc live after they separated?"

"He stayed in Dickson Road for a long time and then he moved in with Marlene. That was after Derek disappeared, then a few months later they both vanished. Didn't say a word to anyone, just went, haven't heard from them since."

"I understand that Bernice was the last person to see Derek."

"That's right."

"And that was on Saturday the 21 July 2001, at about 1am."

"That's right dear; at least that's what PC Adams told me."

"And what can you tell me about Bernice?"

"She's a brazen hussy, always has been and always will be. She used to boast about having a different man for each night of the week, with weekends off."

"Do you think she was having an affair with Derek?"

"What did you say dear?"

"Do you think she was having an affair with Derek?"

"Would you like another cup of tea dear?"

"Did Derek go to The Admiral often?"

"No dear, just on Friday nights."

"Do you remember what Derek was wearing when he went out on that last Friday?"

"Yes dear, his favourite clothes; a tweed flat cap, tweed jacket, green trousers and brown shoes."

"Did he take anything else with him?"

"His Accurist wristwatch."

"And what did that look like?"

"Silver with a square face and stainless steel bracelet; I bought it for him."

"Anything else?"

"His wallet, Zippo lighter; I bought that as well and his tobacco."

"An overnight bag?"

"No. Nothing else."

"And you haven't seen him since?"

"No dear."

"Any telephone calls or letters?"

"No dear."

"I've been told that Derek and your son had a difficult relationship."

"That's not true. They got on just fine. Of course, Derek did have to tan his backside a couple of times but that was soon forgotten."

"It's been suggested that they didn't get on because your relationship with Derek wasn't good."

"What do you mean, dear?"

"That you and Derek were always fighting."

"What do you mean by fighting?"

"That Derek used to hit you, regularly."

"That's not true. Who's been telling these lies? Derek and I were in a loving relationship." She started to cry. "Why are you saying these awful things about my husband?"

"Have you got any false teeth Patricia?" she started sobbing.

"What's that got to do with Derek going missing?"

"It's been suggested that Derek knocked most of them out."

"That's not true."

"You won't mind signing this Medical Disclosure Form then?"

"I don't mind if I do… There, how's that!" Charlie's mobile vibrated and he removed it from his pocket.

"Sorry, I have to take this." It was a text message from Mark Goddard and the rest of his team. *We've got the search warrant and we're waiting outside.* Charlie replied, *Almost done. Let yourselves in using the drop key and wait in the corridor.*

"Were the police ever called to Tower Hamlets Street when you were living there?" She shook her head. "Didn't the neighbours complain about the noise when you were fighting?" She shook her head again.

"I think you should go now," she mumbled.

"Didn't Michael punch his father on the nose, the day before he joined the marines, because Derek was pulling your hair viciously and daring you to scream?" She turned sideways and looked towards the French windows. Charlie looked at his watch. It was nearly 12:30. The conversation was over. He'd have to return later and re-interview Patricia, before asking for her signature on the statement forms. He'd give her one more opportunity to tell the truth.

"Is there anything you'd like to add Patricia?" She looked at him through tear stained eyes and for a moment he felt sorry for her. She was clearly a victim of domestic violence. These days she'd probably get the help she needed due to their positive arrest policy but in the sixties, seventies, eighties and most of the nineties. He shook his head negatively and closed his notebook.

"I'm sorry if I upset you Patricia but I did need to ask those questions."

"That's okay dear. I know you're only doing your job."

"Some other officers are waiting outside to search your flat for Derek's clothing, his wristwatch, zippo lighter and his wallet. Are any of those items here?"

"No dear." Charlie stood up and when it was proffered shook her hand.

*

"Got everything you need." Mark nodded. "Go gently. She's a little upset at the moment. She's been telling lies… Know what you're looking for?"

"Derek's clothing; his wristwatch, lighter and wallet."

"Don't forget to look for the first six pages of Dorothy's Calendar. I know they're not on the warrant but the contents of a wallet are very small, so you can look everywhere."

"Yes Sarge."

"Ring me if you find anything interesting."

"Sarge."

CHAPTER 15

Matt slept like a dead thing after breakfast.

"Time to get up," Rose said, "it's twelve-thirty."

"Already?"

"The boss told me to wake him at twelve-thirty with a strong coffee, so that's what I'm doing. Come on sit up, you've got ten minutes, then into the shower. I've put your best suit out with a smart shirt, tie and your best shoes. Inspection's at one fifteen; parade's at two, when you'll get your updates; then it's off to meet that press reporter, make sure you knock him for six; then to the television studios for the press conference."

"You're giving me a headache."

"I'm just making sure you're awake."

The incident room was eerily quiet. Matt was pleased; that meant the streets were being worked to progress the enquiry. Charlie, Dean and Ed were on their telephones gathering the final updates from their teams and within five minutes they were hovering by his open door, with Roger and Kate.

"Come in." They crowded into his small office. "OK Dean, you first, what have you found out about Marlene?"

"Maiden name Marlene Thackeray, date of birth: 19 April 1942. Born in Dover to Maria and Peter Thackeray who used to reside in De Burgh Terrace, De Burgh Hill, Dover. She attended Charlton Church of England Primary then Dover Grammar School for girls."

"Go on," Matt said.

"Doctor Poole at The Peter Street Surgery was very helpful. He trawled through her medical records which were in paper format as she hadn't attended the surgery since 2001. He discovered she'd had her left kidney removed in 1982, at the tender age of forty, after it had turned septicaemic."

"How did that happen?"

"Apparently Marlene kept attending the surgery complaining of pain in the kidney region but her urine tests showed she had an STD or sexually transmitted disease. Anyway when they eventually removed the kidney they found it contained a massive stone which had effectively killed the organ."

"Anything else?"

"I checked this information against the Pathology report and it turns out that our Dorothy also had her left kidney removed."

"Go on."

"Doctor Poole sent me along to her dentist in Salisbury Road. He was very helpful and gave me her full dental records on the promise that I would return them if our victim wasn't Marlene Johnson."

"Go on."

"Well I've just returned from the morgue after confirming that Dorothy's teeth matched Marlene's dental records."

"Excellent, so there's no doubt our victim is Marlene Johnson."

"Correct."

"Have you informed the pathologist who conducted the second examination?"

"Yes. He's there now, checking the Home Office work."

"Good, that means we should be able to release Marlene's body as soon as we find her next of kin. How did you get on with that enquiry?"

"Not very well. Both of Marlene's parents are dead and her next of kin was listed as Tommy Johnson."

"I see... How did the rest of your team get on?"

"They went to Matthews Place and interviewed everyone who was in."

"Any luck?"

"Dick interviewed a Mr and Mrs Levan, who are the new occupants of number fifteen. They've only been living there for a couple of years but they rent the place. Dick contacted the landlord, Adrian Lloyd. He remembered Marlene but didn't recognize her from the photo we'd been circulating in the press… He said Marlene was a good tenant and always paid her rent on time but in late December 2001 she missed a payment."

"Did he remember the date?"

"No, we asked him to check his records but he only keeps them for seven years, for tax purposes."

"I see."

"He did remember going there in the first week of January 2002 though. He was planning to read her the riot act as she'd been living there on a very reasonable rent since ninety-six, when he'd purchased the property."

"Go on."

"He owned several properties in Dover and collecting the rent after Christmas was often a problem. He had to pay his lenders on time or there'd be no more money for future investments… Anyway, when he arrived at Marlene's he was surprised to find the house in darkness. He hadn't wanted to arrive too early but didn't want to arrive too late and find that she'd gone out for the day."

"Go on."

"He could hear the doorbell ringing from outside and imagined her hiding inside, behind the drawn curtains, so he started to knock as well. Then he started tapping the glass with a pound coin because he'd forgotten his keys. That apparently attracted the attention of the neighbour at number thirteen, a Mr Angry, who shouted, 'What's all the noise about?' When he explained that he wanted to speak to Marlene Mr Angry suggested that he ring her instead."

"Go on."

"He could hear Marlene's telephone ringing inside but there was still no reply. Then Mr Angry told him the curtains had been drawn for a week and he hadn't seen them since before Christmas. Adrian asked who them was and was informed that someone named Patrick had been living with Marlene."

"Go on."

"He thanked Mr Angry for his help and hoped he would go away but he kept gaping, then Lloyd realized he'd have to go home to retrieve the keys. It was Saturday and he was a bit hung over… The door opened easily when he returned. Letters littered the doormat. It was cold inside. The air was stale and confined. He said that it was a bit creepy. The kitchen was unoccupied; oil floated on the dishwater and the bottled milk had gone sour. He remembered seeing one of the Sunday tabloids in the living room; thinks it was the last issue before Christmas. I've checked the date; that would have been the 23 December 2001."

"Go on."

"He told Dick that he nearly left when the stairs creaked on his way to the landing. The bathroom was freezing; the window was wide open. The box room at the front was tidy with a few men's things hanging from the picture rails. He gingerly pushed open the door to master the bedroom. It was untidy; drawers emptied, wardrobe ajar, women's clothes discarded all over the bed."

"Sounds like Marlene left in a hurry," Matt said.

"That was his conclusion."

"Did he say anything else?"

"He searched the house for a note. There were no letters addressed to him. No rent left by a remorseful tenant; just household bills addressed to Marlene. He did admit finding ninety-five pounds in a money box masquerading as a Baked Beans tin. He pocketed that for safe keeping."

"Sounds like a charming individual."

"Then he contacted his handyman; arranged for the locks to be changed and a clean and tidy up, so he could get it back on the market."

"Sounds all legal and above board," Matt said. "Has anyone spoken to Mr Angry at number thirteen? I assume that's not his real name."

"Apparently he's red, rotund and has a surly face," Dean said. A feeble titter escaped from Kate.

"Time for a cup of tea… I think we should carry on in the main office. It's getting a bit claustrophobic in here."

"That's better. Charlie, how did you get on with Patricia Stevens?"

"I spent a couple of hours interviewing her. I don't think she'd know the truth if it came up and punched her on the nose. She was a bit tearful when I left but agreed to see me again to sign a formal statement."

"Did you take notes?"

"Is the Pope a Catholic?"

"Okay, well just summarize what she had to say."

"What about the search of her premises?"

"It's still on-going. I left Mark in charge of that with the rest of the team."

"What about the son Michael Stevens?"

"He's been located at Brooks the butchers in Canterbury. Ron and Audrey visited him at about ten-thirty this morning. Michael's the branch manager; his assistant's taken the day off to run her elderly mother to the hospital."

"So he's not been interviewed."

"Not yet but he's invited the officers to his home address after work."

"Where does he live?"

"St Mildred's Road, Westgate-on-Sea."

"Do we know anything about that address?"

"Michael's on the voters register but aside from that nothing."

"What are Ron and Audrey doing now?"

"They're sitting in the coffee shop opposite the butchers. They've offered Michael a lift home because he travelled in by train."

"What time do they expect to get going?"

"Michael's going to lock-up at five-thirty; they should be back at his place by six. They'll text me when they get there so that we can sort out the search team."

"Excellent."

"Ed, how did you get on at The Admiral Harvey?"

"Can I take you back a stage so that what I say makes sense?"

"Go on."

"Marlene wasn't a particularly good student when she was at the Dover Grammar School but she was very popular with the boys. She had a brief relationship with Trevor Hazelwood which he finished when she became pregnant. She was just over eighteen. Trevor was also eighteen and a bit of a scoundrel. Marlene's parents didn't approve of him and he didn't want to marry her anyway."

"How did you find that out?"

"When I visited Bernice Roberts at The Admiral Harvey," Ed grinned at Dean and Charlie.

"What's so amusing?"

"Bernice Roberts is now married to Paul Adams, the retired Missing Persons Enquiry Officer," Ed continued, "but it appears that she used to be a bit of a goer herself and was in close competition with Marlene when they were younger. Anyway, she was the one that put us back onto Hazelwood and when I re-interviewed him he admitted having a relationship with Marlene. He didn't tell you because he was hoping we wouldn't find out. He's a respectable married man in his seventies with a forty-two year old Thai wife."

"I'm forming the impression that you find that amusing," Matt said, keeping his expression serious.

"Anyway," Ed continued, "in those days falling pregnant out of wedlock was scandalous so Marlene's parents scouted round for a suitable patsy. They suggested Tommy Johnson, a nice boy who'd dated Marlene on and off before he'd joined the Merchant Navy. Well it appears that Tommy wasn't averse to getting married to Marlene and taking responsibility for the baby, even though it would be obvious to everyone that he couldn't be the father. He was at sea at the time of conception."

"Unless she had the gestation period of a manatee," Roger said.

"A manatee, where the fuck did that come from?" Dean said.

"I studied biology at School."

"Gentlemen please," Matt grinned, "I'm short on time and I don't need to know about the gestation periods of manatees." He noticed Charlie wiping tears away from his eyes with the back of his hand. "Please continue Ed."

"Tommy and Marlene married in December 1960. It was a private affair in the local registry office. Marlene was nearly full term. The only guests were Marlene's parents and Tommy's friends. His parents refused to attend the marriage. Tommy's friends were Patraicc Delaney, his wife Margaret, their baby Robin, Derek Stevens, his wife Patricia and their baby Michael."

"Go on."

"After that it gets a bit sad… Marlene's baby was still-born. Tommy was made redundant in 1972 and he died of lung cancer in 1998."

"What did Paul Adams, the Missing Persons Enquiry officer, say about Derek's disappearance?"

"Unfortunately, he wasn't at The Admiral," Ed said, "apparently he's gone on a Jolly Boys outing to Jersey with a load of old crusties. They're on a chartered yacht somewhere in the English Channel and Bernice isn't expecting a call from him until they reach St Helier on Wednesday morning."

"Great," Matt said, "and what about the archived missing person's form?"

"Can't be found. It was moved to Headquarters earlier in the year, due to more of those unnecessary cutbacks. I've got one of my team at Maidstone kicking the librarian up the arse with his size tens but he's getting nowhere. It's a complete mess with unopened removal boxes from all over the county."

"Bloody politicians, they want a five star service but don't want to pay for it," Charlie said, "and this bloody lot are even worse than John Major's. I remember the last time the conservatives were in government. They ran the police service into the ground."

"Charlie, we can do this another time."

"Roger, how did you get on with the CCTV images?"

"We started by looking at all of the good stuff; full images of people we wanted to trace and interview, minus those we'd already found. Then we worked our way through the partial and grainy images. That didn't produce any positive results; there were no images of anyone resembling Derek. Then we started scraping the barrel and hey presto; we've got a left arm and shoulder dressed in a tweed jacket and a left leg in green trousers with a brown shoe." He handed the images to Matt who looked at them carefully.

"When were these captured?"

"At nineteen-thirty on Bank Holiday Monday, the fourth of June."

"Whereabouts?"

"On the minimarket camera in Market Street."

"Where was the subject?"

"Approaching the camera from the direction of Potter Street."

"How many images have you got?"

"Just the one; the camera at that location is on time-lapse and only takes one image every five seconds."

"So jacket and trousers would have been going in the general direction of Marlene's flat."

"That's right," Roger said.

"Has anyone else admitted being dressed like that?"

"No," Roger said.

"Have any of our witnesses described this individual?"

"No, at seven-thirty most were at home watching the start of the Diamond Jubilee Concert."

"Well ladies, it looks like we've got a man-hunt... Roger I want Derek circulated for the murder of Marlene Johnson straight away."

"Yes boss."

"Well, what are you waiting for?"

CHAPTER 16

"Hello… Michael?"

"Hi Denise… How's your mother?"

"She's doing okay… I'm sorry I didn't ring sooner but it's been a bit chaotic; what with the triage, admission, medical examination and x-rays."

"Where are you now?"

"I'm still at the QEQM in Margate; mum's inside having her wrist set; she's broken it and they think she's got Osteoporosis."

"What's that?"

"It's a disease that causes the bones to become weaker and easily broken."

"Like thinning bones?"

"That's right. How are you getting on without me?"

"We're all thinking of you and Adam's cancelled his fishing trip this afternoon; says he can go another time."

"He's such a darling; please thank him for me… I think we'll have to skip our visit to the Carlton tonight."

"I was going to suggest that but I need to talk to you about something else."

"Michael, you sound so serious. Is something wrong?"

"Two policemen popped into see me this morning. They're re-investigating my father's disappearance; apparently it's just routine, nothing to worry about."

"Did they say how long they'd be?"

"No but it must be serious because they've offered me a lift home after work."

"But I thought your father disappeared years ago?"

"He did."

"So why are they making enquiries now?"

"I don't know. I suppose I'll have to wait to find out."

"Will you ring me later; let me know how you get on?"

"Of course I will... Give my love to your mother and tell her, get well soon... I've ordered some flowers from Vanessa; it's very handy having a florist in the village; give her a call when you get home and she'll pop them round. She hasn't seen Yvonne in ages so it'll be a good excuse to catch up."

"That's very kind of you Michael... You must be her best customer... Perhaps you should buy some shares in her business."

"I was thinking that, just the other day... Love you lots."

"I love you too... Bye."

The journey to Michael's house was light on conversation. After a couple of probing questions about his father he'd realized that it was the police that should be conducting the interview and shut up.

"If you pull up on the right just by the tree stump we shouldn't inconvenience the neighbours," Michael said.

"Okee-cokee," Ron replied, as he expertly slid into the kerb outside a 1980s semi. Seagulls screeched and dull grey skies threatened rain as they stepped out of the car.

"Looks like a nice place," Audrey said, noting they were in a quiet residential street of mixed housing which included Victorian and Edwardian Villas.

"I like it," Michael said, "it's convenient for the town centre and the train station." Michael led them through double gates and past his dark blue Ford Mondeo.

"Have you lived here long?"

"Since ninety-seven, about six months after I retired from the Marines." Ron had to remind himself that he was there to interview a witness but couldn't help noticing that the front door was fitted with multi-locks and the plain panelled door leading into the house only had a Yale. The front door would be a problem for a rapid entry team but the inner door would sail of its hinges. He liked the cut and thrust of modern policing but found routine enquiries and paperwork tedious.

"Can I get you a cup of something?" Michael said.

"Two teas, white without sugar," Audrey said.

"Take a seat. I'll be back in a minute."

"I think you'd better conduct the interview," Ron said, "It'll be good practice for you. Have you got a copy of the interview plan?" Audrey threw a copy at him. "I'll sit on the sofa and listen; to make sure that you don't miss anything."

"That's very generous of you," Audrey said, as she scanned the open planned living rooms. It was minimalist and obviously a bachelor's pad. The view from the bay window into the front garden was pleasing; laid to lawn behind a mixed hedgerow. A large flat screened TV hung from the wall over the fireplace which contained a multi-fuel stove; the sofa was brown leather with matching footstool and the cushion opposite looked lived in. Photographs of Michael in full regalia wearing his campaign medals sat in the chimney recesses above shelving containing a digital recorder and surround sound music system. He appeared to have a complete collection of novels and several hardbacks on the Duke of Wellington.

Audrey took a seat at the dining table, between the lounge and kitchen, and closed the cover on her interview plan when Michael returned. He handed one large mug of tea to Ron and put the others on the dining table, before taking a seat opposite Audrey.

"Now, how can I help you?" he said.

"We're here to re-investigate the disappearance of your father."

"Okay. What do you want to know?"

"Perhaps you can tell me when you last saw him?"

"Third of January seventy-nine."

"That's very precise; how can you be so sure."

"That's the day I left home to join the royal marines and they always ask for your date of joining when you apply for anything."

"Have you spoken to him since then?"

"No."

"Why not?"

"We had a difficult time when I was growing up. His relationship with my mother wasn't good. They were always arguing and fighting and making-up."

"What do you mean by fighting?"

"He used to hit her regularly: mostly where it didn't show; on her arms, legs and back. When things got really bad and he was drunk he'd forget and punch her in the face."

"What were the arguments about?"

"His dinner not being on the table when he walked in, the house being untidy, the way she looked, what she was wearing, the way she spoke to him. You name it, there was always an excuse."

"What do you mean by making-up?"

"She was desperately worried that he would leave her and was very clingy, like an abused bitch looking for her master's approval. He'd knock her about and then they'd go into the bedroom for sex... I didn't know what sex was but one of the boys at school brought a strop mag into class to show me."

"I see... Can you describe the noises you heard coming from the bedroom?"

"Well, let's just put it this way; they weren't gentle, like you see in the movies."

"Are you suggesting that your father was raping your mother?"

"Well as far as I'm aware, they never had sex without violence... If you want to know whether he raped her, you'll have to ask her. It's not something we've discussed."

"Was their relationship always like that?"

"No, it was very different when my father was in the navy. He was away at sea most of the time and when he came home he was pleased to see us. He used to take us on day trips to the seaside. We used to visit his best friends Patraicc and Tommy and do things with their families. Have picnics in the garden, go to the park and play on the swings, go to the cinema, to Dreamland in Margate, go cycling and swimming; all those sorts of things."

"Which navy was he in?"

"The merchant."

"Do you remember when he left?"

"Well, I was eleven; born in September nineteen-sixty so I reckon it must have been late December seventy-one."

"Do you remember the name of the vessel that he served on?"

"The Lady Irene but he always called her The Lady… I think my mother's got a framed photograph of her somewhere."

"Do you remember why he left?"

"I think he was made redundant with Tommy and Patraicc."

"And what did he do for a living after that?"

"He was a bit of a wheeler-dealer."

"What did he sell?"

"Mostly duty free cigarettes."

"Where did he get those from?"

"I'm sure you can work that out for yourself." Audrey paused and read through her notes. Michael studied her. She was about thirty years old; with straight strawberry blonde hair touching her shoulders. Her skin was pale and decorated with freckles. Her gingery eyebrows were plucked; black mascara coloured her eyelashes above deep green eyes. She had a thin nose, generous lips, gleaming white teeth and a dimple in her slightly protuberant chin. She was very attractive, power dressed in a navy pin-striped jacket and matching skirt; her armour Michael concluded, a substitute for her uniform, hiding her insecurities. He looked at Ron; no insecurities there. The professional was nodding like a Texan oil well.

"I think your partner could do with a coffee," Michael said.

Audrey resisted the urge to kick Ron.

"Wake up you lazy bastard."

"What's happened? Where's he gone?"

"To make you a coffee."

"I wasn't sleeping. I was just resting my eyes."

"You'll be resting your eyes permanently if you fall asleep again."

"Keep your knickers on."

"I think you'd better sit at the dining table with us, Ron."

Michael returned with the coffees.

"You said earlier that your father was always knocking your mother about."

"That's right."

"Why didn't you call the police when they were fighting?"

"We didn't have to. The neighbours called you the first time they had a fight to complain about the noise."

"And then what happened?"

"PC Plod arrived and spoke to my father. He was very polite and even invited Plod in for a cup of tea. It was as if they were best mates and nothing had happened... They had a nice cosy chat in the living room whilst my mother scurried about making tea and biscuits. Derek admitted they'd been squabbling and promised to apologize to the neighbours in the morning; then in front of my father Plod asked my mother if she was alright. She nodded of course and that was the end of that. Plod drank his tea and made small talk with my father. He didn't even ask if there were any children in the house. He just left. I think it must've been close to his knocking- off time."

"Well, we certainly do things very differently nowadays. We have a positive arrest policy for domestic violence."

"I know all about that," Michael said. "PC Adams filled me in."

"Did your father ever get in touch with you after you left home?"

"No, he wouldn't speak to me because I floored him and wouldn't apologize."

"What do you mean?"

"On my last night at home, he pulled my mum's hair viciously and made her scream. I lost my temper and punched him on the nose. He landed on his backside; banged his head on a doorframe and passed out."

"When did you first realize that your father had gone missing?"

"When my mother telephoned me."

"What day was that?"

"It was on a Monday."

"Do you remember the date?"

"No. It was ten or eleven years ago. You must have a note on your file." Michael stared at Ron. "PC Adams was a very diligent officer." The implied criticism was wasted on Ron. Audrey coloured once more. Michael concluded that Ron was either thick, thick-skinned or both.

"Monday 23 July 2001?"

"If you say so."

"Where were you when you received the call?"

"At Brooks in Canterbury."

"What did your mother say?"

"That she was worried about my father... He hadn't been home since leaving for work on Friday morning... Something about his dinner still being in the oven... She was very upset so I contacted the local police."

"Then what happened?"

"Well, they had no record of him being arrested or involved in an accident so they sent PC Adams over to mum."

"And?"

"I went to see her after work. PC Adams was still there. He told me he'd established that Derek was in The Admiral Harvey on Friday night with Patraicc until closing time."

"And?"

"Then he left to interview, Bernice, the landlady and my father's best friends, Patraicc and Marlene."

"And what happened after that?"

"Eventually we found out that Derek had left the pub at about 1am on the Saturday morning."

"That would be Saturday 21 July 2001?"

"If you say so."

"Where do you think your father is now?"

"I've no idea. I heard the police were making enquiries in France."

"Why would they be doing that?"

"Because my father went missing quite a few times after he left the navy and implied he had another family over there."

"Did he tell you that?"

"No, that's what he told the police."

"Do you have any of his possessions?"

"No, my mother hung onto those but most of his possessions went to the charity shop when she moved into her flat?"

"Any keep-sakes or mementos?"

"No, nothing; look do you think this is going to take much longer?"

"A couple of hours I should think."

"In that case, can we take a break? I'm starving. I've been working all day and was planning to have fish and chips for dinner."

"That's a good idea, Audrey. Why don't we all have something to eat? I could walk up to the chippy with Michael."

CHAPTER 17

The Press Room was like a premier football stadium; all seats were taken. There was a murmur of anticipation from the crowd but the dais was still vacant. Several reporters looked at their watches impatiently ticking off the minutes whilst others studied their tablets and mobile phones.

"Ready?" Joan said. Matt nodded; the room fell silent as he entered.

"Good evening Ladies and Gentlemen," Matt said. "Thank you for coming to this press conference… I'm going to start by reminding everyone why we are here." Matt looked around the room to make sure that he had everyone's attention… "On Sunday the tenth of June 2012 police were called to the top flat above Regal Estates in Market Street Sandwich. At that location they found the body of a seventy year old woman who had clearly been murdered. She was known locally as Dorothy Skinner. She'd been residing in her flat since the thirtieth of June 2010. " Matt paused to make sure those making notes were keeping up and when their pens stopped he continued. "Today, the Home Office Pathologist was asked to re- examine the victim's body and compare her with the medical and dental records of another. The outcome of that examination was positive and we now know that the victim was actually Marlene Johnson… Her maiden name was Thackeray. She was born on the nineteenth of April 1942 and used to reside in Matthews Place, Dover. This is a photograph of the victim when she was much younger, probably in her thirties." Joan smiled at Matt to indicate he should carry on. "Unfortunately the next of kin shown on her medical records died some years ago and we've been unable to trace any other relatives. I would therefore ask anyone who is related to her to contact the Incident Room as soon as possible." Matt sipped from a glass of water.

"Why are you showing us this photograph, Chief Inspector?"

"Because we'd like to hear from anyone who knew her: anyone at all; no matter how long ago."

"What else can you tell us about Marlene Johnson, Chief Inspector?"

"She was living with this man, Patraicc Delaney," a new photograph popped up on the screen, "before leaving Matthews Place. We'd like to speak to Patraicc or anyone else who knows where she went between December 2001 and June 2010. We'd also like to know why she changed her name."

*

Keith Burns was dumbfounded. He hadn't seen that ugly bastards' face for forty years; Patraicc Delaney... So that was his name; suddenly he was a fifteen year old boy again. He'd just cycled up the hill, leaned his bike against the outside wall and rushed into the public toilet on the Dover Road. He'd noticed that someone had been decorating the walls, as he'd emptied his bladder. There were half a dozen raunchy ladies, in a one foot border above the Vitreous China urinal, including one with her legs wide open. Those on either side displayed their buttocks and boobs. MORE THIS WAY directed the reader into the toilet cubicle.

As he put his penis away he realized that he wasn't alone; Patraicc was filling the space between him and the outside world.

"Do you like those paintings?"

He coloured and said, "They're okay."

"They're even better in here," Patraicc said, as he guided him towards the cubicle. When he looked inside he noticed the images were of men having sex. In that instant he understood Patraicc's intention. He backed away. Patraicc tried to push him into the cell. He'd caught him off balance. At first he was easy to guide: then he struck a devastating blow; left hand over right clenched fist driving an elbow under Patraicc's ribs. A loud crack, then the bastard squealed in agony and reeled away.

Patraicc recovered quickly, too quickly. He blocked the exit and shouted, "Get in there, you little faggot." The bastard didn't notice he was up on his toes and couldn't avoid his first punch. It landed solidly on his nose. Keith could still smell the scent of fresh blood. He watched him stagger away. His fists struck again in quick succession. He was terrified and wild with anger but his father had taught him how to look after himself. He'd never expected anything like this to happen but his fury was tempered by his training and strong sense of self preservation. As his fists struck Patraicc's face he knew he could kill him. He'd heard his ribs crack with the first blow and now his face was covered in blood. He struck again at the ribs on the right side and grinned when the bastard squealed; several upper cuts and another blow to that rib finished him. Patraicc banged his head on the rolled edge of the urinal as he fell; his left hand dipped into the wet trough. Keith stood over him; kicked him in the genitals, stamped on his face and heard the cold water from the toilet cistern discharge as he left.

He pedalled furiously for about a mile before he heard the vans' engine roar. He'd sensed him coming and rammed his bike into the hedgerow. He heard a loud crack as the van came to an abrupt halt and Patraicc's head smashed into the windscreen. He ran through the new wheat grasses and didn't look back until he reached the high ground on the other side. He was sore; his bare arms and legs had been torn to shreds by the hawthorn. The Transit van was gone. He recovered his bike and went home. He didn't tell anyone about the incident in the public toilet; he didn't want to be labelled a victim or a pervert.

*

"Chief Inspector, do you have a suspect now that you've identified the victim?"

"Yes we do." A murmur of excitement filled the room. "This is a photograph of Derek Stevens; date of birth: 13 March 1937. We believe that it was taken in 2001 when he was in his sixties. He used to reside in Tower Hamlets Street, Dover and socialize with Marlene Johnson and Patraicc Delaney."

"Can you tell us anything else about him, Chief Inspector?"

"His wife reported him missing some time ago. The last sighting of him was at 1am on Saturday 21 July 2001, when he left The Admiral Harvey in Bridge Street Dover."

"Where has he been for the last eleven years?"

"We'd like him to come forward to answer that question."

"What advice can you give to anyone who knows of his whereabouts?"

"Please don't approach him. He may be dangerous. If you do know where he is, dial 999 and ask for the police."

"Anything else?"

"If you can give any background information whatsoever, please contact the incident room or if you wish to remain anonymous Kent Crimestoppers on 0800 55****."

Keith dialled the number. He wanted to help but needed to speak with someone before giving up his identity.

CHAPTER 18

"Hello Charlie... Audrey here."

"How are you getting on?"

"We're just taking a break... Ron's taken Michael to the Fish & Chip shop. They should be back in a minute."

"What's Michael like?"

"He seems okay... He's been very patient and answered all of my questions."

"How far have you got?"

"I'm about half way through."

"So you'll need a couple more hours?"

"It's six thirty now so I'd hope to be finished by eight."

"I'll have the search team waiting outside... How are you getting on with Ron?"

"He talks a good job but frankly, he's a waste of space."

Audrey felt refreshed after the break. The fish and chips had gone down nicely.

"Ready to carry on Michael?"

"I am but I can't imagine what else you need to know."

"You said earlier that your father was in the merchant navy serving on a ship called The Lady Irene."

"That's right."

"What was his job on The Lady?"

"He was their chef and their first aider."

"Was he a good cook?"

"He was a fantastic cook and an accomplished first aider."

"Really?"

"By all accounts he could've been a medic, if he'd had the right education and background. He used to read medical journals avidly, like you or I would read a novel."

"What did his friends Patraicc and Tommy do?"

"They were proper seamen."

"And where did they live after they were made redundant?"

"Tommy lived with his wife, Marlene, in Matthews Place and Patraicc lived in Dickson Road with his wife Margaret and my best friend Robin."

"Do you know where they are now?"

"My mother told me that Tommy died of cancer."

"What about Marlene and Patraicc?"

"I don't know where they are. Look, when I left Dover it was to start a new life. I wasn't happy there; it was a dump and I had no intention of going back."

"But you did go back?"

"Occasionally, to visit my mother."

"Can you tell me what your relationship was like with Marlene and Tommy when you were growing up?"

"They were my Dad's friends. I used to call her Auntie Marlene, though strictly speaking we weren't related and I used to call him Uncle Tommy. It was less formal than Mr and Mrs Johnson but still showed respect for their seniority."

"And what did you do with them?"

"We used to go out for picnics, go to the park, to the cinema, the beach, cycling, swimming; those sort of things."

"Anything else?"

"Robin and I used to sleep-over from time to time."

"When was that?"

"When we were in our teens and before Robin went away."

"Why did Robin go away?"

"Because his parents split up."

"And where did he go?"

"He went with his mother Margaret; to her parents in Maidstone."

"Did you keep in touch?"

"No."

"Why not, he was your best friend?"

"Margaret didn't want anything to do with us and communication wasn't so easy in those days; people did have telephones but there were no mobiles and no internet, so it was telephone or write a letter. If you telephoned the adults picked up the receiver and if you wrote, your letter could be intercepted."

"Do you know where they are now?"

"Margaret's still living in Maidstone, in her parent's house."

"How do you know that?"

"After I retired from the marines Robin and I met by chance whilst I was working at Brooks. It was remarkable really; all those lost years just fell away and we were teenagers again enjoying each other's company. Well, we've been friends ever since. We get together about once a month for a barbeque with the family or a trip to the seaside, that sort of thing. He's got a gorgeous wife named Sabrina and two beautiful children, Rachel and Maxwell. Quite frankly, he's a lucky so and so."

"Where does he live?"

"In Sittingbourne."

"Address?"

"I'll have to check my address book… Westerham Road. Look, why do you need to know all this stuff about Marlene, Tommy, Patraicc and Robin?"

Audrey considered her answer.

"Because the woman murdered in Market Street, Sandwich, during the Diamond Jubilee Celebrations, was Marlene Johnson."

Michael was silent as the gravity of that statement sunk in.

"But I thought that was someone named Dorothy Skinner."

"No. It was Marlene Johnson."

The room was silent once again save for the breathing of the three individuals present.

"How do you know it's Marlene?"

"We've checked her dental and medical records."

"I see. So there's no doubt?"

"None."

"I'm sorry."

"What for?"

"Being impatient earlier, I didn't realize you were investigating a murder."

"Does that change things?"

"No. I still don't know where my father is… Are you sure it's Marlene?"

"Absolutely."

"So why are you asking me questions about my father?"

Michael felt that he was being scrutinized by the deep green searchlights within the constable's face…

"Because we think he might be responsible for Marlene's murder."

Those words remained suspended in the air for some time while Michael considered their significance and looked steadily at Audrey.

"So where is he, Michael?"

"I've already told you what I know about his disappearance. I've no idea where he is."

"So you won't mind if we search your house for his possessions?"

"Of course not, I don't have anything belonging to him."

"And question your neighbours."

"Of course not, I've got nothing to hide."

"We might question the whole town."

Michael immediately thought of Denise. Their relationship was still in its infancy and he wondered if it would survive the police intrusion.

"Can I ring my girlfriend?"

"Why do you want to do that?"

"Because she's had a rough day; her mother had a fall this morning and broke her wrist. She's been at QEQM for most of the day. They think she's got

Osteoporosis and I don't want her finding out about this from anyone else."

Audrey paused before responding.

"What's your girlfriend's name?"

"Denise Summers."

"And where does she live?"

"In St Nicholas-at-Wade."

"Telephone number?"

"What do you need that for?"

"We might need to speak with her. *This is a murder enquiry.*"

"Can I take this," Michael said, when his mobile started ringing.

"Of course you can; you're not in custody," Ron replied.

"Hi Denise, I was just about to ring you. How's your mother."

"Fortunately she's in bed."

"You don't sound very happy."

"I've just seen the news."

Michael looked at the clock on his digital recorder. It read 20:00.

"So you know the police are looking for my father."

"I already knew that but you didn't tell me he was wanted for that awful murder in Sandwich."

"I've only just found out myself."

"But they've been interviewing you for hours, Michael."

"I know but they only told me a few minutes ago and wouldn't let me ring you until they had your details."

"I see. Do you think he did it?"

"I don't know… He and Marlene were good friends but that was a long time ago."

"They must have some evidence though."

"They haven't told me anything."

"What are you doing now?"

"They're still here, searching my house."

"Why are they doing that?"

"They seem to think I might be harbouring him or know of his whereabouts."

"That's ridiculous; you haven't seen him for years, have you?"

"Not since I left home… Denise, I hope this isn't going to spoil things."

"No Michael… It's not… I was upset when you didn't ring me but now I've heard your voice I'm feeling a lot better."

"Why are you crying then?"

"I don't know; relief probably, that you haven't turned into that monster. Will you ring me when the police finish?"

"Of course."

"And, Michael, the flowers are lovely."

"Everything okay?" Ron said. Michael nodded. "You should expect a few more calls before this evening's over." Michael looked around the room; four officers were searching his house, working in pairs. One from each pair was rummaging while the other looked over his partners shoulder to make sure nothing was missed. They were being very thorough and Michael realized that it might take several hours to search the whole house.

"Would you like a cuppa Ron?"

"Please." They adjourned to the kitchen.

"So how long have you been a murder detective?"

"This is my first proper case. I've been involved with a few others but this is the first sticker; all the others were rolled up within twenty four hours." Michael's mobile rang again. It was his mother this time. He looked at Ron who nodded his assent.

"Hello mum."

"Hello Michael. I'm not very pleased with you. I've had the police here for most of the day, questioning me about your father. They've said some terrible things about him, beating me up, knocking my teeth out, having affairs. I'm not happy Michael; it seems they got most of those ideas from you."

"Well you didn't have the perfect relationship, did you?"

"It suited me and I don't remember you complaining when you were younger."

"Come off it mum; he wasn't a saint."

"And neither were you. I can remember you stealing biscuits from the pantry Michael. I never told your father because he would've taken the skin off your backside. And now they want him for murder and you're making things worse by telling terrible stories about him. I'm not sure I'll ever want to speak to you again. Don't ring me Michael. I need some time to calm down." He heard her sobbing before she replaced the handset. Ron raised a questioning eyebrow.

"My mother," Michael said.

It was just after ten when Robin rang.

"Hello Robin... You've seen the news then... The police are here searching my house... They seem to think I might know where he is... I expect they'll want to interview you as well... About my father, yours and auntie Marlene... Yes, I know you can't help but they'll want to speak with you just the same." Michael noticed that Ron was hovering. "Did you want to speak with Robin?" Ron nodded.

"Hello, Robin, this is Detective Constable Ronald Stanbridge from Operation Carnegie; investigating the murder of Marlene Johnson... I understand that you used to know Marlene... Where will you be during the day tomorrow... At work; where? The Continental Metal Recycling Centre, Ridham Dock, Kemsley Fields Business Park... Telephone number? 01795******. Thanks very much... Do you want to speak to Michael again?" Ron handed Michael's mobile back to him.

"I'll ring you tomorrow." Michael said. His telephone rang again as he terminated the call. "Hello Denise... Yes, they're still here... Is Yvonne okay? Good; I'll pick you up in the morning; usual time... Bye... I love you too."

CHAPTER 19

It had all seemed so simple when he'd met Tony Baraclough, in the piano bar of The Lancaster Hotel. Spill the beans about Derek, the name that appeared on Dorothy Skinner's calendar against the 4 June 2012, the date she'd been so brutally murdered in her bed. Baraclough would surely see his superior's error in withholding that information from the press for five weeks and he would publish a scathing article criticizing the police investigation.

He and Detective Chief Inspector Matt Sanderson would be called before Detective Chief Superintendent Baxter. Sanderson would be on the back foot defending himself and Detective Inspector, soon to be Detective Chief Inspector Brian Kelly, would remind Sanderson of all the times he'd said the name Derek should have been publicized. He'd imagined the chief privately persuading Matt that it was time to take his retirement and offering him the opportunity to act up as Operation Carnegie's DCI.

How differently it had turned out. He'd known that something was wrong when he'd arrived at the station. The yard was already packed, even though the weekly briefing wasn't due to start until 8am. His concern had been heightened as he'd let himself through the outer security door and made his way up towards the first floor. He wondered what was going on. He could hear his DCI speaking, as if to a packed office. As he'd tapped the number into the keypad to gain access to the incident room he'd been able to see Matt looking at him through the wired glass panel. It was obvious that the morning briefing was in progress and he'd been excluded. He'd felt his bile rising as he pushed the inner fire door open.

"And, finally," Matt had said, "it has come to my attention that someone has been briefing the press against my express wishes." All eyes had looked in his direction. Matt had smiled and continued, "Please do come in Brian… That's better… Now, as I was saying; should anyone feel that I'm not capable of leading this investigation I'd be glad to discuss their concerns privately in my office." He'd felt his face redden as he'd realized that he'd been rumbled. "In the meantime, everything we've discussed must be kept out of the public domain until I have decided what should be released… Okay Ladies and Gentlemen I think we've all got enough to be getting on with. Brian, if you'd like to join me in my office."

He'd recognized the type when he'd entered the DCI's office and saw the men in grey suits. He'd done a stint in Complaints himself, when he'd been climbing the promotion ladder. He hadn't given a second thought to the careers he'd ruined on the way to becoming a Detective Inspector. Now it was his turn and he felt like a swimmer drowning under the bows of a super tanker.

"This is Detective Inspector Brian Kelly," Matt had said to the men from internal affairs. "I'll leave him in your capable hands. Good day gentlemen. Good day Brian." They'd stripped him of his warrant card and mobile phone; extracted his confession; there was no point denying it; suspended him and told him to go home.

The humiliation had become unbearable when he'd watched Sanderson putting on his best performance at the subsequent press briefing. There was nothing left for him in Kent. His one bedroomed love nest was rented. He didn't think he'd be able to spend another night there, with or without Kate. It was time to leave this episode of his life behind, return to his family in Clapham and salvage what he could of his career. In a burst of gay abandon he'd gunned his Harley Davidson all the way up Detling Hill, raced past the Kent Country showground and plummeted down the other side. He hadn't noticed the slick from the burst water main until it was too late; now all he could see was his rider-less Harley Davidson, trapped and screaming under the crash barrier, an empty road and his blood stained boots.

*

Perspiration peppered Robin's brow. His heart raced. His arms were pinned to his sides. Legs rooted to the spot. Flight was the instinct that overwhelmed him. His heart missed a beat and he cried out in terror.

"Wake up Robin." A hand shook him vigorously and he kicked out, striking something solid. "Ouch! Wake up Robin, you're having a nightmare." Robin surfaced. The quilt was wet and tightly wound about his upper body…The tension slowly seeped away as he realized that he was safe in his own bed with his wife, Sabrina.

"I'm sorry," he said.

"What was it this time?"

"I was trying to run away from someone but something was holding me back."

"Mum, is Dad okay," Rachel said, standing in the open doorway with her younger brother, Maxwell.

"Yes, he's just had a nightmare... Go back to bed. It's not time to get up."

"Who was chasing you?" Sabrina said.

"I don't know," Robin lied.

"Go back to sleep. I'll rub your back."

"It's my leg that needs soothing."

Robin lay awake with eyes closed. He knew exactly what he was running from. It was always the same dream. He was visiting Brooks in Canterbury when he saw Derek, dressed in a green trilby, white shirt, green tie and overalls; sharpening a knife behind the counter. Fear overwhelmed him; he tried to run but his feet wouldn't move. It was as if they were set in concrete. His legs buckled and mistiness filled his brain. He could hear the blood flowing through his ears, loud like the sound of an underground train running through a tunnel. Michael caught him as he fell and cradled him in his arms.

"Wake up Robin... It's me Michael." Robin felt himself being drawn back towards the light. His mind rejected this information; he was a child again and whispered,

"Don't hurt me Uncle Derek."

"It's me Michael; not Derek. I know I look like him but I'm nothing like him." That had been fifteen years ago, just after Michael had been discharged from the Royal Marines. They'd grown fond of each other since. Michael visited about once a month; sometimes they'd have wonderful picnics in the garden and in the winter Sabrina would cook a roast. The meat always came from Brooks and Michael ensured they got the best cuts.

CHAPTER 20

Matt couldn't sleep. The telephone call from Headquarters had disturbed him. Brian Kelly had been involved in a serious accident and was in hospital fighting for his life. Matt lay awake and wondered if he were somehow responsible. Eventually he decided to get up and after taking a long shower drove into the office through a milky sunrise.

The incident room was quiet. The lighting had been dimmed. A few ghostly spectres tapped away on computer keyboards whilst others slumped in their chairs. Kate was the first to acknowledge Matts' presence with a "Good moaning".

"Hi Kate," Matt said quietly. "How's it going?"

"We had quite a good response to your appeal."

"Really?"

"It seems Derek Stevens is quite a common name. We've had twenty seven nominations during the night. We've been able to eliminate the local ones but we're reliant on other forces to conduct the initial research on the ones outside our force area."

"So how many does that leave?"

"Twenty four."

"I think we'll pass those onto Kelly's old team. They're very keen on Dereks."

"What do you think they'll do to him?" Kate said.

"Why don't we pop into my office?"

Matt was surprised when Kate burst into tears. He'd no idea that she and

DI Kelly were intimate.

"Can I go and see him?" she said.

"I don't think that's a good idea Kate; at least not for the moment. He's very ill and the hospital's only allowing visits from close relatives. Why don't you let him recover a little and then pay him a visit with some of your mates from the office?"

"But I love him. I must go and see him."

"They won't let you in Kate. You're not related so you've no rights."

"I could tell them I was his sister or something."

"You're not thinking clearly Kate. How long would it take his wife to find out and then what are you going to say. I'm his lover; his mistress; his bit on the side? Do you think that's going to help his recovery? No, I think it's best to stay away and visit later, when he's feeling better." She nodded and then looked at him through tear-stained eyes.

"Does anybody else need to know about this conversation?"

"Of course not… Does anyone else know about this relationship?"

"I don't think so. Brian always insisted on being very discreet."

"Well let's keep it that way. Come and talk to me if you have any problems. Okay."

"Yes sir; thank you sir."

Matt was in a sunny corner of the station yard, smoking, when Charlie found him.

"Shit the bed?"

"Good morning to you too."

"You're in early."

"Brian Kelly. Again."

"What's he done this time?"

"Tried to kill himself on Detling Hill… Was putting that flash Harley through its paces and came off in style. He's in intensive care at Maidstone. Critical."

"Does his wife know?"

"The Mets sent an officer round and they drove her to the hospital."

"Have you spoken to her?"

"No and I don't think I should. Normally I really feel it when one of ours is seriously injured or killed; in this country or overseas but on this occasion I don't feel anything. He's just another scumbag, only interested in himself, so how can I offer my condolences?" Charlie didn't respond immediately.

"Do you think he's told his wife about your disagreements?"

"Probably," Matt said.

"Would you like me to speak with her?"

"If you don't mind."

"I'll try before I knock off and let you know how I get on."

"How did you get on last night?"

"We finished interviewing Michael Stevens at about eight."

"Did he have anything interesting to say?"

"He said that his father's relationship with his mother was a violent one which revolved around Derek's appetite for control."

"Good, so we've established that Derek was violent, in the domestic setting at least… Anything else?"

"He was the chef on a ship called The Lady Irene, when Michael was born, and he was the ships' first aider."

"That's interesting."

"Apparently he could've been a medic, if he'd had the right education and background, and he used to read medical journals like they were novels."

"So he'd probably know how to perform a tracheotomy?"

"I should think so."

"Anything else?"

"Derek was made redundant in late 1971 and went into the smuggling business with Tommy and Patraicc."

"What were they smuggling?"

"Duty Free cigarettes."

"Hence the Calais connection. Anything else?"

"He re-iterated not seeing his father since he left home in 1979."

"Confirming what he told Paul Adams?"

"That's right. Audrey did a good job. There's a lot of detail concerning family background; his relationships with Marlene and Tommy, Patraicc, his wife Margaret and their son Robin. His statement's on your desk with the results of the other enquiries."

"Anything come of the searches?"

"No, we didn't find anything."

"Okay Charlie, send your team home. I'd like them back at three to conduct house to house, in Sarre Village initially and then Westgate-on-Sea. Let's see what we can find out about the Stevens family."

The office was quiet. Kate and Roger's teams had been sent home with Charlie's; Dean's were working through the house-to-house enquiries in Dover; Ed's were contacting all the witnesses who'd been traced in Sandwich, with a view to finding any who might remember seeing flat cap man. That enquiry was going surprisingly well, in a negative sort of way, as most could remember exactly where they were at the beginning of the Diamond Jubilee Concert.

After reading through some of the reports on his desk Matt rang Customer Services at Dover District Council. He and the Coroners' officer had spoken to them several times before about a public burial for Dorothy, as no relatives could be found.

"Hi Marilyn; Matt Sanderson speaking… I'm ringing regarding the funeral arrangements that we've made for Dorothy Skinner this Friday… Are you aware that we've now identified her as Marlene Johnson? …You are, good. Okay, I've been told that her late husband Tommy Johnson died in 1998 and was buried in The Old Charlton Cemetery. Would you run their names through your database? I'd like to locate Tommy's grave and find out if she's purchased a grave space… I'll hold."

"Sorry to disturb you Matt."

"Come in Ed. I could do with a break anyway."

"We've just received this report from Crimestoppers. It's about Patraicc Delaney. Apparently he tried to entice a fifteen year old boy into a toilet cubicle for gay sex back in 1972."

"Where was the toilet?"

"It was a public convenience on the Dover Road between Dover and Deal. According to the source it isn't there anymore."

"What was his modus operandi?"

"He followed the fifteen year old into the toilet, engaged him in conversation about some raunchy paintings of women above the urinal and guided him into the cubicle where there were paintings of men having gay sex. When the boy realized what Patraicc was about he decided to leave. Patraicc tried to stop him. There was a set too and the boy gave him a good hiding before cycling off. He was subsequently run off the road by Patraicc who was driving a navy blue transit van, a bit like one of our old meat wagons."

"Did the boy make a complaint?"

"No, he was worried about being labelled a victim or a pervert."

"What's his position now?"

"He still wishes to remain anonymous." Ed passed the docket to Matt who studied it carefully.

"This enquiry has more twists than a helter-skelter. Leave it with me." Matt dialed the direct number for DC Boyle, the contact at Crimestoppers.

"Hello sir. I thought you'd find that report interesting… No, the source wasn't willing to disclose his personal details… He did give a contact telephone number and we provided him with a pseudonym."

"Would you ring him on my behalf and let him know that I'd really like to speak to him, confidentially of course. I'll give you my office and mobile numbers."

"Sorry to disturb you again," Ed said, "there's a solicitor on the telephone; sounds very cultured. He's asking for you personally." Matt hated solicitors, like the press they often frustrated his enquiries but what really pissed him off were there incredible salaries. How could anyone be worth three hundred pounds a bloody hour; the Prime Minister didn't command that sort of remuneration and he was running the country for Christ Sake.

"What does he want?"

"He wouldn't tell me but said you'd be interested."

"Okay, put him through."

"DCI Matt Sanderson."

"Paul Smythe, Bentley, Rolls and Smythe Solicitors."

"Smith: obviously a junior partner," Matt thought.

"How can I help you?"

"It's more of a question of how can I help you officer."

"Go on."

"My firm is in possession of certain documents that might be of interest to your enquiry." Smythe was already irritating Matt with his airs and graces.

"Go on."

"Well a certain lady attended our practice in January 2002."

"Go on."

"One Marlene Johnson to be precise."

"Go on."

"She wanted to make a Will and sought our advice."

"And?"

"Well, it's here in our offices at Folkestone; quite frankly we didn't recognize her when you were circulating the photograph of Dorothy Skinner but when you circulated her under her correct name, Marlene Johnson, and showed the earlier photograph the penny dropped. We realized the deceased was one of our clients."

"Can you tell me what's in her Will?"

"The partners and I discussed that this morning with the only beneficiary and as they have no objection I can send you a copy."

"Who was the beneficiary?"

"The King Georges' Fund for Sailors."

"Never heard of them."

"It was established in 1917 and is now known as Seafarers UK. It's the UK's leading charity for seafarers in need; in fact we helped her choose The King Georges' Fund."

"Why did she choose that particular charity?"

"When we were taking instructions she said she had no family to leave money to so she wanted to do something for the Merchant Navy; you see her husband Tommy was a sailor and so were her best friends. They found it really difficult settling into civvie street when they were made redundant and nobody offered them any assistance."

"Why didn't they go to Seafarers UK?"

"God knows; ignorance probably."

"Anything else in her will?"

"Her funeral arrangements."

"Which are?"

"She wishes to be buried with her husband Tommy Johnson in The Old Charlton Cemetery in Dover. She's paid Dover District Council for her plot. Her choice of prayers, hymns and music. What she'd like to be buried in, clothing wise. There's specific mention of her wedding ring. She wanted the service to take place in the cemetery's chapel. Her choice of flowers and the inscription for her headstone."

"Did she leave any money to pay for those things?"

"She purchased a top of the range funeral plan at the time of signing her Will to cover the full cost of her funeral arrangements."

"And her legacy?"

"She appointed our firm to act as the executors of her Will but you're probably in a much better position than I to judge whether there will be a legacy."

'And a fat-fee for your firm,' Matt thought.

"Where was she living when she made her Will?"

"In Matthew's Place, Dover."

"Did you correspond with her at that address?"

"No, we did everything within the office. She came seeking our advice, liked what we had to say, instructed us to produce the Will, returned the next day, signed it and left it in our safe custody."

"How did she pay for the work and the funeral plan?"

"Now that was unusual; she turned up with nearly five thousand pounds in cash."

"Probably part of the proceeds of her husband Tommy's smuggling activities with Derek and Patraicc," Matt thought. He made a note to instigate Financial Investigations into each of their affairs.

"Did she list any guests to be invited to the funeral service?"

"Two; their names will please you; Derek Stevens and Patraicc Delaney."

"Did she provide their contact details?"

"Two telephone numbers 0776739****, for Derek, and 0788031****, for Patraicc." Matt noted the numbers. He handed them to Ed with a note to run them through their database and if there was no trace initiate subscribers' checks. Ed nodded and left the room.

"What was her choice of music?"

"Just one song, 'Only the Lonely,' by Roy Orbison." Matt knew it well. It was released in the year that he was born; his father used to play it regularly when he was growing up.

CHAPTER 21

Matt was standing in the corner of the station yard, smoking, again. He'd tried giving up the dreaded weed several times with nicotine replacement therapies including chewing gum: he didn't like the taste, patches; they gave him nightmares, and a nicotine pipe which satisfied his cravings but not his taste buds. He was considering the latest devices, electronic cigarettes, when the late shift started to arrive. He'd already decided to debrief the early turn and brief the late turn together. There'd been a few interesting developments during the day which had included a conversation with DCS Baxter regarding Kelly's replacement. Charlie joined him in smokers' corner.

"How you doing?" Matt said.

"I'm bloody knackered but looking forward to a day out in Sarre Village and Westgate- on-Sea." Matt liked Charlie's positive humour. He was the most reliable member of his team and they both spoke the same tongue.

"How did you get on with Kelly's wife?"

"She seemed okay; obviously very concerned about Brian but his condition was stable when I spoke with her."

"Any recriminations?"

"No, none at all, she seems to be very level-headed. Any interesting developments?"

"DCS Baxter rang me earlier. He doesn't have an immediate replacement for Kelly. I told him that I did need a deputy but I'd prefer to select my own man."

"Who do you have in mind?"

"Well, I was actually thinking of you. You're qualified and you've completed the junior command course."

"That's very kind of you, sir."

"And I need someone reliable to review my work whilst I go through Kelly's with a fine tooth comb. Are you up for the challenge?"

Charlie smiled. "You can always rely on me, sir."

"That's why I'm asking you. I can give you some time to consider."

"That won't be necessary. We get on well and this is a very interesting enquiry. I'd be a fool to turn down your offer."

"Good. I'd hoped you'd say that." Matt proffered his hand and Charlie accepted it with a grin. "Now we only need to find a replacement for you. Who would you suggest?"

"Audrey; she's qualified."

"She's very young."

"Yes, but she's smart and very thorough; not like some other people that I could mention."

"Go on."

"She had a run in with Ron yesterday. Apparently he fell asleep when she was interviewing Michael Stevens." Matt could feel the colour coming to his face. This wasn't the first time Ron's name had been mentioned negatively. He decided that he'd review his actions and results before any others. "Don't worry I'll sort him out," Charlie said, "assuming you want me to bring Kelly's team back together."

"That was my intention. Six teams are better than five; under the correct supervisors, of course."

"Anyone else on your team likely to have issues with Audrey?"

"None, she's well-liked and respected."

"In that case you won't be getting your day out in Sarre and Westgate." Matt spotted Audrey arriving in her black mini cooper. She appeared to be as fresh as a daisy, was smartly turned out, as usual, and smiled when she saw Matt and Charlie.

"In the naughty corner," she said, with reference to their smoking habits. Charlie beckoned her over with a nod of the head.

"Something wrong?" she said, adopting a serious expression.

"Matt's asked me to replace Kelly."

"Oh, I see, and who's going to look after us once you're gone?"

"We'd like you to take on my role," Charlie said.

Audrey smiled. "Does that mean I'll be supervising Ron?"

"No, we're reforming Kelly's old team under my supervision."

"That's a shame. I was looking forward to punishing him for the sexist remarks he made yesterday."

Matt decided that it was time to call it a day. He'd been up since 4am and he was shattered. The teams were now aware of Audrey and Charlie's promotions. The day shift had been debriefed. Charlie's new team had worked diligently on the actions to research the outstanding Dereks and they'd reduced that number from twenty four to eighteen subjects.

Dean's team had located Mr. Angry and interviewed him as part of the house to house enquiries. He'd been very helpful and confirmed what they already knew about Marlene's household. They'd also made several appointments with other householders living in Matthews Place, Tower Hamlets Street and Dickson Road to further the enquiries into the Johnson, Stevens and Delaney families.

Audrey had been tasked with re-interviewing Patricia Stevens after obtaining her medical records. She was a SOIT, fully trained in Sexual Offences Investigation Techniques and considered to be the best person for the job. Mark Goddard was working on the financial investigations for Derek Stevens and Patraicc Delaney and the telephone numbers supplied by Marlene's solicitor. The Missing Persons form for Derek had been found at Maidstone HQ; another member of her team had been dispatched to collect it. Matt was hoping he'd be able to speak with Paul Adams in the morning.

Ed's Team had spoken with most of the witnesses who'd been traced in Sandwich regarding the sighting of flat cap man at 7.30pm on Monday 4 June but their responses had remained negative. One member of his team had started checking the crime report archives for allegations of sexual assault in public toilets, going back as far as December 1971, looking for suspects who matched Delaney's description. This enquiry had been passed onto Roger's Team.

Kate had been tasked with printing off all the actions completed by Ron and leaving them on Matt's desk. Her team were inputting the new intelligence and statements onto the HOLMES database and manning the phones. After 23:00 any calls to the incident room would be re-directed to the Control Room in Dover.

Matt tried to hide his amusement as he was leaving the station yard. Ron had already been taken in hand by Charlie. He'd been given a humiliating choice; sweep the yard with a broom up your arse or report to HQ Maidstone on Monday for a new uniformed posting. He'd chosen the former and was making the best of it dressed in a sou'wester, soaking wet green overalls and wellington boots that were too big for him.

After a few hours rest and an early dinner with Rose, Matt was collected by Audrey. She'd made an appointment to interview Robin Delaney at his home address in Westerham Road, Sittingbourne. Matt waved to Rose as he settled into the passenger seat of the firm's Vauxhall Astra. He was looking forward to being a passenger; for a change. This was Audrey's opportunity to impress. He had an hour-long drive to look forward to then it would be his turn to sit and listen whilst Audrey conducted the interview.

"How did your team take to your promotion?" Matt said.

"Very well, considering they know I'm only acting up." Matt remembered when he'd had his first temporary promotion. He was a little older than Audrey but he'd still found it tough going. Most of his colleagues had accepted his promotion without question. He was the natural choice, an experienced police constable, the first five years in uniform, another five with the CID, before passing the promotion exam; very pro-active; always suggesting ways of catching the local villains perpetrating burglaries and vehicle crime, a priority in their force area.

He'd returned to uniformed duty on interchange; a pre-requisite to promotion to Police Sergeant in those days. Some of the senior constables had given him a hard time until that incident with Samantha Springer and Stewart Baxter. They'd been called to one of their many domestic incidents. Baxter had clearly been stabbed in the stomach. He had a small entry wound but refused to go to hospital with the paramedics. They'd obtained a disclaimer from him and he'd left before Matt arrived. The medics advised Matt that Baxter wouldn't get far with his injuries. They'd found a small blood stained knife at the scene and Springer had admitted stabbing him.

It was the opinion of one of his senior constables that Baxter deserved what he'd got. He was always knocking Springer about and she'd ended up in hospital on several occasions. Matt immediately recognized this to be a "critical incident." He'd instructed the senior constable to arrest Springer for grievous bodily harm with intent, one down from attempted murder. The officer had refused at first but thought better of it when Matt stood his ground.

Matt had managed the crime scene, as if there'd been a murder. Whilst doing so a call for police assistance had been received to a male stabbed, ambulance on way. He'd dispatched one of his team; a reserve medic from one of the public order teams. When he'd arrived, he'd found Baxter slumped on the ground. His heart had stopped. He'd performed CPR until the ambulance had arrived. The medic had gone to hospital with Baxter and marveled at the efficiency of the crash team in A&E, who'd brought him back from the brink of death.

"If it had been one of us we'd definitely be dead but that lucky bastard has more lives than a stray tom cat," was the report he'd received. Baxter had been interviewed, refused to press charges and said that he deserved it. That had been the first time he'd admitted being in the wrong.

Matt's team had taken him for a drink afterwards. The senior constable, Rafferty, who'd initially refused to obey his instructions, bought the first round. He named Matt "The Daddy" and thanked him for saving their bacon. They were his piglets now and if he had any trouble from anyone, he Rafferty would sort it out.

"It's not that easy acting up but it does get easier," Matt said. "Where's your team now?"

"In Sarre Village, questioning Patricia's neighbours in Sarre Court and then working their way out from there."

"Shall we drop in on them?"

"No, I think we should leave them to it. I need to show that I trust them and don't want to appear to be sucking up to the guv'nor." Matt considered her response.

"Very wise; you'll be able to judge how well they've done when you go through their returns in the morning."

"Precisely."

"How's Ron getting on with his tasking?"

"He's taken it really well. The humiliation I mean. He's had a lot of leg pulling to put up with and it rained all the time he was out there. Charlie praised his work. He'd been very thorough and swept in all of the corners."

"Not up to his usual standard then?"

"And he's apologized to me. Charlie's sent him home to dry out and promised to forget it providing there are no more shenanigans."

CHAPTER 22

The house in Westerham Road was very ordinary looking; a modern mid-terrace; double glazed with tiled walls to the first floor and a capped storm porch. The front garden had been sacrificed for parking; red block paving with a black border led up to a semi-circular step and the front door. The boundaries were marked out with low raised beds, planted with mauve hebes; not one of Matt's favourite plants. They got too big and woody after a few years. A Silver Skoda Estate car was parked on the drive.

"Looks like our man's at home," Audrey said.

"Let's take a final look at your interview plan, before we go in… I don't think we should ask about his father's activities in the public toilets. He would have only been eleven or twelve in 1972… I think we should keep that to ourselves and save that for his mother Margaret. It'll be a nice surprise for her and we might learn something that we don't know already."

"I wasn't sure about that; that's why there's a question mark in the margin."

Robin had been worrying about the police interview all day. His past experiences with the police had rarely been positive. He'd been caught speeding a couple of times. The first officer was pleasant enough and accepted an apology but the second, a traffic cop, treated him like a criminal. He wondered what they'd be like now they were dealing with something far more serious.

He spotted them sitting in their Astra outside and didn't know what to do; should he go out and introduce himself or wait for them to knock? The car doors opened, making the decision for him. He recognized the man immediately. He'd been on the TV several times in connection with Marlene's murder. The girl was new; much younger; in her late twenties perhaps and very attractive.

"You must be Robin Delaney," Matt said. Robin nodded. "This is Audrey McCullock; one of our Detective Sergeants and I'm Detective Chief Inspector Matt Sanderson."

"Please come through," Robin said, waving them into the hallway. Matt noted the layout; staircase to the first floor on the left, kitchen straight ahead, living room door on the right. "I thought we'd go into the conservatory, just in case Sabrina comes home with the kids before we're finished."

"Good idea," Matt said.

"She's gone to a friend's house to watch a movie and have supper. Can I get you something to drink? Tea, coffee?

Robin noticed that his hand was trembling when he poured the hot liquid into the cups. He took several deep breaths to calm down and placed the cups on a tray. He was relieved that his hands didn't shake as he carried them into the conservatory whilst the two officers gazed at him.

"This is a nice room," Matt said. "I've always fancied a Victorian style conservatory to complement my house but never had the time to get round to it."

"We had it built last year. It only took the company six days and that included digging out the footings…" Matt let him rumble on. He could see that Robin was very nervous and wanted him to calm down before they got down to business.

"Is it difficult to heat?"

"No, we went for under-floor heating. We have to top it up with an electric radiator when it gets really cold but we're only in here for short spells, now that we use it as a dining room."

"That's a nice photograph of you and?" Matt said.

"My wife Sabrina, my daughter Rachel and my son Maxwell."

"Have you lived here long?"

"About thirty years."

Matt sipped his coffee. "This is very good. I've been up since the crack of dawn and needed something strong." Robin smiled. "Can I use your little boy's room before we get started?"

"It's at the top of the stairs."

*

Matt had a good look round as he made his way upstairs. The bathroom was small; there were two main bedrooms off the landing and a box room at the front. He now had the full layout of the premises in his head and would draw a sketch plan later for his team and the local intelligence officer. You never knew when it would come in handy; during this enquiry perhaps or when another family move in.

He found Audrey seated opposite Robin when he returned. Her notebook was open and the cups had been cleared away.

"May I sit in the wicker chair?" Matt said. He wanted to study this man from a different viewpoint and make his own observations. Besides it looked far more comfortable that the wooden chair he'd been sitting on.

"Go ahead, make yourself comfortable," Robin said. Sometimes Matt liked to listen with ears open and eyes closed. As he settled into the chair he wondered if Audrey would kick him if he appeared to be sleeping. She'd picked up on Robin's nervousness and decided to start with the easy stuff.

"Can I have your full name, please?"

"Where do you work?" Audrey said.

Robin really enjoyed his work at the Continental Metal Recycling Centre. It was only a short drive from his family's home in Sittingbourne and he could usually get there within fifteen minutes. He always loved the last bit of the journey; driving along the access road which followed the Swale Estuary to Ridham Dock, opposite the Isle of Sheppey. The mixture of fresh and sea water, together with tidal movements made this a great place for bird watching and he'd often stop to admire snipes, redshanks, curlews and bitterns feeding on the mud flats.

The recycling centre dealt in ferrous and non-ferrous metals and often paid the best prices in the local area. It was a slick operation. Punters would usually arrive early, their loads would be sorted and weighed and sold immediately on international markets. This was a multi-million pound operation; the owners co-operated with the police as they wished to discourage criminals visiting the site, with lead from church roofs, copper wire from the railways and plaques stolen from War Memorials. Even a shut down for an hour could cost thousands of pounds.

Robin was familiar with all of the equipment on site. The massive grab loaders, which were like cranes sitting on raised platforms, between huge mounds of ferrous metals waiting to be dropped into substantial ribbed containers or loaded onto ships. JCB's collecting product that had just arrived or been turned into metal chippings at the end of long rubber conveyor belts. Compactors used to compress car bodies into small cubes of steel ready for smelting in the UK or overseas. He'd been working there for thirty years now and promoted to Yard Manager. He never tired of the frenzied activity within the yard, the vast skies overhead or the movement of the tides and spoke enthusiastically about his workplace.

"How long have you been the yard manager?" Audrey said.

"About fifteen years. Tom, the last yard manager, always wanted me to have the job when he retired. He took me on at twenty-two, passed his knowledge onto me and prepared me for the job. He was a fellow twitcher so we had something in common right from the start… Would you like another coffee?"

"I'd now like to ask you some questions about your extended family," Audrey said.

"Okay."

"Mothers name?"

"Margaret Delaney."

"Date of birth?"

"She's seventy three on the 29 July, so 29 July 1939"

"Where does she live?"

"Brunswick Street, Maidstone."

"How long has she lived there?"

"Ever since we left Dover."

"And when was that exactly?"

"In 1973, when I was thirteen."

"Where did you live in Dover?"

"Dickson Road."

"Who with?"

"My mother and Patraicc." Matt noted the unusual response. Why Patraicc? Why not, my father or my dad?

"And when was he born?" Audrey said.

"I don't know."

"Why's that?"

"Because we left him when I was thirteen."

"Both of you?"

"That's right."

"Why was that?"

"Because my mother and Patraicc didn't get on."

"Is Patraicc your father?" 'Good girl,' Matt thought.

"Yes… Yes he is."

"So why don't we just call him dad?

"Because I don't think of him in that way." Robin noticed Audrey staring at him and felt obliged to continue. "After we left Patraicc my grandfather brought me up as if I were his son, so I think of him as my dad."

"So you left Dover in 1973?"

"Correct."

"How many times did you see Patraicc after you left?"

"I never saw him again."

"How many times did you speak?"

"I never," Robin said.

"You never spoke with him again?"

"No."

"Did you write?"

"No."

"Did he ever try and get in touch with you?"

"I think he contacted my mother a couple of times but she warned him off."

Matt opened his eyes. Audrey stared. Robin wanted to bite his tongue off.

"Why did she warn him off?"

… "Because she hated him."

"Why was that?"

… "Because he hurt her."

"How did he do that?"

… "I don't know… You'll have to ask her."

"Did Patraicc ever try and get in touch with you through your grandparents?"

... "I don't know."

"What are their names?"

"They're dead."

"I'm sorry... Did Patraicc ever do anything to hurt you?"

"No."

"So why didn't you look him up when you were older?"

"I didn't want to."

"Why not?"

... "Because I didn't want to hurt my mother or my grandparents... That would be disloyal." Robin noticed that his palms were sweating; perspiration ran down his spine and leaked into the cleft between his buttocks; globules peppered his scalp beneath his thick black hair and threatened to run down his temples. "Can we take a break? I need to use the bathroom."

"Of course," Audrey said. She smiled at Matt, as Robin left the room, and listened to Robin's hurried footsteps as he climbed the stairs. "He must be desperate."

"To get away from you," Matt said. "His behaviour's been a bit bizarre since you started questioning him about Patraicc." Audrey flicked back a page.

"It started with his response to, "Did he ever try and get in touch with you?"

"I think he contacted my mother a couple of times *but she warned him off,*" Matt said.

"Then his answers became stilted as if he'd said something ill-considered."

"Which is exactly what he had done. Now, why would his mother warn Patraicc off?"

"Is that something I should pursue?"

"Let's save that for Margaret. It'll be another nice surprise for her. In the meantime, let's see what else you can tease out of Robin."

If they hadn't been conversing Matt and Audrey might have heard Robin vomiting in the bathroom. He was doing his best to retch quietly with little success. After three or four spurts of hot liquid he felt terrible. A pale mask looked back at him from the mirror and he was covered in perspiration. He rinsed his face in the sink and after taking several deep breaths his colour began to return. He checked his clothing for vomit; cleaned the toilet and opened the window to let the smell out.

"I wonder what's taking him so long," Audrey said.

Matt grinned. "Must be doing number two's."

"Too much information."

Matt chuckled. "Or number three's."

"Enlighten me."

"Both ends."

"That's disgusting."

"I fancy a fag break. I'll be by the front door, if you need me."

Audrey slipped up to the bathroom when she heard Matt engage Robin in light hearted banter about the merits of smoking. The window was wide open but the room smelt disgusting; a bit like the cells after a football match. She lifted the lid and the toilet seat to find what she was expecting; diced carrot and tomato skins under the hinge mechanism. Why did they always appear in vomit?

Matt and Robin were seated in their former positions when she returned to the conservatory.

"Do you feel well enough to continue?" Audrey said.

"Why wouldn't I?" Robin replied.

"Because there's vomit in the bathroom," Audrey said.

CHAPTER 23

"What was Patraicc like when you were a child?" Audrey said.

"He was at sea most of the time," Robin said.

"What was he like when he came home?"

"It was a long time ago."

"Sometimes it helps if you close your eyes and think," Matt said. Robin obliged. Matt winked at Audrey and smiled.

"He was a happy drunk most of the time, out every night with Uncle Tommy and Uncle Derek."

"Were you related to Tommy and Derek?"

"No, we just called them uncle because that was less formal than Mr Johnson or Mr Stevens."

"Who are we?"

"Michael and me."

"What did Patraicc do during the day?"

"Sleep mostly."

"All day?"

"No, just in the mornings… Sometimes we went cycling or swimming."

"Anything else?"

"We used to go to the park and play on the swings."

"Which Navy was Patraicc in?" Audrey said.

"The Merchant."

"What did he do?"

"He was a sailor."

"What was the name of his ship?"

"I don't know."

"When did he leave?"

"When I was eleven."

"Month, year?"

"Christmas."

"Why did he leave?"

"They let him go. He was very bitter about that."

"What did he do after that?"

"He had a van." Robin hated that van.

"What did he do with that?"

"He worked for Uncle Derek."

"Doing what exactly?"

"I don't know."

"Did anyone else work for Derek?"

"Uncle Tommy."

"What did he do?"

"I don't know. I was eleven or twelve."

"Most boys take an interest in their fathers' work," Matt said, opening his eyes. "Some even choose to follow in their footsteps."

"I must be different then because I didn't want to join the navy, drive my fathers' smelly old van or work for Uncle Derek."

"Time to take a break," Matt said.

"Can I ring Sabrina and the kids?"

"Of course; we'll be out front polluting the atmosphere."

Audrey waited. Matt lit a cigarette and inhaled deeply. He exhaled slowly through his mouth and nose and disappeared in a shroud of smoke.

"He really doesn't like his father," Matt said, "and he doesn't appear to have a lot of time for Derek and Tommy. Let's move onto one of the women, someone safe, Patricia, Michael's mother. He might empathize with her as her relationship with Derek wasn't good. Then I think we'll go back to Derek or Tommy and see what happens."

"You think he's hiding something sinister?"

"I know he is, just keep going. We need to get his first account down on paper. We can always come back at a later stage and challenge anything we're not happy with."

"What can you tell me about Patricia and Michael?" Audrey said.

"Patricia's Michael's mother; she lives in Sarre. Michael's one of my best friends and he lives in Westgate-on-Sea."

"How long have you known them?"

"Forever. Michael and I were born within a few days of each other. We must've been conceived at Christmas when our fathers were on leave. We grew up together, that is until I left Dover. Then we met by chance when I was shopping in Canterbury. We've been friends ever since."

"How do you get on with Patricia?"

"She's a nice old lady, a bit of a fruit and nut case but that's not surprising."

"Why's that?"

"Because she had a terrible time with Uncle Derek."

"How do you know?"

"Michael told me about their relationship."

"When was that?"

"Snippets when we were growing up, a little more when we got back together."

"What did he tell you?"

"That they used to fight all the time."

"What about?"

"Anything and everything."

"Go on," Audrey said, mimicking one of Matt's favourite phrases. She'd start sounding like him if she wasn't careful but then he was a Detective Chief Inspector, so maybe that wouldn't be a bad thing.

"Did you ever witness any of these fights?" Matt said.

"Not that I can remember."

"A cross word maybe?"

"Not that I can remember. People didn't wash their dirty laundry in public. We didn't have TV talk shows for dysfunctional families, in those days."

"How often did you see Patricia?"

"We used to see her and Auntie Marlene regularly before they left the navy."

"Who are they?"

"Uncle Tommy, Uncle Derek and Patraicc."

"And afterwards?"

"Auntie Patricia was always tired."

"Why was that?"

"I don't know."

"What did you do with your aunties before your uncles left the Navy?"

"We used to go on day trips to Ramsgate and Margate, have picnics in the garden, go to the park and play on the swings, go to the pictures, all sorts of things."

"And after they left?"

"We didn't do so much?"

"Why was that?"

"Because Patraicc spent most of his money on drink and cigarettes."

"When was the last time you saw Derek?"

"Just before we moved to Maidstone."

"When was that?"

"When I was thirteen."

"Do you know where he is now?"

"I'd tell you if I did."

"Does Michael talk about him?"

"Rarely."

"Why's that?"

"Because he hasn't seen him for donkey's ears-years."

"Where do you think he is now?"

"I've no idea; didn't you say he'd disappeared in 2001 during your press conference."

"Reported missing by his wife Patricia," Matt said.

"Is there a difference?"

"Sometimes; what did Michael tell you about Derek's disappearance?"

"That the police gave up looking for him a long time ago. Of course, that was before he murdered Marlene."

"And what do you think of that?"

"It's possible I suppose, but that's your job, I think I'll stick to scrap metal and bird watching, if you don't mind." There was a commotion at the front door. Matt looked at his watch. It was 9pm and already dark outside. Robin rose.

"May I?" Matt nodded and smiled; diffused voices drifted in from the hallway.

"How much longer do you think we can carry on?" Audrey said.

"Until he says he's had enough and starts making excuses about having to go to work in the morning."

Robin re-appeared in the living room followed by his entourage.

"This is my wife Sabrina." Matt looked up and saw a very attractive pair of slender legs dressed in purple high heels approaching. They were complemented by a purple mini-dress with pencil thin belt over a slender waist, shapely breasts behind a plunging neckline. Her shoulders were covered in a short black leather jacket with studded shoulder pads.

As Matt climbed to his feet he noticed that Sabrina was at least 5'10". Straight blonde hair cascaded down her back. Chocolate brown eyes stared at him. Long lashes and a thin nose complemented the perfectly formed mouth which had been painted with bright red lipstick. He thought that he was seeing double before Robin introduced his daughter Rachel.

"Pleased to meet you," Matt said, noting Rachel had a mouth full of braces, which she was trying to conceal. "This is Audrey."

"Where's Maxwell," Robin said.

"I'm coming Dad." Maxwell was good looking; slim and athletic with a shock of jet black straight hair, neatly trimmed at the sides and back with a parting on the left and a quiff at the front. His fine features and olive skin contrasted with his white shirt, which was buttoned right up to the collar, with sleeves rolled up and tails hanging out of his grey green trousers. Robin tousled his hair affectionately. The family was like chess pieces; two white queens and two black kings.

"Say hello to the officers."

"Where's your car?" Maxwell said.

"Sorry," Sabrina said, "he's always been fascinated by police cars."

"It's parked outside."

"Not that ropey old Astra?"

"I'm afraid so."

"Can you come in something a bit smarter next time?"

"Hopefully, there won't be a next time," Sabrina said. "Are you going to be much longer? I need to get the kids off to bed and Robin's up at six in the morning."

"We've just a couple more questions for tonight."

"Can you tell me where you were during the Queen's Diamond Jubilee concert on Monday 4 June?" Matt said.

"I was here with Sabrina, the kids and the next door neighbours, Carol and Herbert. We had a cocktail party and watched the concert together. Wasn't it great?"

"So what do you make of the Delaney family?" Matt said.

"Robin seems to be very nice. He's obviously hard working and has the same ambitions as most people of his age, a better house being the top of the list. He adores his wife and children. She wears the trousers, metaphorically speaking, and is very protective… Something happened to him when he was a child and Patraicc was involved. I think that he might have been abused."

"Go on."

"He had to hurry off to the bathroom just after I asked him if Patraicc had ever hurt him." Audrey was replaying the scene in her head, "And then I found the vomit. That was your fault; talking about number twos and threes. How did you know?"

"Instinct, intuition, experience, a lucky guess."

"Do you always follow your instincts?"

"Pretty much. The brain is a wonderful thing, much more complex than the greatest computer. It doesn't always dot the i's and cross the t's when inputting the information but often tidies up later."

"Is that why you read absolutely everything?"

"That's right. I can't always see the links as I input the information but later, sometimes much later, the brain unravels the mysteries for me. It was something that I practiced when I worked on the intelligence side of the business, tackling burglaries and vehicle crimes. Posting patrols in the right areas with a good intelligence package often produced excellent results. Sometimes arrests for the patrolling officers who would eagerly return for more briefings: sometimes a good stop fed back into the system, which I could analyse; a modus operandi identified from the subjects criminal record; a search warrant obtained; an early morning call with the investigation team; an Aladdin's Cave; a good result and so it went on; round and round in a perpetual circle."

"Do you think that can apply in a case like this?"

"Of course; if you can investigate a burglary proficiently, you can apply the same techniques to investigating a murder. The only difference is the nature of the offence."

"Who's the beautiful girl you've been dating all night?" Rose said, as Matt let himself in through the barn door.

"That's Audrey, my new Detective Sergeant. Would you like to meet her?"

CHAPTER 24

Michael hadn't had a good day. He was tired after being kept up half the night by the police officers searching his house and when he'd collected Denise she'd been grumpy. He'd never seen her like that before. His heart sank, "Was this the beginning of the end?" he thought.

"How's Yvonne?"

"She's very upset, Michael."

"She's heard the news then?"

"That's right."

"What did she say?"

"That she doesn't want to be related to a murderer, especially one who kills old ladies in their beds." He noticed that she was weeping.

"I'm so sorry, Denise."

"She wants me to stop seeing you," she sobbed. Michael was devastated. "The whole village is gossiping about us," she bawled, "and not in a nice way."

"How things had changed," Michael thought, "they'd been the talk of the town when they'd started dating and now on the turn of a sixpence…"

When they arrived at Brooks things went from bad to worse. There was a trickle of water at the front of the premises. When the roller shutter was raised Michael saw that the windows were steamed up. He felt like laughing in the face of his misfortune when he saw the lake inside as nothing could compare with his sense of loss.

"Looks like we should have brought our bathing suits," Denise said, cracking a hesitant smile.

"Just when you think things couldn't get any worse, luck pops up and kicks you in the balls."

"We'll get through this, Michael; you just need to let the dust settle."

"And in the meantime?"

"You can see me at work."

It had taken the best part of the day to stem the leak which was actually coming from the flat above the shop. The water main had been turned off, once it had been located in the street outside; then they'd forced entry into the flat. All of the ceilings were down. The galvanized steel water tank in the loft had corroded with age and hundreds of gallons of water had flowed through the premises into the shop below.

The insurance company had been very good, when their offices had eventually opened, and sent an engineer from a dehumidifier company along to assess the damage. He'd put arrangements in place for removal of the debris. Everything had been written off and the staff had been sent home. The story had been reported in the local press and on the radio. It was going to take months to re-instate. In the meantime the staff, including Denise would be deployed elsewhere. Michael rang his mother during the late afternoon.

"Hello mum."

"I thought I told you not to ring me, Michael."

"I know you did but I thought you might have calmed down by now."

"How can I calm down, Michael, the police are here interviewing the neighbours, the people who own the pub and they're knocking on doors on the main road. They're all over the place; everyone's gossiping. I feel so ashamed. I can't go out."

"Can I get you anything?"

"No, not today Michael; just stay away."

When Michael got home he felt very lonely. He couldn't ring Denise. She was looking after her mother. He'd already tried his mother and Robin was waiting for the police to arrive. As he scanned the TV schedules he noticed that the only programme that would interest him was a drama set in a city hospital. That wasn't on until 8pm so he had two hours to kill. After sipping a hot cup of tea he changed into his running kit and had a solitary jog along the seafront to Plumpudding Island, a big mistake given the circumstances.

*

The house was decorated with rather gruesome looking balloons. Each had a face with a crescent shaped scar over the right eye in black felt tip.

"They're much better looking than you," Marlene said, when Patraicc explained their relevance, "and the white ones are the right colour; you really didn't look well when you pitched up that night."

"I can't believe it was just a year ago; so much has happened since then," Tommy added.

"Thanks to you and Derek… Now what would you like to drink?"

"I fancy a Babycham," Marlene said.

"What about you, Tommy?"

"I think I'll try some of your homebrew."

The boys were pretty drunk. The homebrew was going down well but there was always an inch of ale left in the bottle, before the sludge. They couldn't fit it into the guest's glasses and felt it was their duty not to waste it. Robin was unsteady on his feet and giggling stupidly when Marlene walked into the kitchen for another Babycham. "A Lovely Way to Spend an Evening," played in the living room. She was feeling amorous. She was a little taller than the boys and draped her arms around their shoulders, pulled them together and kissed each of them affectionately as they danced a threesome.

"I feel sick," Michael said, as the record came to its end.

"Fresh air and exercise is what you need." She guided him through the kitchen door and said, "See you in a tick Robin; don't drink any more home-brew."

Michael's head ached; his mouth was dry and he was very sweaty when he woke the following morning. He was in his own bed but he'd no idea how he'd got there. The last thing he could remember was dancing with Robin and Marlene in Patraicc's kitchen; everything after that was a little hazy. Had he gone for a walk with Marlene or was that just his imagination. Images of Marlene's smiling-laughing face filled his consciousness before he realized that he needed to go to the toilet.

It was very quiet outside for a Monday morning and he thought it must be early. His mother and father were still in bed. The sun was already up and it was very warm. He drank a large glass of water in the kitchen before heading back to his bedroom. He wasn't ready to get up. He opened the bedroom window a little more and his curtains billowed in the breeze as he reclined onto his bed. Marlene's smiling-laughing face filled his consciousness again. She was like a big sister, dragging him round the streets; leading him by the hand, encouraging him to take deep breaths to clear his head and gently rubbing his back as he vomited in the gutter.

"There, there; you'll feel much better now; better out than in, that's what I say when I've had too much to drink."

Then they were standing in an alleyway. Michael thought it was the one leading to Patraicc's back gate but he couldn't be sure. It was getting dark and Marlene was encouraging him to kiss her on the lips, not in the way that you'd kiss your mother's best friend but a kiss with tongue in it. He could remember the buttery taste of her lipstick; the heady smell of her perfume and the tickling sensation that he experienced when she ran her tongue over his white piano keys.

"Did you enjoy that, Michael?" She gazed at him steadily with those big brown eyes. He'd nodded diffidently… "Why don't you have a go on me this time?" Their teeth clashed but she didn't pull away; he continued; this time running his tongue over her pearly white pegs. He'd been startled when their tongues had started their courtship but soon got the idea and was struck by the electric sensation they produced.

He became aware of a tightening in his trousers. He wanted to cover his groin with his hands. He hadn't become accustomed to the fluctuation of his penis. She guided his hands to the middle of her back before gently rubbing her groin against his. His penis flared and he groaned as it stretched to new lengths.

"It's alright, darling, it's perfectly natural; nothing to worry about. Would you like me to relieve you?" He'd nodded nervously, wondering what she meant. Beads of sweat peppered his forehead as she gently teased his member out of the fly and massaged it between thumb and forefinger. His heart raced, his breath was sharp and shallow, his face burnt as he discharged his load into the palm of her hand.

"There, there, darling. That wasn't so bad, was it?" She wiped her hand on a paper napkin. He was lost for words and couldn't express how he felt. She tucked him back in and said, "I think we'd better get back or they'll be sending out a search party. Now, not a word to anyone. It'll be our little secret, okay?" He nodded, still dumbfounded.

When they got back to the party Michael was sure everyone knew what they'd been up to. He felt terribly guilty and wasn't able to relax until he got home to his bedroom. Then his mother and father started fighting. He'd often wondered about the shouting, screaming and the silence before the gentle groaning but now he understood a little more.

The following day Marlene telephoned.

"That was a great party," his mother said… "That's a really nice idea, Marlene. It'll be good for the boys to spend some more time together… Michael would you like to go to Auntie Marlene's on Friday night with Robin and stay over until Saturday?" Michael felt his skin burning. He was sure that he must be bright red but if he was, his mother said nothing. He nodded. "Michael would like that… We'll see you at six then."

CHAPTER 25

Margaret naively hoped the police would go away if she kept ignoring their messages. She'd realized early on that their calls always came up number withheld. She'd stopped taking calls on the house and mobile phone unless she recognized the number. She was in no mood to discuss her former life with Patraicc. She thought she'd left that behind her years ago.

She rang Robin early Wednesday morning and was shocked to learn that the police had been taking his statement for more than three hours on Tuesday night.

"Why did it take so long?"

"They wanted to talk about everything, my parents, where did we live, why did you split up."

"What did you tell them, Robin?"

"That you and Patraicc didn't get on."

"Anything else?"

"They asked about Uncle Derek, Uncle Tommy and Aunty Marlene."

"And?"

"I didn't tell them anything."

"You must have, they were with you for hours."

"They picked me up for calling my father Patraicc."

"How did you deal with that?"

"I told them my grandfather brought me up as if I were his son, so

I didn't think of Patraicc in that way."

"And that's the truth. Anything else?"

"I told them Patraicc contacted you but you warned him off."

"What did they make of that?"

"They asked why you'd warned him off and I said you hated him; he'd hurt you. Then they asked me if Patraicc had ever hurt me and I said no."

"Good… Anything else?"

"They wanted to know why I hadn't looked him up when I was older and I said that I didn't want to hurt you or my grandparents. It would be disloyal."

"Excellent."

"I'm not making it up mum. That's how I feel."

"So you remembered what I told you all those years ago?"

"Yes mum, tell the truth but leave out the sticky bits."

"Did anything else happen?"

"I was sick in the toilet just after they questioned me about Patraicc."

"Oh Robin, I'm so sorry. If only I'd realized sooner."

"And Audrey, the lady detective, found the evidence."

"How did you explain that away?"

"I said I'd been feeling ill all day. She asked me if I felt well enough to continue. I said that I felt much better; better out than in, so we just carried on. Then they asked me what Patraicc was like when I was a child. I told them he was at sea most of the time and when he came home he was a happy drunk, out every night with Uncle Tommy and Uncle Derek. Then they started asking questions about them."

"And what did you tell them?"

"The truth, what I could remember. They thought it a bit strange that I didn't take an interest in my father's work."

"And how did you respond to that, Robin?"

"I'm afraid that I did mention his smelly old van."

"Not in those terms?"

"I'm afraid so… Then they started asking about Auntie Patricia and Michael."

"Any problems?"

"I don't think so. I told them where Michael and Auntie Patricia lived and mentioned Patricia's difficult time with Uncle Derek. Then they asked me about Derek. The last time I saw him, that sort of thing."

"Anything else?"

"Where I was during The Queens' Diamond Jubilee Concert... What should I say about this conversation if they come back?"

"Just tell them we've spoken about it, in general terms."

"Have they rung you yet?"

"A couple of times but I haven't got round to ringing them back."

*

The telephone in Matt's office was ringing when he arrived.

"DCI Matt Sanderson."

"Hello Sir, DC Boyle, Crimestoppers."

"Thanks for coming back to me Bob. How did you get on with our man?"

"We spoke at some length about the incident and your desire for a chat."

"And?"

"Well it's clearly a case of indecent assault in the toilet and possibly attempted murder when Patraicc ran him off the road... You could start there but the CPS would probably accept pleas for common assault and dangerous driving."

"Go on."

"Well the victim's worried about coming forward because he gave Patraicc a good hiding. He thinks he may have gone overboard towards the end; a little bit more than self-defence. He kicked Patraicc in the genitals and stamped on his face after he'd knocked him out."

"We've checked the crime books and Patraicc made no complaint; the victim was a fifteen year old boy and the assailant a thirty-six year old adult. I can't see that being a problem with a carefully crafted statement. Have you recorded these concerns on your paperwork?"

"No. I've just left it as it was. He gave Patraicc a good hiding and cycled off."

"Is he willing to talk to me?"

"He is. Wants to ring you from a caller withheld number."

"That's OK; give him my mobile number. What name is he using?

"Keith, his first name, we still don't know his surname."

*

Paul Adams was happy. They were safely berthed in St Helier Marina. The last seventy two hours had been exciting, a bit too exciting at times. They'd left Dover with calm seas, favourable winds and a good forecast. A pleasant days sailing had followed. They'd been escorted by a pod of dolphins racing down the sides of their yacht and frolicking in the waves created by their bow. They'd sat on the gunwales for nearly an hour, their legs dangling over the sides and marveled at the water aerobics. Then the first signs of trouble had appeared; a mackerel sky, a hazy sunset, a falling barometer. They'd ploughed on into increasing winds and moderate seas.

The barometer had fallen quickly during the night and they'd shortened sail. The crew of six had done well, during their four hour watches. It had been cold for the time of year and everyone had been seasick at some stage. Paul had lived through several uncomfortable moments when a car ferry overtaking from astern had suddenly turned towards them; her profile had taken an age to change. Why she hadn't crossed their bows in complete safety was a mystery to him. They hadn't even acknowledged their presence when he'd illuminated their mainsail with a floodlight.

The following day they'd climbed mountainous waves and raced into green watery canyons. Adrenalin pumped through their veins and heightened their senses, fear and elation with each peak and trough until it was the norm and they believed in their vessel and their own endurance.

The wind and cloud had faded throughout the night to reveal a million stars against a jet black sky. Dawn had brought an amazing sunrise and diminishing seas. They'd had a close encounter with Moby Dick in the middle of the day. He'd surfaced about two hundred yards away on their port side spraying water thirty feet into the air. He'd been in one hell of a hurry to get somewhere. He'd dived and they'd waited anxiously to see if he'd mate with their keel but he'd popped up on their starboard side spouting water before waving his tail at them and disappearing forever.

The last hundred miles had been a chore. The wind had died completely and they'd had to listen to the monotonous drone of the diesel. Now it was time to wash, drink and party. The serious business of taking on water, fuel and provisions for the return could wait for tomorrow.

"Hi Bernice. Did you miss me?"

"Hello Paul. How was your voyage?"

"Exciting at times."

"Everyone okay?"

"We're all in one piece."

"Good. I was worried about you. You've had some awful weather... Did you have any fun?"

"We've all fed the fish at some time."

"You as well?"

"Afraid so. Geoffrey chundered over the windward side; the wind whipped it back into the boat and I ended up wearing most of it. Some of it got lodged in my beard and,"

"Don't tell me anymore. You're making me feel sick."

"I had a good clear out and Barry threw a bucket of water over me. Geoffrey's been fined. He's buying dinner tonight. How are things with you, business as usual?"

"Do you remember Derek Stevens?"

"The missing person that brought us back together?"

"That's the one."

"How could I forget him? If he hadn't buggered off our paths probably wouldn't have crossed again. He hasn't pitched up for a drink has he?"

"No. He's wanted for that murder in Sandwich."

"The old girl?"

"That's right. Turns out she was Marlene Johnson."

"Who?"

"You remember, the good looking girl from Matthews Place. You interviewed her and Derek's best mate Patraicc."

"The black widow and the ginger pig?"

"That's right."

"The couple who ran off together later in the year?"

"That's right."

"I wouldn't have recognized her from the photo the police were circulating. She hadn't aged well and she looked fat whereas Marline was slim, like a coat hanger."

"Like a model you mean."

"No good to me. I like my women to have a bit of meat on them."

"Like me you mean?"

"You've got a beautiful figure… just like Marilyn Munroe."

"Thank you."

"I'm glad we've cleared that up; for a moment I thought I was in trouble."

"You could be."

"Why's that?"

"DCI Matt Sanderson wants to speak to you."

"Does he know where I am?"

"I told him you were on a jolly boys outing to Jersey."

"I hope he hasn't sent anyone to meet me."

"I don't think so but I did promise to give you his number when you rang."

"Best give it to me then but I can't promise I'll ring before I get back."

*

"Roger," Matt said.

"Yes boss."

"Bring your notepad and a pen. I've got a list of jobs for you to do."

"Number one; contact The Shipping Register and find out where The Lady Irene was registered. Two; find out who owned her between her commission and disposal. Three; find out who her Masters were and whether any of them are still alive."

"How would I do that?"

"Merchant Officers used to receive generous pensions upon retirement. Four; arrange interviews with any who served with Patraicc, Derek and Tommy. I want confirmation that Derek was a Chef and accomplished first aider. I also want to know what they were like. Were they well behaved or were they sex tourists." Roger raised a questioning eyebrow. "We know that Patraicc, at least, was a sex-offender so why not the others."

"Yes boss."

"And send Mark Goddard into see me."

"Yes boss."

Charlie appeared at Matt's door.

"How are you getting on, Charlie?"

"My heads spinning. I don't know how you manage to read all the reports coming in and still get out of the office."

"I have to get out for my sanity. Do you fancy a smoke? Mark, why don't you join us? How did you get on with those subscriber checks on Derek and Patraicc's mobile phones?"

"They've both been re-allocated. The bills weren't paid and the numbers appeared inactive."

"When was Derek's last call made?"

"Just before he went missing. Paul Adams was very thorough and checked his itemized bills right up to the point where his contract was cancelled."

"And Patraicc's?"

"That was a little more difficult; the provider closed the account in June 2002 after the bill remained unpaid from January. As it was more than ten years ago they no longer have the billing information." Matt proffered Mark and Charlie his Bensons and they disappeared into a pall of smoke.

"How are the Financial Investigations progressing?"

"All done. Very little on Derek both before and after he disappeared. Hardly any credit agreements, his mobile phone of course and the utility companies but that was it. They were settled by his wife who took over as payee."

"And Patraicc?"

"Same, mobile phone and the utilities, only difference his were outstanding for a long time before being written off."

"Your conclusion?"

"They were either cash rich from their smuggling activities and managed to change their identities like Marlene."

"Or they're no longer with us," Matt said.

"That's an interesting proposition," Charlie said, through a plume of smoke, "a serial killer?"

"Possibly. We need to look for someone who knew Marlene, Derek and Patraicc," Matt said. "Mark, I want you to make a list; make sure they've been run through our systems. Then check the customer databases of the businesses in Dover, Deal and Sandwich. Report back to Charlie and me but keep this conversation under your hat. I don't want this getting out of hand. It's just a thought at the moment."

"Right you are sir." Mark ground the dog-end under the heel of his shoe and marched off towards the incident room. Matt lit another cigarette. Charlie joined him.

"A penny for your thoughts," Charlie said.

"What if Marlene, Derek and Patraicc were active sex-offenders who fell upon their own swords. Bad things do happen to bad people from time-to-time."

"Ain't that the truth," Charlie said,

"So what do we do now?"

"We carry on; keep dotting the i's and crossing the t's. How are you getting on with the Dereks?"

"We're down to half a dozen."

"Any promising ones?"

"No, we're just going through the motions; should be finished by Friday."

CHAPTER 26

Details from the news conference had finally filtered across the channel and found their way into the Calais tabloids. Alphonse read an article with interest. He'd often wondered what had happened to his friends from Angleterre. The last time he'd seen Derek and Patraicc was at Tommy's funeral in the late nineties. That had been the only time he'd been to Dover. It wasn't a pretty place. The yacht basin and the seafront were okay but the town was very run down; the suburbs occupied by his friends were even worse. The only attraction had been Tommy's widow, Marlene. He recognized her photograph on the front page of the newspaper, next to those of an older Marlene, Derek and Patraicc.

So Derek was wanted for the murder of Marlene Johnson, who'd changed her name to Dorothy Skinner. He wondered what could have happened during the intervening years to bring about such an event, and this after the three had disappeared in 2001. He remembered the Admiral Harvey, the pub where they'd had Tommy's wake, manned by a rather seductive landlady. It had been a sombre affair in a small bar not far from their home. He'd been glad when it was over and he'd been able to return to his yacht Mistral.

So a Detective Chief Inspector Matt Sanderson wanted to speak with anyone who knew them. Alphonse wondered if that would include a crusty old sea dog in his mid-seventies. He decided to give the incident room a call to satisfy his curiosity.

"Operation Carnegie, Detective Sergeant Roger Maxted speaking."

"Bonjour, this is Alphonse of The Mistral."

"How can I help you, Sir?"

"I have just read of the assassiner of Marlene Johnson in the Calais Comet and I want to speak with detective chef inspecteur Matt Sanderson."

"Can I say why you are calling?"

"Of course, the chef inspecteur want to speak with me. I knew Madame Marlene et Monsieurs Tommy, Derek and Patraicc."

"When was that?"

"A long time ago."

"Can you hold the line?"

"Of course."

"Matt, I've got a mad Frenchman on the phone asking for you. He claims to have known our victim as well as Tommy, Derek and Patraicc."

"Okay, get his number and put him through."

"Detective Chief Inspector Sanderson."

"Bonjour, this is Alphonse of The Mistral."

"Bonjour; good day to you. Where are you calling from?

"Le Bassin Ouest, Calais."

"Would you like me to call you back?"

"Oui s'il vous plait. The telephone calls are expensive."

"Alphonse?"

"Yes, it is I… I need to practice my English, no?"

"You're doing very well. You're English is much better than my French."

"Merci."

"I understand that you used to be acquainted with Marlene Johnson."

"Oui."

"How did you know her?"

"She was married to mon ami Tommy."

"How well did you know her?"

"I only met her once."

"And when was that?"

"At her husband's funerailles."

"At his funeral?"

"Oui."

"How did you know Tommy and his friends Derek and Patraicc?"

"They used to come to Calais to buy tabac and cigarettes."

"How often?"

"Every three weeks."

"They must have smoked a lot."

"Non, they were contrebandiers."

"Smugglers?"

"Oui."

"How did they travel?"

"They had a bateau a moteur."

"What was her name?"

"Spartacus. She was a Freeman 30 cruiser, looked like she made for James Bond 007 but that was a long time ago."

"So she was fast?"

"She was well built, solide, she had two powerful engines and one hundred and twenty horses."

"Top speed?"

"Sixteen knots."

"How did you meet?"

"They a little bit crazy. Arrived in Calais and look around the bars trying to, how do you say, suss-out the locals who stared at them over their blonde beers. Then they stumble into Alphonse; a retired marin and we like old friends."

"I bet they couldn't believe their luck."

"We chat and they ask for sixty thousand cigarettes. I nearly cough to death. I take them to a few bars and we discuss l'enterprise. Then they come back a couple of weeks later. Cash on delivery as you English say."

"When was that?"

"In 1973."

"Aren't you worried about being prosecuted?"

"I an old man… It a long time ago… I only want to help my friends. In the seventies, eighties and nineties everyone a smuggler in Angleterre and France."

"Who was in charge of the enterprise?"

"Derek the boss. Tommy and Patraicc do as he say."

"Do you know where they travelled from in the UK?"

"Sandwich. I went there once in Mistral. C'est beau?"

"It is very pretty."

"Le canal tortueux."

"It does snake back and forth."

"That a good description… La Douane; Customs, they like their bier and always in Le Red Cow, a long way from the 'arbour."

"When was the last time you saw them?"

"At Tommy's funerailles. In the late nineties."

"Where do you live?"

"Sur mon bateau Mistral, un antique Contessa 26, in the west basin."

"Do you fancy another trip to Sandwich?"

"I like to stay in Lord Nelsons Hotel before I die. He another great sailor, like me."

"You mean the Royal Hotel in Deal."

"Precisement. Why you want me to come?"

"It's less complicated than interviewing you in France."

"You don't want to apprehend me?"

"No, I'm investigating a murder. I'm not interested in smuggling."

"I look forward to meeting you."

"Roger."

"Yes boss."

"Task someone from your team to contact Highway Marine and The Harbour Master in Sandwich. Find out what they know about a Freeman 30 motor boat named Spartacus. It used to belong to Derek and his cronies when they were smuggling cigarettes, from 1973 until Tommy's death in the late nineties."

"Yes boss."

"I want to know where they used to moor her and what happened to her. Did they sail her away, leave her to rot or sell her."

"Yes boss."

"Identify the Customs Officials from that period. I want them interviewed tout suite; also the licensee of The Red Cow; apparently they used to drink there when they were supposed to be on duty."

"Yes boss."

"And contact The Royal Hotel in Deal. I want to know when they have a room available for a special guest."

"Yes boss."

*

Audrey had never been so busy. She was enjoying the challenge that promotion afforded her but finding it a strain. She'd arrived early and examined the returns from the house-to-house enquiries in Westgate-on-Sea. Michael was well known. He was often seen going to work in his car, visiting the shops and cinema in the village and running along the seafront.

He was well liked and respected by his neighbours who considered him to be both hardworking and caring. He'd helped most of the elderly ones with little tasks, shopping for them when they were ill or when it was bitterly cold, tidying their gardens when they'd been overwhelmed, putting their bins out and taking rubbish to the dump for them when he was going for himself.

There'd been a great deal of excitement recently when he'd introduced his girlfriend, Denise Summers, and a lot of speculation about marriage. She'd been unanimously described as beautiful, on the outside by all of the elderly gentlemen and on the inside by their wives.

All were shocked by recent developments. They could hardly believe he had a father who was wanted for the dreadful murder of Marlene Johnson. None had ever seen Derek at Michael's address but many had met his mother Patricia during her frequent visits.

Like everyone else they could all remember where they were during the Diamond Jubilee Concert. The next door neighbours could remember speaking with Michael that day. He'd been returning from a World War II event at Dover Castle and waxed lyrical about the Wehrmacht Infantry re-enactors; the Queen Mother and Princess Elizabeth inspecting the troops, Sergeant Bannon drilling the children and the highlight of his day, The Spitfires Fashion show. They'd even seen photographs of him with the ladies on his mobile phone, smiling happily.

None could remember him going out again but then most were distracted by the TV. The neighbours opposite could remember seeing the lights go out in his house whilst they were preparing to retire just after the concert had finished. They'd not seen anyone else arrive or leave and his car was still parked behind his double gates. Audrey initialed the supervisors section of each form after considering what to write in the supervisor's comments and was already exhausted before her team arrived for their briefing. She'd praised them for their hard work; sent them on their way for another day in Westgate and deposited the returns on Matt's desk.

She'd strived to identify the PC referred to in Michael's statement as Plod who attended the first domestic at Patricia and Derek's house to no avail; the police archives didn't go back that far. Dean's team had also failed to find her neighbours from that era so there were no witnesses to corroborate Michael's account.

She'd driven to Patricia's GP in Minster and her Dentist in Wingham; both had studied Patricia's medical records prior to her arrival and come to the same conclusion; either she was very accident prone or she was a victim of domestic violence prior to Derek's disappearance in 2001. The frequency of her visits had normalized after that and none of her subsequent treatments appeared consistent with being assaulted.

She'd tried ringing Patricia before driving to Cleven Lodge to re-interview her but there'd been no reply. She'd buzzed her intercom on arrival but there'd been no response. She'd eventually found her in a neighbour's flat.

"Patricia Stevens?"

"Yes dear."

"I'm Detective Sergeant Audrey McCullock from Operation Carnegie."

"What do you want?" Patricia said.

"I'd like to speak with you privately."

"What about?"

"The statement you gave Charlie Speck on Monday."

"You're not going to search my flat again?"

"No, of course not."

"See you later Bobby."

"Take care," Bobby said. Audrey followed Patricia into her flat.

"You can sit at the dining table."

"I can see that you're upset Patricia but it's important that we get your statement right. Can I make you a cuppa before we get started?"

"No thank you; just say what you've got to say."

"Okay, well first of all I'd like you to read the declaration under your name which says that this is your statement and that the content is true to the best of your belief. Can you do that for me?" Patricia read the words and although they were spoken quietly they were audible.

"Do you understand the declaration?"

"Yes. This statement is true and if I've told any lies I could be prosecuted."

"Good. Well before I ask you to sign it I would just like to clarify a few points."

"Okay, dear."

"I think the best way for me to do that is to read it to you." Patricia nodded and Audrey started to read... "Everything okay so far?"

"Yes dear."

"You said previously that Margaret moved to Maidstone with Robin after she split up with Patraicc."

"That's right dear."

"And you hadn't seen them for nearly thirty years."

"Is that what I told Charlie?"

"Yes."

"Well that was a mistake. I've seen Robin at his house in Sittingbourne but I haven't seen Margaret for nearly thirty years."

"Why's that?"

"I don't know. I've asked about her but she's always too busy to see me." Audrey amended the statement then continued reading.

"You told Charlie that you and Derek were in a loving relationship."

"That's right dear."

"And Charlie put it to you that Derek used to fight with you and hit you regularly."

"That's not true. My husband never laid a finger on me."

"Do you remember signing a Medical Disclosure Form?"

"No." Audrey showed Patricia the form.

"Is that your signature?"

"Yes. I do remember now, dear."

"Well I've just come from your G.P and your dentist after examining your medical records."

"Yes dear."

"And they show that you frequently attended both practices with injuries which were consistent with being assaulted or beaten up."

"That's not true. They've obviously got me mixed up with someone else."

"And that the frequency of your visits normalized after Derek's disappearance in 2001."

"My husband never assaulted me or beat me up."

"So your G.P, your Dentist and your son are all mistaken."

"They're lying."

"Are you sure you don't want to change this part of your statement; remember this is your statement and it must be true to the best of your knowledge and belief or you could be prosecuted?"

"I'm the one telling the truth. The rest of them are lying."

"Did Derek ever force you to have sex with him?"

"No. I already told you; we were in a loving relationship."

"It's not too late to investigate these things Patricia. We can still help you put these demons away. Michael can corroborate what you have to say. We can offer counselling and witness support throughout the whole process."

"I already told you; WE WERE IN A LOVING RELATIONSHIP."

"Where do you want me to sign?" Patricia said.

"Here under the declaration to say that you're telling the truth. Initial the amendments and sign at the bottom of each page and after the last word on the final page... Thank you."

CHAPTER 27

The road was bathed in hazy sunshine as Matt made his way through the deep cleft in the hills separating Dover's cemeteries. Cast iron gates suspended between stone needles greeted his arrival at The Old Charlton Cemetery. There was death and decay among the trees. Headstones peppered the earth in tidy rows, behind short post and rail fences.

As he passed the old Victorian Gatehouse he noticed that it was sentry-less. Overgrown cultivated plants marked its domestic border; bright green mosses endowed its tiled roof, strips of pale green paint peeled from the woodwork. It was cold for July but Matt was warm after the steep climb up the dark tarmacadam road to the twin chapels. He admired the Victorian Gothic architecture, the tall tracery windows; stained turquoise and gold, the dressed stonework and the porches linking the Anglican and non-conformist Chapels. He noticed that the paintwork was gleaming and the box hedging neatly trimmed. 'It must be the Grade II listing,' he thought as he walked around the buildings.

It was Friday and he hoped this would be the last job of the week. A dead end job in a grave situation was how he'd described it to his team; bury Marlene Johnson and speak with anyone attending her funeral. He was early as usual. The rest of his team weren't due to pitch up until 10am, an hour before the Commendation and Committal.

He'd already decided to look for Tommy's grave. He'd been informed that it was the only one behind the chapels without a headstone. He was surprised to find a small group of mourners, standing with their backs towards him, as he turned the corner and wondered what they were doing there.

"Good morning," he said, to attract their attention. The group parted and there it was; an oblong black marble border with short ironwork fence; spiked in the corners. No headstone.

"You're the detective investigating Marlene's murder, aren't you?"

"Matt Sanderson and you are?"

Steely grey eyes betrayed a sharp mind; they were alert and focused, in complete contrast to the fading body that presented them, thinning grey hair, liver spots on the temples and back of the hand that shook his, a little too firmly, crow's feet in the corners of his eyes, veined cheeks and harsh grey stubble, a pinched mouth, which reminded him of a dog's bottom and a protuberant chin. He was the only one not dressed in black, wearing a faded denim baseball cap, worn jacket, torn jeans and Doc Martens. Matt got a whiff of body odour, unwashed linen and whisky.

"Ken. Ken Cartwright."

"Did you know Marlene?"

"Sure did. She was a bonny lass. We often bumped into each other. Why are you here?"

"I'm attending the funeral and wanted to see where Tommy was buried."

"You're looking at his plot."

"So I see. Why doesn't he have a headstone?"

"Why don't we go for a walk?" Ken said, turning away from the other mourners. Matt fell in step with Ken as they slowly walked away. Their pace was suited to the occasion; a slow death march. He waited in silence as they followed the path further into the cemetery. "I remember the last time I saw Marlene here," Ken began. "It was just like today. Marlene found a group of Sunday mourners standing opposite Tommy's grave. She said good morning, to attract their attention and the group parted like the oceans separating for Moses; their eyes turned away and she noticed the graffiti on Tommy's headstone. It was beneath the photograph of him embossed onto the marble. Paedophile painted in neat white script, the same size as the engraved words Tommy Johnson, which had been picked out with the same white material. There was no doubting the malice of the writer. She looked questioningly at the mourners, whispering, hovering; a few feet away, out of harm's way. She recognized me straight away. I was the only one not dressed in black. A couple of the others looked vaguely familiar, neighbours perhaps, people we exchanged pleasantries with; in the supermarket or at the bus stop, no-one that we really knew... She pulled the cleaning things she'd brought with her from her bag and went to work furiously trying to remove the paint from the headstone but it was no use. Tinned silicone polish and a duster weren't up to the job. Eventually, she took a house key from her pocket, scraped away at the paintwork and the word paedophile became a scratched illegible mess... I said, ' Come away, love. Let me walk you home.' She turned to me, I took her in my arms and she cried uncontrollably. That was the only time I got to hold her. She smelt as good as she looked... She couldn't escape the feeling that we were being watched as I led her back down the tarmacadam drive, through the gates and along the ravine leading to Frith Road. Then we were past The Admiral Harvey and up to her front door. Patraicc was in when we got there, looking through the sex adverts in the Sunday paper. He said, 'Why are you back so early?' That was before he noticed me and the mascara running down her cheeks. Then she threw her arms around his wide girth and sobbed. Patraicc looked at me and raised his left eyebrow. 'Someone's put graffiti on Tommy's headstone,' I said. 'Marlene got most of it off but you can still see what it says if you look carefully.' He said, 'What does it say?' I said, 'Just one word, paediatric.' I'd never heard the word paedophile. I wasn't good with big words. You didn't need to spell to work in the mines, so I never really learnt. Then I said, 'I think I should be off now; leave you two to get on.' I offered to have a go at the graffiti with some paint stripper. I had some Nitromors in the shed and I was going back to the cemetery to have a little chat with Hilda. She's been gone for fifteen years now. I still miss her... Anyway Patraicc said, 'That's very kind of you Ken. I'll meet you up there in about half an hour. We can work on it together; then I think I'd better take you to the Admiral for a Whisky or two.' 'That's very kind of you,' I said. 'I hope you feel better soon, Marlene.' She looked up at me through reddened eyes and said, 'Thank you Ken, you've been an absolute angel. I don't know how I would have coped without you.' Then she smiled at me and my heart melted. I doffed my cap and was gone... I was very pleased with myself when Patraicc caught up with me at Tommy's grave. 'Almost as good as new,' I said proudly. Paedophile had become a shadow of its former self. It was less noticeable from a distance but it was still there peppered into the fine perforations of the marble. Patraicc said, 'You've done a fantastic job Ken. No one could have done better. Let me buy you a drink.' We had a little pub crawl; a couple of whiskies in The Admiral and The Dewdrop. I asked him how Marlene was doing and he said, 'She's much better now; gone to bed for a lie down.'"

"Are you sure it said Paedophile on Tommy's grave?" Matt said

"I thought it said paediatric at the time but I now know that's the study of medicine dealing with children and their diseases."

"So you're not down the coalmines now."

"No, I've learnt to read and write since then if that's what you mean. I like to read poetry and passages from the Bible to my Hilda. "

"So what's your understanding of the word paedophile?"

"That's the sexual love by an adult of a child."

"Sounds like you looked that up in a dictionary."

"I did. I've been thinking about speaking to you since Monday when you announced Dorothy Skinner was Marlene Johnson."

"Do you know why Tommy no longer has a headstone?"

"The word paedophile was daubed over it a few days after I cleaned it off. I can only presume that Marlene had it removed."

"Why do you think someone would deface his headstone in that way?"

"I've thought about that long and hard. Either Tommy was a paedophile or the writer got the wrong grave or someone wanted to upset Marlene."

"How long have you lived in Dover, Ken?"

"Most of my life."

"And in this community?"

"Same."

"Did you ever hear anything untoward about Tommy when he was alive?"

"It was rumoured that he was a bit of a nancy-boy when he was growing up."

"Gay you mean?"

"Yes, a queer; a poofter; a homosexual."

"How did those rumours start?"

"Well, he was a pretty boy with a mop of thick curly blonde hair. He had intense blue eyes and fine features, a square jaw and a light down that covered his face and an agile body. He looked like a male model."

"Anything else?"

"His best mate Eddy was the same. They used to go everywhere together before the rumours started."

"When was that?"

"When they were teenagers."

"Did they have girlfriends?"

"Tommy dated a couple of girls, including Marlene but they were always the same, skinny with boyish figures."

"Why did Tommy marry Marlene?"

"Because she was pregnant."

"With his child?"

"No, the baby was Trevor Hazelwood's. He still burns a candle for her."

"What do you mean?"

"He always regretted not marrying her and always took an interest. That's probably why he recognized her when no one else did."

"What happened to Eddy?"

"Still lives here. He's as bent as a nine bob note."

"Would you be willing to introduce us?"

"I'd have to ask him first."

Matt realized they'd come full circle. The grave diggers were at Tommy's grave removing the soil with a mini JCB and preparing the site for Marlene's burial.

"Are you staying for the funeral Ken?"

"I was planning to."

"Can we talk some more when it's over?"

"Of course."

"One last thing… Have you seen Derek or Patraicc today?"

"No… I haven't seen them for years."

"I'll see you later then."

"Morning Charlie."

"You're a bit chipper today, Matt. Who's the old boy?"

"An old friend of Marlene's. We've just had a very interesting conversation. Apparently Tommy's headstone was removed because someone kept defacing it with the word paedophile."

"So that makes two out of four; Patraicc and Tommy."

"Everything in place?"

"Yes boss. The whole place is staked out. Do you really expect Derek and Patraicc to attend?"

"No, of course not but we'd look very foolish if we weren't prepared. Interview teams?"

"On standby, waiting to speak to anyone who attends the funeral."

"Good. Tell them to ignore, Ken, the old boy who looks like a tramp. He and I are going for a walk once the service is over."

CHAPTER 28

"Only The Lonely" signalled the end of the service. The doors of the chapel opened. Ken emerged, wiping tears from his eyes with the back of his sleeve, accompanied by Trevor Hazelwood. They were the only mourners. Dylan Barry, the press reporter followed at a respectable distance. He nodded to acknowledge Matt's presence. They'd spoken before the funeral and Matt had re-iterated his appeal for Derek and Patraicc to come forward. Dylan, together with the editor of the East Kent Chronicle had joined the quest to solve Marlene's murder.

"Thanks for coming Ken," Trevor said. They shook hands.

"Ready Chief Inspector?" Ken said.

"Not staying for the burial?" Matt said.

"No, Trevor's going to see her off." Matt gazed in Trevor's direction.

"You go on ahead. I'll join you later."

"How was it Ken?"

"Dreadful, only two mourners and that song summed it up for me. She must've been very lonely at the end, pretending to be someone else."

"I am sorry."

"Join me for the wake?"

"What did you have in mind?"

"A walk down to The Admiral, a couple of whiskies, then a walk up to The Dewdrop and a couple more. You're not allowed to drink on duty are you?"

152

"No but I'm sure I could manage a couple, purely for medicinal purposes you understand." Ken grinned. Matt nodded to Charlie. "I'm ready when you are." Ken marched down the tarmacadam driveway. Matt followed. They passed through the gates and onto the Old Charlton Road, the ravine separating the two cemeteries. Matt waited for Ken to speak and they were soon on the Frith Road approaching the Admiral Harvey.

"Would you like me to show you where Marlene used to live?" Ken said. Matt nodded. "It's only just past the pub and then I can introduce you to the lovely Bernice."

"The landlady?"

"That's right."

"That's very kind of you Ken."

Matthews Place was just as Matt had imagined it; a nondescript small terraced Victorian house in a cul-de-sac.

"You must've seen a lot of changes in this area," Matt said.

"The housing hasn't improved a great deal but the industrial estates have been replaced with superstores and supermarkets, plus everyone burns gas instead of coal so the air's a lot cleaner. Seen enough?"

"Yes, thank you."

"Hi Bernice," Ken said. Matt noticed a voluptuous woman standing behind the bar, legs apart with hands on hips. She looked to be in her sixties but he knew that she was actually in her early seventies. Thick curly auburn hair cascaded onto her shoulders. Her forehead was high and featureless; eyes sparkled with mischief above a rather long bony nose and bright red lipstick framed a dazzling smile. She had a magnificent chest over a narrow waste and nicely tapered legs. "No wonder Alphonse had described her as seductive and Paul Adams had married her," Matt thought.

"Who's your friend?"

"This is Detective Chief Inspector Matt Sanderson," Ken said.

"Oh," Bernice replied, "come to chase me up regarding my errant husband?"

"Not at all, Ken's just showing me around."

"I did give Paul your telephone number but he didn't promise to ring you."

"When's he back?"

"Tomorrow, I expect he'll give you a ring then. So what can I do for you two gentlemen?"

"I'll have a large whisky," Ken said.

"And a pint of Spitfire," Matt added, handling a tenner between thumb and forefinger. "So this is where Tommy used to drink with Derek and Patraicc?"

"That's right; very convenient wouldn't you say?" Bernice said.

"It couldn't be any closer."

"Any of their old friends pop in nowadays?"

"They didn't have many friends," Bernice said, "kept themselves to themselves. Cheeky Charlie still pops in from time to time but you already know all this from your colleagues who've been pestering me all week." Matt smiled and handed her one of his cards.

"Can you give this to Charlie with my compliments and ask him to ring me?"

"Will do, he normally pops in over the weekend."

"And what does he do?"

"Nothing now but he used to run a breakers yard and repair cars."

"Can I get you another Ken?"

"Cheers guv'nor." Ken smiled. "I'm feeling better already… Do you still want me to ring Eddy?"

"Please." Ken retired to a table.

"So Chief Inspector, what do you think this is all about?"

"Marlene's murder?" Bernice nodded. "We're still working on it."

"I'm surprised that you want to speak to Derek about it."

"Why's that?"

"Because he was very fond of Marlene. I can't imagine why he'd want to hurt her. They were as thick as thieves. She was as close to him as she was to her husband Tommy, and she adored him."

"Do you have a theory of your own?"

"Well, my husband and I always thought Derek's sudden disappearance was very suspicious. It was so unlike him to just vanish like that, leaving his wife and best friends without a word."

"So you don't buy into him having another family in France?"

154

"No, of course not, Paul would have found him if that had been the case but his boss, Detective Chief Inspector Baxter, wasn't prepared to widen the enquiry not even when Marlene and Patraicc disappeared." Matt wondered if Baxter was now his boss, Detective Chief Superintendent Baxter; the chief of detectives within the force. If so he would have to tread very carefully; Detective Chief Superintendents were not happy when they got egg on their faces.

"So what do you think happened to Derek, Patraicc and Marlene?"

"I think they were all done in and the only one you found was Marlene."

That tallied with Matt's recent suspicions.

"And who do you think might be responsible for their deaths, if that's what actually happened?"

Bernice crossed her arms, leaned on the bar and plonked her ample breasts on her forearms.

"Someone they upset, the father of a child they'd interfered with," she whispered.

"Do you have anyone in mind?"

"No, but you must know about the graffiti on Tommy's grave by now." Matt didn't acknowledge that he did and said.

"Go on."

"Well first Derek disappears then Tommy's headstone is desecrated with the word paedophile," she whispered, "not once but twice. The gossip starts and then Patraicc and Marlene disappear."

"Go on."

"Well it all adds up doesn't it?"

"What does?"

"That they were done in."

"And what did Paul tell Baxter?"

"Exactly that."

"And what did Baxter say?"

"You'll have to ask Paul about that but he wasn't happy, was spitting feathers when he came home. He wanted Baxter to assign the case to the CID so it could be properly investigated but Baxter refused, saying he wasn't going to send a team of his detectives on a wild goose chase. Then he started to put pressure on Paul by discussing our relationship; perhaps they should drag me in for a good grilling as I was the last one to see Derek.

Baxter made his life a misery because he wouldn't let it go then picked him up for a minor misdemeanour and forced him to take early retirement," which was exactly what he'd do to Matt if he wasn't careful.

"Why didn't you tell this to the other officers who interviewed you?"

"Because I didn't want them to go through the mill like my Paul; it's different for you. You're all in the same club, aren't you, senior officers. I mean; you're not going to take any shit like that, are you?" Matt looked steadily into her eyes and shook his head. "I thought not... I'll ask Paul to ring you as soon as he comes home."

"Thank you."

Matt bought Ken another whisky and joined him at the table.

"How are you getting on with Eddy?"

"Just finished, he'll meet us at The Dewdrop and if he likes the look of you he'll talk. He doesn't generally like the police but I've told him that you are okay. He had a lot of trouble with them when he was growing up due to his being a Homosexual."

"The law was an ass before they decriminalized homosexuality in 1967."

"And so were a lot of coppers," Ken said.

Matt spotted Eddy as soon as they walked into The Dewdrop. He was seated with his back to the door. Long light grey, almost blonde, straight hair hung down to the middle of his back; it was feathered at the ends and gently caressed his buttocks which were tucked into skin-tight black leather trousers. His upper torso was similarly dressed in a fine black leather jacket and his feet tucked into black high heels.

"Hello officer," he said, turning towards them, his deep booming voice betraying his sexuality. Matt smiled and proffered his hand.

"You must be Eddy."

"That's right but you can call me Edwina, like the Currie."

"Matt Sanderson."

"I told you he was a character," Ken said.

"What can I get you?" Matt asked.

"A Babycham. George always keeps a few cases for his favourite customer, don't you George?"

"That's right Eddy."

"Edwina when we've got company, if you don't mind. I don't want to give the officer the wrong impression." George's laughter filled the bar.

"Right you are Edwina. And what would you two gentlemen like?"

"A whisky for Ken and a pint of Spitfire for me," Matt said.

"Okay Mattie. I can call you Mattie can't I?"

"Of course, I've been called far worse." Eddy raised a manicured eyebrow.

"Why don't we go over to the corner for our little chit-chat and you can tell me all about it." Matt laughed and followed him to a dark corner of the bar. "I don't like your outfit, it's a bit grey. I thought you worked for the boys in blue."

"I do."

"Let's see it then, Mattie." Matt wondered what he was referring to. "Your truncheon," Eddy laughed at his own joke, "no seriously, your warrant card. A girl can't be too careful these days." Matt smiled and handed the document over. "Not very photogenic are you?"

"I haven't been airbrushed if that's what you mean."

"Now how can Edwina help you?"

"I understand that you and Tommy Johnson went to school together."

"Ken, what have you been telling the officer," Eddy shouted. He looked back at Matt and said, "That's right."

"And that you were very close when you were teenagers."

"That's right. Some might say we were teenaged lovers."

"Were you?"

"Now that would be telling deary." Eddy sipped his Babycham. Matt waited; all in good time. "We were experimenting. Tommy wasn't sure about his sexuality. We played about a little, then he had a few goes on Marlene, then he came back to me, then he had a few more goes on Marlene. He was what you might call AC/DC."

"So he liked men and women."

"Boys and girls; we were boys and girls then."

"How long did this go on for?"

"Most of the summer of fifty-six."

"And then what happened?"

"The rumours started and we had to stop seeing each other. It was another eleven years before, you know, they legalized sex between consenting males over twenty one."

"And what happened after that?"

"Nothing, Tommy was married to Marlene and in the merchant navy by then."

"Did you see much of him after he joined the navy?"

"We did see each other a couple of times but the flames of desire for me had left him. Then I caught him ogling young boys. It was pretty disgusting, a twenty year old man looking at youngsters in that way."

"When was that?"

"At Christmas, at the end of his first year at sea, just before he wed Marlene."

"So you noticed a profound change in him?"

"Yes, he was clearly into young boys."

"How did that affect your friendship?"

"Destroyed it. I didn't mind Marlene. I could've been his bit on the side. It would've been safer that way. He was a respectable married man so no one would suspect that we were carrying on. Of course, I didn't dress like this in those days. That would've been asking for trouble."

"Did he tell you anything about his travels?"

"He hinted that he'd had sex with a couple of rent boys, in Bombay I think."

"What do you mean by rent boys?"

"Young boys, children. I wasn't interested. Told him that was disgusting."

"What did he say in response to that?"

"That the whole crew was at it."

"Did he mention anyone in particular?"

"No, he wasn't stupid. He could see I was upset and dropped the subject."

"Did you hear any rumours about him subsequently?"

"No, nothing; until a few years after he died. Then I heard about the graffiti on his headstone."

"Who told you about that?"

"Ken. Silly bugger thought it said paediatric on his headstone but I knew straight away and then I started thinking about Derek's disappearance and about the boys who used to go to Marlene's house. Derek's son, Michael and Patraicc's son, Robin. They were good looking boys. I'm sure Tommy would've fancied them. Another Babycham? For a babe."

"George, another baby for Edwina, please."

"You're alright Mattie. A good listener; I hope you catch the bastard that murdered Marlene." Matt sensed that the conversation was over. "What are you doing tomorrow night?"

"I've got to spend some time with the missus."

"Shame. What a waste. I always fancied a man in uniform. There aren't enough gays in this town to keep a man like me occupied."

CHAPTER 29

Matt was enjoying a lie in for the first time in two weeks when Rose appeared with a mug of tea and Saturday's newspaper.

"Hello sleepy head. Caught up on your beauty sleep?" Rose said.

"I think I'll need another week in bed before I can say that."

"I doubt if you can be spared that long," Rose said, as she placed a large pillow behind his back and put the mug down on the bedside cabinet. "So Chief Inspector, how's it going?"

"I think we're getting there. Had a bit more luck. Hit it off with an old fella at the cemetery yesterday." Matt sipped his tea. "He took me for a walk. It was very revealing. Tommy Johnson, Marlene's husband, might have been a paedophile. So that makes two sex offenders. We already knew about Patraicc." Rose smiled and nodded to show that she was paying attention. She could see that Matt was thinking carefully before speaking as if vocalizing his thoughts for the first time. "But we still need to find out whether Derek and Marlene were the same way inclined. He introduced me to the landlady of The Admiral Harvey as well. An interesting woman, very attractive for her age, married to the missing person's officer who first looked into Derek's disappearance. She has her own theory; thinks that Derek, Patraicc and Marlene were all murdered but we only found Marlene's body. I'd been thinking the same myself. Thinks it was probably by the father of someone they'd interfered with. Her husband wanted Baxter to treat Derek's disappearance as a murder but he refused. They fell out and Paul was forced to retire over something minor. Should find out what that was later on today."

"You're not going back to work?"

"I might have to, luv. I'm not sure Paul will speak to anyone else."

"Why's that?"

"A matter of trust. He's got an axe to grind and that axe involves the most senior detective in the Kent Police. He'll want to be sure that I'm not going to bury what he has to say."

"Can't Charlie deal with it?"

"No, he and David are interviewing Eddy or Edwina, another colourful character I was introduced to yesterday. He's gay and an ex-boyfriend of Tommy's. That was before Tommy got into young boys."

"That's enough! It's bad enough talking about murderers but paedophiles. They just make me sick. Should be castrated as far as I'm concerned... Now what would you like for breakfast?"

"You could come back to bed."

"Hello, Chief Inspector Matt Sanderson?"

"That's right."

"Sorry to disturb you on a Saturday morning. It's Cheeky Charlie. Bernice said to give you a ring on this number."

"Thanks for ringing. Did Bernice tell you why I wanted to speak with you?"

"She said you wanted to speak with anyone who knew Marlene."

"That's right. How well did you know her?"

"Quite well I suppose."

"And what about Tommy, Derek and Patraicc?"

"Better."

"Can you tell me how you met?"

"I met Tommy, Derek and Patraicc in The Admiral. They were a bit cliquey at first. Then Patraicc had an accident in his van and Derek asked me to repair it."

"When was that?"

"A long time ago, just after they left the navy."

"Can you describe the circumstances?"

"I can remember that it was in the summer, at the weekend. Patraicc's van was parked in the trading estate in Granville Street, not far from The

Admiral, among a load of old Bedford and Comma vans. The front end was stoved–in and the windscreen had gone."

"What type of van was it?"

"A navy transit van, like a copper's old meat wagon."

"Anything else?"

"There was a lot of blood in the cab and all over the steering wheel, and a mattress in the back, which I thought a bit strange."

"Why did Derek ask you to repair it?"

"Because I ran a breakers yard, I suppose."

"Why didn't Patraicc ask you himself?"

"Because he'd been injured in the accident."

"Which accident?"

"The one involving his van."

"Do you know where that was?"

"No, I'm afraid not but he ended up with a nasty scar on his forehead."

"The crescent shaped one?"

"That's right and he had a broken nose; must've taken a nasty knock to do that much damage."

"Do you know which hospital he went to?"

"I don't think he did. He stayed at Marlene's until he was better."

"Didn't you think that was strange?"

"Not really, people went into hospital to die when I was a nipper."

Rose appeared at Matt's side and looked over his shoulder at the notes he was scribbling down. She pointed her left hand skyward, crossed it with her right and mouthed the word Tea. Matt nodded.

"What did you do with Patraicc's van?"

"Popped it into a lock-up until Patraicc was better."

"Why did you do that?"

"Because Derek asked me to."

"Before or after you'd repaired it?"

"Before."

"So Derek asked you to hide it?"

"No. He asked me to lock it up but I suppose it could be construed that way."

"How long did you have it before they asked you to repair it?"

"A couple of weeks, Derek wanted to make sure Patraicc made a full recovery before paying for the repairs."

'More likely they wanted to be sure the police weren't looking for it before bringing it out again,' Matt thought. Thanks luv, he mouthed as Rose put his tea down on the table.

"Did you see much of Derek and co' after you repaired Patraicc's van?"

"I continued to service his van and they also employed me to look after the engines on their boat."

"What was the name of their boat?"

"Spartacus."

"What type of boat was she?"

"A Freeman thirty cruiser fitted with twin sixty horsepower Bedfords; a bit like having two bus engines in a boat."

"Where did they keep her?"

"She was moored near the Gazen Salts Nature Reserve in Sandwich."

"What did they use her for?"

"Smuggling cigarettes across the channel."

"Who did they sell them to?"

"Most of the small shops in Kent kept duty free cigarettes under the counter."

"Did you ever see them socially?"

"Once, about a year after Patraicc's accident, he had a party to celebrate his resurrection and the new life he was enjoying with his best pals Derek and Tommy. He said he hadn't been that happy since leaving the merchant navy."

"Where was it held?"

"At his house in Dickson Road."

"Who attended?"

"Derek, his wife and son, Tommy and Marlene, Patraicc's wife, of course and their son."

"So it was a small affair?"

"That's right."

"Anything happen?"

"No we all drank too much. I got pissed on Patraicc's home-brew, woke up the next day surrounded by balloons. Thought I was having a nightmare. They all had faces with crescent shaped scars over the right eye. I screamed and was thoroughly embarrassed over brunch when they took the piss out of me."

"Apart from their smuggling activities and concealing the fact that Patraicc had been involved in a road traffic accident, is there anything else I should know about?"

"No. I don't think so."

"When did you last see Derek and co'?"

"At Tommy's funeral in ninety-eight."

"Hello, Charlie. How did you get on with Edwina and Ken?"

"I've got Ken's statement. David's still interviewing Edwina. Edwina's treating it like a date. Any contact from Paul Adams?"

"He's expecting us at five thirty. I've just finished chatting to Cheeky Charlie."

"Did he have anything interesting to say?"

"An interesting tale about Patraicc having an accident in his van and concealing it from the police; seems to corroborate Keith's allegation about being run-off the road. He also gave me some info about their boat, where it was kept and their smuggling activities."

"How are Audrey and Mark getting on with Keith?"

"They're with him now, in the video interview suite, taking his statement."

"Good, so everything's coming together. See you at five thirty."

*

"Hi Bernice, this is Detective Inspector Charlie Speck; my number two." Bernice eyed the man standing in front of her. Tall, six foot two at least, dark with a matt of jet black hair, of Caribbean or African descent, broad, fit, handsome and beautifully attired in a jet black suit.

"Hardly what I'd call a speck," she said, grinning mischievously. "Paul, they're here," she shouted up the stairs. "He'll be down in a minute."

Paul's blue eyes burned like cold steel.

"So which side are you on?" he said.

"I'm searching for the truth," Matt said, "I'm too old to be taking sides."

"What about your friend?"

"He can speak for himself."

"I'm here to solve a murder and if I have to upset the detective chief superintendent so be it."

"I can see that my wife's been blabbing," Paul said.

"She did tell us that you had a falling out with Baxter regarding Derek's disappearance," Matt said.

"Don't you mean Detective Chief Superintendent Stanley Baxter?"

"If you like," Matt replied.

"Baxter doesn't sound very respectful," Paul said.

"Well he has to earn my respect like anyone else," Matt said.

"Hasn't he done that already?" Paul said.

"I hardly know him," Matt said, "he sits in his ivory tower at headquarters. We never see him unless there's a problem with priority crimes or the overtime budget. Then he usually sends one of his heavies and if that doesn't work he comes himself."

"What about you? You're not his snitch, are you?"

"Do I look like a snitch?" Charlie said, inflating his lungs and filling his suit to full capacity. Paul had to admit that he didn't. He wouldn't like to bump into Charlie on a dark night.

"Look we're here to do a job and we don't take shit from anyone," Matt said, "including you, for that matter." Paul considered that response.

"What would you do if I told you Baxter refused to investigate Derek's disappearance as a murder because he was worried about the crime figures, the overtime budget and his next promotion?"

"I'd listen and then decide whether to believe you," Matt said.

"And what would you do if I could produce documentary evidence?"

"I'd consider that evidence."

"Cup of tea?" Paul said.

"Why not," Matt winked at Charlie, "looks like we might get what we came for," he whispered.

"So where would you like to start?" Paul said.

"The beginning is usually a good place," Charlie said.

"Would you mind if I referred to my original notes?"

"Your notes?"

"Sorry old habits die hard," Paul said.

"Are you telling me that you have your original notes?" Matt said.

"I know I shouldn't," Paul said, "but I knew that TBB, That Bastard Baxter, was after me so I took the originals and posted them to a care of address."

"That would explain why we only have the front sheet," Charlie said.

"You should have a very good copy of all my notes," Paul said. "I could hardly tell the difference between my original and the photocopy."

"We've only got the computerized record and your handwritten front sheet," Charlie said.

"And what does the computerized record say about my consultations with DCI Baxter?" Paul said.

"Nothing about you suspecting Derek had been murdered or you wanting Baxter to assign the case to the CID."

"I knew it," Paul said, "someone who was computer literate and of supervisory rank must have doctored it."

"Can we see your original notes?" Matt said.

"In for a penny: in for a pound." Paul retrieved a brown envelope from a sideboard. "This is a photocopy. The originals are somewhere safe. You can have them when the case goes to court."

"You do know that you could be arrested for theft?" Charlie said.

"Couldn't you say you found them at headquarters?

"That's called noble cause corruption these days," Matt said.

"That's what it used to be called. Now it's just corruption," Charlie said.

"It used to be called practical policing in my day."

"Perhaps it could be dealt with by means of a caution," Matt said.

"Best you look in that envelope then." Matt opened the envelope and examined the spidery writing that had crawled across the pages.

"Is this your best handwriting?" he said.

"They taught me to write like that at the training school." Paul said.

"So the defence couldn't read it?" Matt said. Paul grinned and nodded.

CHAPTER 30

"I was asked to attend Tower Hamlets Street on Monday the twenty-first of July 2001," Paul said. "The call had come via the son Michael Stevens. The wife Patricia was extremely worried and upset. I'd spent some time calming her down and was chatting to her when I sensed someone else was present, listening to our conversation. I hadn't heard the front door. We were in the dining room at the back." Paul closed his eyes. "I can see it so clearly. They say that your memory improves with age. Long term memory perhaps but my short term memory is terrible. 'You told me earlier that Derek was drinking in The Admiral Harvey in Bridge Street on Friday night,' I said. 'That's right,' she said. 'He went out with his best mate Patraicc. They've been friends ever since they were in the merchant navy. They used to go out with Tommy as well but he died of cancer a few years ago. He was such a nice man.' 'Have you spoken to Patraicc since Friday,' I said. 'Oh, yes. I rang him on Saturday and he said the last time he saw Derek was on Friday night,' and then in a quieter voice she said, 'I'm not sure that I should be telling you this but the landlady, Bernice, had a lock-in after-hours.' 'Is there anything else you shouldn't be telling me?' I said. Then Michael, the son, tapped lightly on the dining room door and said, 'May I come in?' I was a little startled; the intensity of the interview was interrupted." Paul opened his eyes and said, "How am I doing; not going too fast for you?"

"I learnt shorthand in an earlier occupation so you're doing just fine."

"Not just a pretty face then?" Paul said. Charlie grinned and Paul closed his eyes once more. "'You must be Michael the only son,' I said. I stood up and extended my hand. 'PC Adams,' I said. We shook hands and I took a good look at him." Matt remembered Paul's cold blue eyes scrutinizing him earlier. "'That's right,' Michael said, 'how are you getting on?' 'I've got all of your father's personal details,' I said. 'Your mother's given me a recent photograph and we've just established that your father was in The Admiral Harvey on Bridge Street on Friday night with his best mate Patraicc.'"

"How can you re-call this in such detail?" Charlie said.

"I've got a photographic memory." Paul said, "Once I've written something down I can re-call it word perfect. I studied my notes carefully before you arrived."

"Please carry on."

"'Can you add anything to that,' I said. 'No, I'm afraid not. My father and I haven't spoken for over twenty years,' Michael said. 'Why's that?' I said… 'Mum, go and put the kettle on,' he said. 'I'm parched.' 'Okay dear, can I get you something officer,' she said. I asked, for a strong cup of tea without sugar."

"Surely you didn't write that down as well?" Charlie said.

"No but it came back to me when I was reading my notes earlier," Paul said, as he carefully appraised Charlie.

Charlie held up both hands in surrender. "No more interruptions, I promise."

Paul closed his eyes. "'Why don't you make a pot?' Michael suggested as she left the room 'and bring some of those nice biscuits you've been saving for visitors,' he shouted. 'You were saying that you haven't spoken to your father for over twenty years,' I said. 'That's right,' Michael interrupted, 'not since the third of January 1979.' 'How can you be so sure?' I said. 'I left home that day and joined the Royal Marine Commandos; you probably know that the armed services always ask for your date of joining when you apply for anything,' he said. 'Why haven't you spoken to him since?' I said. 'We had a difficult relationship when I was growing up, especially during my teenage years. His relationship with my mother wasn't good. They were always arguing and fighting and making-up.' 'What do you mean by fighting?' I said. 'He used to hit her regularly, mostly where it didn't show, on her arms and legs and back. When things got really bad and he was drunk he'd forget and punch her in the face,' he said. 'She doesn't have a full set of teeth you know; she wears a plate which she soaks in a glass of Steradent every night. It's really disgusting. She's had that for more than thirty years.'"

Paul opened his eyes. "It's time for a cup of tea and a fag. Do either of you smoke?" Charlie reached into his pocket and offered Paul his silver cigarette case. "Craven A's; I haven't seen those for years; very posh." Rain beat against the sash windows. "There's no need to go outside," Paul said.

"Won't Bernice mind?" Matt said.

"She will. Let's pretend it's 1982."

"When you could smoke wherever you wanted," Charlie said.

"Do you remember what we used to do with the dog-ends?" Matt said.

"Throw them on the floor at the station to keep the cleaners busy," Paul said.

"Do you remember the spittoons?"

"Bloody disgusting, when you think about it," Paul said. Charlie looked bemused. "Tins for spitting in," Paul added. "I think we'd better open a window before the smoke alarm goes off."

Charlie settled back into his seat opposite his notebook with pen poised.

Paul closed his eyes once more and said, "Where was I?"

"She doesn't have a full set of teeth you know; she wears a plate which she soaks in a glass every night. It's really disgusting. She's had that for more than thirty years."

"'Why didn't you call the police when they were fighting?' I said. 'We didn't have to. The neighbours called you the first time they had a fight to complain about the noise,' Michael said. 'And what happened then?' I said. 'PC Plod arrived and he spoke to my father who was very polite. He even invited him in for a cup of tea as if they were best mates and nothing had happened. They had a nice cosy chat in this room whilst my mother scurried about making tea and biscuits. My father admitted they'd been squabbling and promised to apologize to the neighbours in the morning; then in front of my father PC Plod asked my mother if she was alright. She nodded of course and that was the end of that. Plod drank his tea and made small talk with my father. He didn't even ask if there were any children in the house.' 'Did your father ever try to get in touch with you after you left?' I said. 'No, he wouldn't speak to me because I floored him and wouldn't apologize.' 'What do you mean?' I said. 'He was pulling my mum's hair viciously and daring her to scream that last night. I lost my temper and punched him on the nose. It was a beauty. He landed on his backside, banged his head on a doorframe and passed out.' Patricia returned with the tea. 'How are you two getting on?' She said. 'We're just about finished,' Michael said. 'For now, but before I go I'll need to take your name, address, date of birth and contact details for my records,' I said. 'Why do you need so much information?' Michael said. I lied. 'It's standard procedure.' I wouldn't normally take a date of birth but I really didn't like Michael. I sensed he was hiding something and decided to come back later and have another little chat with

Patricia, unless I found Derek in the meantime. 'I'll be off now,' I said. 'I need to speak to Bernice at The Admiral Harvey to find out what time Derek left and after that I'll have to interview his best friends Patraicc and Marlene.' 'Thank you, Paul,' Patricia said. 'There's no need to get up,' I said. 'It's alright mum,' Michael said. 'I'll show him out. Thank you for being so thorough and taking the time to listen to my mother. She's not used to dealing with people in authority and you've really put her mind at ease. Hopefully, you'll find my father soon and then we can all get back to normal.'"

Paul opened his eyes. "I noticed a grey metallic Vauxhall Vectra parked outside that wasn't there when I arrived and noted the registration number. When I got back to my car I sat in the passenger seat with the missing persons form and recorded my misgivings about Michael. That was a bit unconventional for 2001; to record opinions, I mean, as the report could be disclosed in court but they were my original notes and I had my own style of recording things. Whilst I was topping and tailing the first entry on the free text page I noticed Michael leaving in the Vectra. I ran him through the PNC later and checked the intelligence database but didn't find anything untoward… Do you fancy another cuppa and one of Charlie's Craven A's Chief Inspector? "

Matt laughed.

"How did you get on at The Admiral Harvey?" Charlie said.

"Touché." Paul said, "My shout but I'm afraid I only have Duty Frees."

CHAPTER 31

"How did you get on at The Admiral Harvey?" Paul mulled over that question while the kettle boiled and the tea diffused into the cups.

"Hello stranger. What brings you here?" Bernice had said, standing with legs apart and hands on generous hips. She was just as Paul remembered, brassy but full of fun and amazing for sixty. She still retained her hour glass figure; large breasts over a thin waist and long shapely legs. Curly auburn hair fell onto her shoulders. Her eyes sparkled with mischief and bright red lipstick framed her cheerful smile. "It must be trouble because I haven't seen you in?" "Four years," he'd said. "It is good to see you Bernice. You haven't changed a bit; still as cheeky and sexy as ever." She'd pouted at him and said, "So why did you stay away so long?" "You know why," he'd replied.

He'd been passionate about her but monogamy was not her thing. She liked to play around. That wasn't his style. He didn't want to share her with anyone and when he told her he couldn't, she'd finished it. Their affair hadn't lasted long and he'd never been into the pub during opening hours. He hadn't really thought it through either. If you were on the force you could have a wife who was a publican but you couldn't live on licensed premises. He was sure that infringed his human rights but he was on the wrong side of the law for anyone to care.

He'd explained he was there on official business and she'd invited him in, asking one of her regulars to mind the bar. "So what's this all about?" she'd said, as she drowned two tea bags in milk and hot water.

"How are you getting on?" Matt said, bringing him back to the present.

"Sorry... I was day dreaming. I'll be through in a minute."

"So how did the interview with Bernice go?" Charlie said, with a wide grin.

"Once we'd got over the pleasure of seeing each other, much the same as any other," Paul replied. "We'd dated previously but things hadn't worked out and we'd wasted four years."

"Was she expecting you? Charlie said.

"No, she was surprised."

"Did she behave normally?"

"She did."

"What did you say to her?"

Paul closed his eyes. "'I believe that Derek Stevens is one of your regulars.' 'That's right,' she said. 'He was in here on Friday night with his best mate. Patraicc was pissed but Derek was on really good form so I asked him to stay behind and help me clear up. He left at about 1am on Saturday morning.' 'Did he say where he was going?' I said. 'No but I presumed he was going home to his wife Patricia,' she said. 'They don't live very far away. You can walk it in five to ten minutes when you're sober.' 'Was he sober?' I said. 'No, he was reeling by the time he left,' she said. 'Have you heard from him since Saturday morning?' I said. 'No but I wouldn't expect to; he only comes in on Friday nights,' she said. 'Does he socialize with anyone else?' I said. 'Not really. There used to be three of them, Tommy, Derek and Patraicc. They were inseparable but Tommy died a couple of years back. Do you think something's happened to him?' She said. 'He hasn't been home since Friday and his wife's worried about him,' I said. ' Poor thing; I hope I'm not a suspect,' she said. 'Should you be?' I said. 'No,' she said, 'but if I am, I want the full works, handcuffs and all.'" Charlie grinned at Matt.

Paul looked thoughtful. She'd continued. "You do remember the handcuffs don't you Paul?" He'd handcuffed her to the Victorian bedstead in his house on one occasion before realizing the keys were at the station. She'd remained tethered for half an hour while he'd gone to fetch them, was like a mare on heat when he'd returned and the pub didn't open that night. "You do remember don't you?" He'd grinned at her. How could he forget? "Now back to business," he'd said. "Oh, do we have to?" she'd said.

"This isn't a social call, Bernice," I said.

"She must've been disappointed," Charlie said.

Paul opened his eyes.

"What happened after that?" Matt said.

"It was 9pm by the time I finished typing up my report. I was already in my own time. Nobody would have thanked me for doing any more; in fact, I would've got a bollocking if I'd submitted an overtime claim for a Low Risk Misper. I'd discovered that Derek had gone on walkabout before. Patricia had reported him missing in ninety-one and ninety-five and on both occasions he'd returned when he was ready. He'd been interviewed by my predecessor and hinted that he had another woman in Pas-de-Calais. The archives only went back ten years so he could have been reported missing on other occasions. I'd already circulated him as Missing on the PNC and noted his PNC ID number on the pro-forma. I'd placed the form in the relevant binder and put the binder in its cubby hole. If Derek had been found during the night he would have been cancelled, the pro-forma would have been removed from the binder and I would have found it in my tray in the morning."

"Do you think Bernice had anything to do with Derek's disappearance?" Charlie said.

"I'm sure she didn't. I fancied a good drink after work. I walked back to the Admiral and the rest, as they say, is history."

"What would you have done if you thought she'd done anything wrong?"

"Nicked her just like anyone else."

"I believe you interviewed Marlene and Patraicc the next day," Matt said.

"That's right," Paul said. "They were at Matthews Place. I'd had a busy day. It was getting dark and they were in a sombre mood. I confirmed a lot of what I already knew over their kitchen table and a pot of tea. '"Where do you think he's gone?' I said. 'It beats me,' Patraicc said. 'I've no idea,' Marlene said. 'Did he tell you that he was going?' I said. 'Not a dicky-bird,' Patraicc said. 'Marlene?' I said. 'Patraicc knows him better than anyone else,' she said. 'Is there another woman in his life?' I said. 'Only Bernice in The Admiral Harvey but that's restricted to Friday nights,' Patraicc said. I nearly choked on my tea. 'Are they in a relationship?' I said. 'No,' Patraicc said, 'but it doesn't stop the rumours.' 'What about hobbies and pastimes?' I said. 'We used to own a boat and go to Calais quite often,' Patraicc said, 'but we gave that up when Marlene's husband Tommy died, nearly three years ago.' 'Does he have any friends in Calais?' I said. 'Not that I know of,' Patraicc said, 'but this isn't the first time he's gone missing.' 'Really,' I said. 'If you check your records you'll find that he's gone missing on quite a few occasions,' Patraicc said. 'Did he tell you where he'd been when he returned?' I said. 'No,' Patraicc said, 'but he told PC Fredericks that he had another family in Calais.' 'How do you know that?' I said. 'PC Fredericks told me when he went missing on subsequent occasions.'"

"What did you make of Patraicc?" Matt said.

"He was quite glib. I didn't like him at all."

"What about Marlene?"

"She seemed anxious, didn't say anything unless I addressed her directly but was willing to follow Patraicc's lead."

"Did you come to any conclusions?"

"I felt they both had something to hide."

"Did you return on any subsequent occasion?"

"About six weeks after the first when the enquiries in France proved negative."

"What were they like on that occasion?" Matt said.

"Same as before, the only difference being that Patraicc had moved in with Marlene. He'd given up the tenancy on his flat after his landlord put the rent up and moved into her spare room. It was a Friday night and they were having dinner when I called. They knew all about the enquiries I'd been making across the channel, thanks to Patricia, but didn't seem surprised that I hadn't found him. It was as if they'd written him off. I went to Baxter after that and asked him to treat Derek's disappearance as suspicious; suggested he might've been murdered. He told me to go away and come back when I had a bit more to go on. Marlene and Patraicc disappeared about six weeks after that, just after Tommy's grave was desecrated but that still wasn't enough. He threw me out of his office even though I'd found a motive. He wasn't going to waste his money on a missing person's enquiry. His money: not Kent Police's money; his money. He had budgets to worry about and didn't want another unsolved murder on his books. In my opinion, he was more interested in his next promotion."

"What happened after that?"

"I made waves, got an appointment with the Detective Superintendent who told me to go away. He had complete faith in Stanley Baxter and accused me of going behind Baxter's back. I'd invited Baxter to attend the meeting but he denied receiving the invitation. Then I tried to make an appointment with the Detective Chief Superintendent but he refused to see me. Then the trouble really began. I was warned to mind my back by the Chief Super's bag carrier, a Sergeant I'd worked with earlier in my career, but I wasn't worried as I'd always behaved myself and done things properly. Then they threatened to arrest Bernice for Derek's murder and search The Admiral. She told me to let them, she had nothing to hide. Then I was dragged in on my day off and told they'd discovered a number of discrepancies with my mileage claims. I was given a choice. I could take early retirement or face prosecution for obtaining money by deception. I was sure that my mileage claims were above board but not sure that I'd never made a mistake. I didn't want to risk twenty nine years of pensionable service."

"So you took early retirement?"

"Yes."

"Any regrets?"

"Only that TBB made it to Detective Chief Superintendent."

*

"So what's your assessment of Paul Adams," Matt said, as Charlie drove back to the incident room.

Charlie smiled. "I liked him. He's a bit of a character, like all the best coppers I've met."

"Do you believe him?"

"Yes, I do. I've heard that Baxter's a ruthless swine and only interested in one person, himself. What about you?"

"I've had first-hand experience. When I was much younger he took all the credit for solving a murder. There were a number of street robberies in Tunbridge Wells which were getting increasingly violent. Then one of them went wrong and the victim died. An officer from the intelligence unit contacted Baxter as soon as he learned of the murder and put up four suspects from the Met, who'd been stopped in Tunbridge a couple of weeks earlier. They all had previous convictions for violent muggings. Baxter asked the Mets to pay them a visit and got lucky; four arrests for Armed Robbery and Murder. They still had the victim's property, a Rolex Oyster, and were wearing the same clothes. They hadn't expected the police to be so quick off the mark."

"Was that you?"

"No, it was my best mate. I asked Baxter to write him up for a commendation but he denied all knowledge of the conversation."

"Bastard... What are we going to do about him?"

"That's a good question," Matt said.

CHAPTER 32

"I feel like a naughty child, Michael, creeping around like this," Denise said, into her mobile phone.

"I'm sure it will only be temporary."

"You mean until my mother forgets that your father's wanted for murder."

"That's hardly likely to happen. She's not got dementia. No I meant until she gets over the shock," Michael said.

"She's not god, punishing the children for the sins of the fathers to the third and fourth generation."

"I sincerely hope not."

"I've got to tell her I'm meeting you, Michael. She'll never forgive us if I lie to her. Like father like son, she'll say. You'll get all the blame for leading me astray."

"What are you going to do if she forbids it?"

"Defy her. She'll respect me for that and realize how much I love you."

"See you at one-thirty then."

*

The sky was dark when Michael drove into Seasalter looking for The Sportsman. Heavy rain dashed against his windscreen. His wipers beat back and forth in their futile attempt to clear his view. The restaurant suddenly appeared at the end of the Faversham Road, a scruffy Victorian Pub with grey slate roof matching the sky above. His car bounced and splashed in the puddles as he turned off. He found the car park at the foot of a steep green embankment, typical of the sea defences along the north Kent coast. He parked in a small pond ground out of the shingle and waited. There was no sign of Denise and her little black Citroen. He was disappointed and wondered if she'd managed to escape.

The rain swirled overhead and drifted inland over the saltmarsh obscuring the electricity pylons that marched off into the distant hills. Michael switched the radio on. "Crazy," was being played and he sang along. Denise flashed her headlights when she saw him and pulled up alongside. Michael wound his window down. "I hope you're wearing wellingtons," he shouted. She grinned infectiously, pushed her seat back and showed him her jodhpurs and boots.

"Best we swop places. It was very kind of you to park in the puddle, Michael."

They ran hand in hand into the conservatory and shouted simultaneously, "I missed you," as thunder rumbled overhead. They clung onto each other as if their very existence depended on it.

"I hope you didn't lie to Yvonne," Michael said, looking skyward. "I wouldn't want to anger the gods on a day like today."

"Gooday and you must be?" A man with a beard said.

"Mr and Mrs Stevens," Denise said.

"Would you like to step this way or would you rather eat in the conservatory?"

"It's very atmospheric in here," Denise said, as another clap of thunder rumbled overhead. "What do you think, Michael?"

"On this momentous occasion," Michael looked skyward, "the conservatory it is. Can we have it all to ourselves?"

The man with the beard nodded and indicated a table.

"Have you been here before?" he said.

"No, never," Denise replied.

"Okay, well once you're settled just come into the bar. The menus are on the chalk board. Choose what you like. If you need any help or advice with the food or wine just ask, and enjoy."

Michael pulled out a battered Lloyd Loom chair for Denise.

"What made you chose this place?" she said.

"It's got wonderful reviews and a Michelin Star."

"You are joking. It's so shabby."

Michael looked at the décor, cream walls, peeling, bubbled with rising damp. Red bricks, blown. Grape vines, painted. Red geraniums on the window sills. Double oven, painted. Upper oven containing a black knight, white king and a mahogany box. Lower a brace of mallards, half full wine glass and half empty bottle of wine. He considered his response.

"Haven't you heard of shabby chic?" he said, smiling. Denise laughed with delight then covered her mouth going red with embarrassment. "Don't you like it?"

"I love it, Michael and I love you." She clutched his hand across the table. "We are going to get through this, aren't we?"

"Depends what's on the menu." She was off again.

"You're so funny Michael." Background chatter filled the room together with the clatter of plates, laughter and the metallic sound of cutlery.

"What do you think of the view?" Denise looked out of the window at the rain sodden car park, the embankment and the clouds rolling overhead.

"It's like a Constable, on a bad day."

"Shall we take a look at the menu?" Denise nodded and they walked into the bar. Michael noticed an immediate improvement in the décor. The place was spotlessly clean and nicely furnished. He held onto Denise's hand and stared at her face. She was just as beautiful as he'd remembered.

"You're supposed to be studying the menu; not gawping at me," she said. "What are you going to have?"

"The smoked mackerel in apple jelly sauce with horseradish, beetroot sliced and warmed in balsamic vinegar with scoops of goat's cheese and spring onion caramelized in olive oil sounds nice."

"Okay, we'll have two of those... What about the main course?"

"You choose."

"I'm going to have pork chop, creamed potatoes and apple sauce and I think you should have ox cheeks, spinach, creamed potatoes and gravy."

"Agreed and I think we should have a large glass of the Pascal Bouchards Chablis with the starter and a large glass of the Chateau Puybarbe Cote de Bourg with the main."

"How was the food," the bearded man said.

"Wonderful," Denise replied, "just like the company."

"Can I get you anything else?" Denise shook her head. "I couldn't eat another thing."

"You sir?"

"Ditto, those ox cheeks were enormous… I don't suppose you can do anything about the weather?"

"It's stopped raining. I can lend you an umbrella just in case it starts over."

The wind was still blowing when they stepped outside.

"Let's go for a walk," Denise said.

"Where to?"

"Up those steps for starters; let's see what's on the other side." Denise ran ahead, leaped into the watery potholes and giggled like a carefree child. She turned and kicked spray in Michael's direction and shouted, "Catch me if you can." They soon reached the apex of the embankment and ran across the top. Michael let her run ahead and when he got to a gate she said, "This is a kissing gate. You do know what that means don't you Michael?"

"That I have to kiss you to pass through?" She nodded and they smooched.

Beach huts, black tar, white and blue lined the shore together with wooden swings and upturned boats. "Why don't we go for a walk on the beach?" Denise nodded and they walked hand in hand. Cows wallowed in flooded fields separated by drains filled with bulrushes. A farmer tended them, dumping hay from his Mitsubishi Pajero.

A gap in the sea wall revealed the Isle of Sheppey and a pebbly beach. Couch grass clung to a wave-shaped lip where recent storms had eroded the land. The beach huts looked different from the seaward side, somehow smarter. There was even a very swanky one with a wood burner.

"I wish we had a key for that one," Denise said.

"Why's that?"

"So I could lie in front of the fire with you and pretend that we'd been shipwrecked on a desert island. I don't want to go home Michael and I don't want to go back to work without you. I miss you so much."

"I don't want you to go home either but you have to, at least until we are married."

"Will you marry me Michael?"

"You know I will. I just need to ask your mother's permission and buy you an engagement ring."

"What will you do if she says no?"

"I'll wait whilst you talk her round." They kissed again.

"I'm so excited, Michael, ask me now."

"Will you marry me Denise?"

"I do. I mean I will."

The sea sizzled as the heavens opened but they didn't hurry to return to their cars.

*

"Okay, okay, you can get engaged," Yvonne said, "on one condition."

"What's that?" Michael said, anxiously.

"That you wait until this business with your father is over."

"Okay, that seems more than fair," Michael said. He hesitated then kissed Yvonne on both cheeks. He was relieved when she didn't pull away.

"I never did thank you for the flowers," Yvonne said, "they really were beautiful."

"How's your wrist?"

"On the mend, thank you. Now then, shall we have a nice cup of tea?"

"I'd love one," Michael said.

"Thank you mother," Denise said, smiling and kissing her affectionately. Yvonne grinned. She was pleased to have her darling girl back.

CHAPTER 33

Matt had been looking forward to this day out for some time but now it had arrived it wasn't terribly convenient. His duty to his wife, Rose, and the two boys in their charge was, however, far more important than Operation Carnegie, at least for today. He'd left Charlie Spec in charge. He was doing very well even though he'd only been acting up, as his number two, for one week. Matt was very pleased with his choice. He'd found a strong ally and had no worries about leaving him.

As they turned into the car park at New Romney Station Stuart screamed with excitement, raised both arms, arched his back in the child seat and stretched his skinny little legs. Matt smiled looking at him through the rear view mirror. This wasn't their first visit to The Romney, Hythe and Dymchurch Railway. It had become something of an annual pilgrimage over the past couple of years and they were looking forward to it.

"There's Doctor Syn," John said, pointing to a black type, 4-6-2 Pacific Engine taking on coal from a siding within the car park.

"What's her number?" Matt said.

"Ten," John shouted. He'd memorized the names and numbers of all of the trains on the world's smallest public railway.

Rose held John's hand firmly as they crossed the car park to the engine. Matt lifted Stuart's stiff little body into his buggy and strapped-him-in tightly; he arched his back once more in excitement. 'Cerebral Palsy was not a nice condition,' Matt thought, 'still Stuart didn't know any better and like most disabled children appeared to be unaware that he was different to anyone else.' Matt was rewarded with a glowing smile. He joined the others and slipped a hand into Rose's.

They met their host, Peter, in the station office and breakfasted in the Heywood Buffet. The sun was shining as they watched Dr Syn Depart for Hythe.

"We have two diesels, John Howey and John Southland," Peter said. "Southland is named after the founder of the school in New Romney and is virtually funded by them. The railway serves the children travelling from Dymchurch and St Mary's Bay. This is her now."

"The Romney Sands and Dungeness train is now approaching Platform 2." John Southland, a black diesel, dressed with yellow chevrons, the number 12 and RH&DR pulled into the station.

"It's Roger," John said.

"Hello John. How are you?"

"Looking forward to my Grand Day Out... This is Matt. He's a policeman."

"We met last year," Matt said, shaking his hand.

"This is Stuart," John said, gliding an opened hand in his direction, "and this is Rose."

"My wife," Matt said.

"Pleased to meet you both. I've tidied the cab up for you John."

"You'd better get on board," John said, pointing at the carriages behind the engine.

"We'll see you at Dungeness." Rose said, "Have a nice time."

"He's forgotten us already," Matt said, as he watched John drag his six foot bulk awkwardly into one of the front seats. Stuart held his hands aloft urging Matt to lift him into one of the carriages and then sat stiffly on Rose's lap. A blast of the whistle followed by an acknowledgement of the horn and they were off. Stuart gabbled, making no sense but expressing his excitement. In the close confines of the carriage, with headroom similar to that of a car, he kicked Matt in the shins. He sat back in surprise as they passed through the dark tunnel under the main road and smiled as they burst out into the bright sunshine.

The train gathered momentum, passing the rear gardens of houses to their left and open fields on the right. Matt smiled at Rose and mouthed the words I love you. The carriages rocked rhythmically; the horn sounded as they crossed a road; the sound of the diesel engine roared in the confined space between gardens; the horn sounded again as they crossed another road; clackety-clack, rock and roll went the train.

The train began to slow; the horn sounded as they crossed another road and arrived at Romney Sands Station, a cabin more than a station, opposite a caravan park. Young couples with pre-school children smiled infectiously as the train came to a stop. There was a murmur of voices within the carriage from a loving couple and a middle aged quartet. Red poppies, yellow rapeseed, pink and white flowers lined the trackside. Green Goddess, a steam train named after a theatre production by Captain John Howey; the founder of the railway, arrived. Stuart waved his arms catching them in Rose's blonde hair.

Moments passed as the token for the single track to Dungeness was exchanged and the line opened for John Southland. The horn be-burred once again, clackety-clack, rock and roll. The train pulled away between gardens, walls, fences, outbuildings, pink daisies, cowslip, red hot pokers, iris and dandelion. Suddenly the terrain changed to pebbles, pylons and poppies. They were on the road to Dungeness, a large shingle headland renowned for its plants and wildlife.

Caterpillars quarried shingle onto black escalators as the train reached top speed. The squat bulk of the nuclear power stations appeared behind a row of Victorian terraces. Black tarred fishermen's huts presented themselves left and right, their gardens pebbles, flowers and telegraph poles. The black Victorian lighthouse towered over a rotunda of white cottages with red and black chimneys and dwarfed Dungeness Station.

"Well that was exciting," one of the quartet exclaimed when they arrived.

"We can stay here for twelve minutes or get out," a lady said.

"Doesn't look like there's much to do here," a man said.

"There's a thriving artist's colony, depicting local scenes, on the beach road," Matt said. "The old lighthouse is worth a visit. If you go in about fifteen minutes before the next train arrives it's quite impressive; you'll see the steam first and then the train racing out onto the pebbles. There's a board walk as well, just past the artist's colony, on the way to the new lighthouse, which takes you down onto the beach and The Britannia Inn serves excellent Fish and Chips." Rose rolled her eyes at Matt. "He's so enthusiastic about Kent and he's not even a native," she thought.

"Thank you," the lady said, "I'm showing my Australian friends around and didn't realize there was so much here." Matt stepped out of the carriage and met John and Roger by the engine.

"Well, how was that?" Matt said.

"Excellent, really excellent," John replied.

"John. What did we have the green token for?" John looked blank. "We have to have that to leave Romney Sands and travel on the single track to Dungeness."

"Yes, but why?"

"It's for safety John. You can only have one train on a single track."

"Yes, but why?"

"To prevent accidents; if you had two trains on the track you could have a head-on once you've gone round the loop."

"Oh, I see," John said. He nodded his head. "I get it now."

"I've got to speak to the station master," Roger said.

"Why don't you show me the token, John?" John escorted Matt to the cab, an arm behind his back, as if he was old and needed support.

"This is the token, it's green and says, Rom... ney Sands and Dunge... ness."

"That's good reading." John beamed at Matt.

"Can I take a photo of John in the cab," Matt said, when Roger returned.

"Of course you can. Be careful of the horn as you climb in John. All of my recruits tend to sit on the horn button as they climb in," Roger whispered. BE-BURRRRRR.

"Oops," John said.

"Having a nice time?" Rose said. Matt smiled and nodded, "You're like a child; one day out on the railway and it looks as if the weight of the world has been lifted from your shoulders."

"And, how are you doing young man?" Matt tickled Stuart. He laughed and shot up like a jack-in-a-box, just missing the roof.

"Be careful," Rose said, sinking her hand into Stuart's curly hair and gently easing him back onto her knee.

"You'll be standing up and walking soon," Matt said, smiling.

Peter was waiting with orange tabards when they arrived at New Romney Station. "Would you like to look around the station with John?" he said.

"You go. Stuart and I'll wait for you in the café."

Matt and John crossed the tracks with Peter.

"This is big Al," Peter said. "He's working the signals today. Come in and he'll show you how everything works."

"Good morning sir," John said, shaking Al's hand.

"This is the signal box. These levers operate the signals and the points. If you look out of the window you'll notice that the signal facing John Southland is down showing red. That means stop."

"I've just been driving the diesel with Roger," John said.

"The signal down in the lower quadrant is the Great Western way of doing things whereas the other railways adopted up for green or go. The other method is safer."

"Why's that?" Matt said.

"If the signal cable breaks the signal drops. On our railway that means go but on the others that would mean stop. John Southland's leaving. John, would you like to operate the lever to make Dr Syn stop?"

"Yes, please. He's taking us to Hythe."

"How was your trip to Hythe?" Peter said, when they returned.

"Really, really, good," John said.

"How did you get on with Mark?"

"Really well… He's a bit dirty though."

Mark grinned; his pale blue overalls were covered in soot and his face and hands were filthy.

"He really enjoyed taking on water at Hythe, backing up onto the turntable, spinning round and chatting to the new passengers joining the train," Mark said.

"Oh he excels at chatting. I wouldn't be surprised if you had a headache," Rose said.

"Okay John, we have to say goodbye now. I've got to take Dr Syn to Dungeness. I hope to see you again next year."

John proffered his hand. "It's been my pleasure… Thank you, sir."

The station master's whistle blew. The engines pistons see-sawed and the carriages groaned as the train got underway.

"See you next year," John shouted and waved… "I'm really sad now."

*

"How did you get on," Eva said, when they returned Stuart.

"We've had a wonderful time," Matt said.

"And Stuart really enjoyed himself," Rose said.

"And how about you John?" Gordon said.

"It was splendid."

"That's John's new word for today," Rose added.

"Would you like to come in for a cuppa and a slice of cake before you take John home?" Eva said.

"Why not, I think we've got time." The two ladies disappeared inside with Stuart and John.

"How was he really?" Gordon said.

"No trouble at all, you know that Rose and I adore him. Did you have a nice day off?"

"We relaxed a little and I did some gardening. Would you like to come through. We could have the tea and cake in the garden."

*

"I'm knackered," Matt said, as he settled down onto the sofa.

"Well just think how lucky you are," Rose said. "Can you imagine what it must be like to have all that responsibility every day?"

"Exhausting but it would be nice to have a couple of sprats of our own." Rose sat down next to him, rested her head on his shoulder and quietly wept.

CHAPTER 34

It had been an incredibly tough week, Charlie thought to himself, but very productive. He was still getting used to being catapulted into the rank of Detective Inspector and being the second in command of a complex murder investigation. He'd known from the start that the time would come when he'd have to helm the ship but hadn't expected the responsibility to come so soon. Monday had gone well but he was looking forward to handing the wheel back to Matt. As the clock on the wall of the DCI's office ticked past the seventh hour he wondered where he'd got to.

*

"Good morning," Matt said, lighting a cigarette.

"Morning Sir," Mark said. "How was your day off?"

"Wonderful, the wife and I took a couple of disabled children to The Romney, Hythe and Dymchurch Railway."

"My kids love it there."

"And it didn't rain for a change. How are you getting on with that onerous task I gave you?"

"Progressing slowly, none of the close friends and family has come up trumps in Dover, Deal and Sandwich and you'll be pleased to know that I've put some more Data Protection Forms on your desk for signature."

"Oh."

"Charlie signed a tranche of them yesterday."

"Did I hear my name being mentioned?" Charlie said, as he joined them.

"Hello Charlie. How did you get on without me?"

"I was on a vertical climb all day. I'm glad to have you back. How was your day off?"

"Wonderful… Are you ready for this morning's de-briefing?"

"I am."

The incident room was packed. Officers lined the walls, reclined on seats and leaned against window sills. Charlie was a little anxious. He was in the chair. Matt didn't believe in mollycoddling those he'd promoted. A respectable hush fell upon the office as he exited the DCI's office.

"Good morning everyone," Charlie said.

"Good morning, sir," the officers replied.

"This morning we're going to review the actions allocated to you last week. There will also be an opportunity for you to express any opinions you might have about those tasks and the progress of this enquiry. I appreciate that you've all been working extremely hard and hope those of you who were fortunate enough to have a day off over the weekend feel refreshed. Okay, I think we'll start with the DCI." There was a murmur of amusement within the room as Matt's nonchalant expression changed. "How did you get on at the Cemetery?" Charlie said.

Matt summarized his attendance. He described Tommy's grave; his chance encounter with Ken Cartwright; the details of their conversation and their subsequent visit to The Admiral. His conversation with Bernice Roberts, excluding the allegations made against DCS Baxter, his visit to The Dewdrop and his chat with Eddy regarding Tommy's sexuality and unhealthy interest in young boys.

"Anything else?" Charlie said. Matt summed up his conversation with Cheeky Charlie including the accident that Patraicc had in his van, the boat owned by Patraicc, Derek and Tommy and their smuggling activities.

"Thank you," Charlie said. "David, how did you get on with Edwina?"

"Everything he'd told the boss was confirmed in writing."

"And Ken did the same," Charlie said. "Mark, how did you get on with Keith, the man who was assaulted by Patraicc when he was a fifteen year old boy?"

"Audrey and I video interviewed him on Saturday. He confirmed that he was the victim of an indecent assault and that Patraicc tried to kill him by running him off the Dover Road with his Transit van."

"Audrey, how did you get on with the press release?

"Joan Armstrong handled that for me. She managed to get it out in most of the Sunday newspapers and on the south east news this morning, quite an achievement considering all the excitement surrounding the build-up to the Olympics. We've already had a good response. Three other males have come forward, two alleging rape and one indecent assault. They're going to be video interviewed later on today."

"How old were the victims?" Charlie said.

"Fourteen, fifteen and sixteen," Audrey said.

"Have we got any leads on Patraicc?"

"No Sir."

"No mistaken identities?"

"No Sir."

"Not surprising I suppose given that he's so distinctive; with that ginger hair, broken nose and scar above his right eye."

Charlie smiled at Matt then summarized the interview that he and Matt had conducted with Paul Adams, including his dislike of Michael Stevens, Patraicc Delaney and Marlene Johnson and Paul's theory that Derek had been murdered in 2001.

"Quiet please," he said, holding his hand up like a stop sign when several officers started speaking simultaneously. Gradually the voices faded away. Matt raised a hand.

"Yes Sir," Charlie said.

"How many Derek Stevens remain to be eliminated?"

"None sir, we got rid of the last one yesterday."

"Roger, what did you find out about Spartacus, the Freeman 30 cruiser?" Charlie said.

"I contacted Highway Marine in Sandwich. They checked their records and discovered they'd bought her in September 2001. The vendor was Patraicc Delaney and they paid two grand for her."

"Do you know who owns her now?"

"Yes, I found the new owners through the Freeman Cruiser Fan Club. She's changed hands a few times since Patraicc sold her."

"How did you get on with the harbour master?"

"He remembered seeing Tommy, Patraicc and Derek on their frequent jollies. Said they weren't very friendly and he generally gave them a wide berth."

"How did you get on with the Customs and Excise enquiry?"

"Not very well, there were several customs officers between 1973 and 2001. All admitted drinking in The Red Cow and denied neglecting their duties."

"What about the landlord?"

"There've been a few during that period. As you'd expect they all denied supplying alcohol to the customs officers when they were on duty."

"What about Alphonse?"

"He's booked into The Royal Hotel on Friday."

"Audrey, how did your team get on with the house-to-house enquiries in Westgate?" Charlie said.

"Michael's well known. He's often seen going to work in his car, visiting the shops and the cinema in the village and running along the seafront. He's liked and respected by his neighbours who consider him to be both hardworking and caring. He's recently started dating his assistant manager, Denise, and there's speculation of marriage. No one's ever seen his father Derek but many have met his mother."

"Anything else?"

"He has a sort of alibi for the night of the Diamond Jubilee Concert. His next door neighbours remember him coming home from a world war two event at Dover Castle. None could remember him going out again. His car remained on his drive and his lights went out just after the concert finished."

"What about the automated number plate readers?"

"There's nothing to show that he took his car out after he returned."

"What about Robin Delaney?

"His alibi checked out. His next door neighbours confirmed they'd attended a cocktail party at his house and watched the Diamond Jubilee Concert with him and his family."

"Roger, what did you find out about The Lady Irene?"

"She was registered in Southampton in 1957 by the Indian Ocean Steam Navigation Company and remained in service until 1972. Then she was broken up as she was too small to be commercially viable. As a British registered ship she had to comply with English Law no matter where she was in the world. I checked with Lloyds List, one of the world's oldest running journals providing shipping news, and obtained the crew lists and ports of call for the period fifty-seven to seventy-two. As you might expect that was quite a long list so I asked for a list of casualties."

"Go on," Charlie said.

"Something very interesting caught my eye. It was an article detailing the loss of a Sri Lankan sailor named Princey Rupasinghe. Rupasinghe stands for beautiful Lion, by the way. It appears that our Princey wasn't happy with his life on The Lady Irene and jumped overboard, not near the shore as you'd expect but in the middle of the Indian Ocean. There was an inquest. The star witnesses were Patraicc Delaney and Derek Stevens. Both were cross examined extensively by the coroner after claiming they'd seen Rupasinghe jump overboard. They allegedly raised the alarm immediately but Princey never surfaced after going into the water. The interesting thing was the age of the victim. He was only just sixteen."

"What was the coroner's verdict?"

"Suicide."

"Did you manage to contact any of the crew?"

"Yes, I spoke with the ships master, who was mentioned in the coroner's report. He confirmed that Derek was a chef and an accomplished first aider. I told him that we wanted to know what Derek, Patraicc and Tommy were like when they worked for him. He considered them to be a bad lot, good at their jobs but always getting up to mischief. When pressed he admitted hearing rumours about them paying rent boys for sex. I also asked about Princey. He said that was a bad business and he'd no doubt that Patraicc and Derek was instrumental in the boy's demise."

CHAPTER 35

"That seemed to go very well," Charlie said.

"I'm not surprised," Matt said.

They were joined by Audrey in smoker's corner. "Well done, Charlie," she said. "That was an excellent debriefing. I loved the way you brought Matt in right at the start. He obviously wasn't expecting it."

"Everything else was expertly choreographed," Matt said with a smile. "I'm glad you're here Audrey. You interviewed Michael Stevens and searched his house, didn't you?"

"Yes sir."

"Did anything about him or his home strike you as peculiar? The reason I ask is because I haven't, as yet, had the privilege of meeting him." Matt regarded Audrey with a faint smile as she considered her answer.

"He had a complete collection of novels and several hardbacks on The Duke of Wellington. They seemed to be in pride-of-place, below photographs of him in dress uniform." Audrey stopped speaking when she saw Matt's wide grin.

"You're a genius," Matt said. "Thank you, Audrey. Charlie there's a pile of DPA forms on my desk that need your signature." Matt spotted Mark Goddard walking in their direction.

"Mark, come with me."

"Where are we going?" Mark said, as he climbed into Matt's car.

"On a local history tour," Matt said.

*

The house, in Brunswick Street, Maidstone, seemed empty from the outside. The curtains were open but there was no visible activity inside. Ron couldn't see into the first or second floor rooms from the street. A rat-a-tat-tat on the front door provoked no response; neither did the monotone ring of the doorbell. He tried phoning Margaret Delaney, the house phone could be heard clearly but again no response. He tried her mobile and listened through the opened letterbox. Nothing, maybe she'd put it on vibrate. He decided to check with the neighbours.

"Hi, I'm DC Ronald Stanbridge from Operation Carnegie," he said, when confronted by a young lady wearing a red dress.

"Have you got some ID?" He showed his warrant card. She smiled. "Not a very flattering picture. You're much better looking in the flesh. So how can I help you?" she said, pushing her chest out and drawing her stomach in.

"I'm looking for the lady next door, Margaret Delaney."

"Oh. I haven't seen her today. Would you like to come in and wait?" She winked and gave him a knowing look. Ron considered for a moment. He was tempted but he'd only just redeemed himself with his boss and didn't fancy sweeping the yard again, or worse putting his uniform back on.

"That's very kind of you but I'd better go and have a look around first."

"Okay, suit yourself, pop back for a cuppa if you get no joy."

"Thank you, I might just do that."

"See you later then." She grinned.

Ron decided that he'd better make sure Margaret's house was secure. He could let himself in if it wasn't, on the pretext of preventing or detecting crime. He didn't need a warrant to do that or to save life and limb. He already knew that the front door and sash windows were secure so made his way to the back gate which was only secured with a latch.

Margaret was still in no mood to be interviewed by the police. She'd been dodging their phone calls for several days. She'd picked up her voicemail messages, whenever she'd declined a call from a withheld number. There'd been a large number from a DC Ronald Stanbridge, one from a company offering to recover her Payment Protection Insurance and another from a finance company offering to write off any debts that she might have over five grand. All were bloody irritating. She would speak to the police eventually but not until she was good and ready.

She'd seen the detective arrive in a Vauxhall Astra whilst brushing her hair and gazing out of her bedroom window. He wasn't hard to identify, dressed in a smart grey suit, white shirt and plain tie. She'd withdrawn into the room and lain quietly on the bed. She'd heard her front gate's familiar screech, as the rusted surfaces ground over each other. She'd listened to the rat-a-tat-tat on the front door, her doorbells boring ring and watched her mobile vibrate angrily. She'd heard the front gate again and heard the officer conversing with Racquel, the young strumpet from next door. He'd been lucky to get away from her so quickly. Then the clip of marching feet died away. She'd thought he'd gone and sighed with relief.

The crash of her side gate dashed her reverie. He'd been caught out by the vicious spring. He would be in her back garden by now, checking the doors and windows. Had she locked up properly, after putting the washing out? She'd hardly dared to breathe. If he found the back door unlocked he'd feel obliged to investigate, then he'd find her lying on the bed, fully clothed, with no explanation for her bizarre behavior. She'd heard him trying the door handles of the kitchen and patio doors; then silence. He must be looking up at the windows or picking the locks, she'd thought. Crash; the side gate again... The clip of marching feet... A car door slammed... Dare she look out? No, she was quite comfortable thank you.

The seconds ticked by, growing into minutes, swelling into hours. Ron was bored and uncomfortable. He'd finished his lunch, a meal deal hastily bought from a Sainsbury's Local, a BLT, packet of salt and vinegar crisps and a bottle of juice. He was on his third cigarette when Racquel re-appeared in her red dress and waved him over. She'd been busy with her hair and face paint. She seemed more attractive; a sure sign that Ron was tired. He needed to use the bathroom anyway. He flashed five fingers at her and mouthed the words five minutes then dialed Charlie's number.

"Any luck?" Charlie said.

"If she's in, she's ignoring me."

"Premises secure?"

"I'm afraid so."

"Where are you parked?"

"Opposite."

"Okay, take a break and walk back after dark. If there's still no sign of life, ring me and we'll knock it on the head for today." Ron smiled. He'd park the car around the corner; slip his jacket and tie off, put a casual one on and have tea with the neighbour. He had several hours to kill.

*

Charlie's mobile rang.

"Hello Charlie; how are you getting on with that enquiry to trace Margaret Delaney?" Matt said.

"Ron's camped outside her address but there's no sign of her."

"Is he on his own?"

"Yes sir."

"Okay, send another officer to keep an eye on him. I want to interview her before I go home."

"Has something happened?"

"Yes, Mark and I have been on Castle to Castle enquiries. It would appear that Michael Stevens was in the area on Sunday the third of June visiting Deal and Walmer Castles. We've checked the CCTV at Deal Castle. He left at thirteen-twenty-five and arrived at Walmer Castle half an hour later. He must have walked along the seafront. It would've only taken ten minutes in the car."

"And Marlene's movements can't be accounted for between thirteen-hundred and thirteen-fifty-five."

"Exactly."

"So you think he might have met her during that promenade?"

"Precisely, and another thing; he looks just like his father Derek on the CCTV."

"But he's twenty four years younger than Derek."

"Yes, but Marlene left Dover in 2001 so Derek would have only been sixty five and Michael's fifty two."

"That's still a thirteen year difference."

"Well let's just imagine that they did meet and… She was a very lonely old woman. We know that from our enquiries and the choice of music for her funeral and let's say she meets Michael and desperately wants him to be Derek. He goes along with her and they make a date. Voila!"

"Sounds like an interesting theory. All we've got to do now is prove it."

"Well that's where you come in. Mark's got a list of staff and visitors for both Deal and Walmer Castles for Sunday 3 June. He's faxing it to you now. I want everyone not on urgent enquiries re-called to the office and briefed. I know that some of them might think I'm mad but I'm willing to take that risk. Then I want them dispatched to the four corners, if necessary, to interview all of those witnesses ASAP."

"Yes sir."

"Mark and I are going to take a nice stroll along the seafront whilst you do that and see if we can't find someone to put the finger on Michael Stevens."

"What exactly are we looking for?" Mark said.

"Witnesses of course, someone missed by Brian Kelly's team, someone overlooked because of their appearance, disheveled or disabled perhaps. What I would call one of the invisible people," Matt said, "like that old boy over there." Matt pointed to a bearded old man sitting in the storm shelter next to the paddling pool.

"Looks like an old soak."

"Does that mean you should ignore him?" Matt said.

"No, of course not but he obviously likes his drink."

"There's no law against that as long as you don't make a nuisance of yourself."

"Good afternoon," Matt said. "Do you mind if I join you?"

"Don't mind if you do. Would you like a drink?"

"I'd love one but I'm on duty."

"What about your mate?"

"He's too young to drink," Matt said.

The old boy's face cracked into a smile. "James Selbourne's me name."

"Pleased to meet you," Matt said. He proffered his hand and James accepted it. "That's a nice strong grip you've got there."

"They taught me how to shake hands properly when I was in the services. 'No one trusts a man with a grip like a wet fish,' they said."

"That's very true."

"So what's this? Official business or did you just decide to drop in for a chat?"

"Official business."

"Copper?"

"That's right. Detective Chief Inspector Matt Sanderson but you can call me Matt."

"I wondered when one of your lot would get round to speaking to me. Watched them wandering up and down the seafront, calling door to door and speaking to passers-by but nobody seemed to notice old James or Jimmy drowning his sorrows in the storm shelter. Anyone would have thought I had leprosy. Most of them looked like your young whippersnapper."

"Mark, Mark Goddard. Pleased to meet you James."

"He has nice manners, your boy. Will go far if he watches the big cheese. If you know what I mean." James tapped the side of his nose with his right forefinger. "So what can I do for you fine gentlemen?"

"We're investigating the murder of Marlene Johnson."

"Who?"

"The old lady murdered in Sandwich during the Diamond Jubilee Celebrations," Matt said. "This is her picture."

"I don't believe it," James said. "I met that old girl when the Medway Brass Band was supposed to be playing. It wasn't a very nice day, drizzled a bit and it was very windy. What I'd call a dreary day. No passers-by to chat or wave to. BORING. They cancelled you know."

"The Medway Brass Band?"

"That's right. It was too cold for the old folks to sit out. More likely it was too cold for the band. Us old un's are made of tougher stuff. Brought up in the war you know. I was five when it finished. Can still remember it clearly; as if it was yesterday."

"How did you meet the old girl in the photograph?"

"I was sitting here when she appeared and asked if she could sit with me for a while. I was proper chuffed. Thought I'd pulled." James laughed at his own joke. "Anyway, to cut a long story short, I offered her one of my tinnies. She declined, already had two pints of Guinness in The King's Head. Said she had a long journey home… Sandwich that was it. Was very fond of Sandwich, she was. Anyway, to cut a long story short, we had a nice little chat and then she wandered off, back towards Deal Castle."

"Did you see her again after that?"

"When I was on my way round to The Heads."

"The toilet?"

"That's right; on the other side of the paddling pool. I see her talking to a young man, younger than me anyway. They appeared familiar."

"Why was that?"

"Because he kissed her on the cheek and patted her bottom. Lucky sod."

"Would you recognize him, if you saw him again?"

"I might. I'm a people watcher you see. Recognize most of the passers-by but I hadn't seen him before. Haven't seen him since neither."

"Are you here every day?"

"Most days."

"Would you call me on this number if you see him again?"

"Of course."

"Would you participate in an identity parade if we asked you to identify him?"

"Course I would."

"You'd better describe him to me then."

"Are you listening to this Mark?" James said.

"I am."

"Watch and learn my boy. Watch and learn… That's what I say."

CHAPTER 36

Margaret had grown tired of Ron Stanbridge's calls to her mobile and his persistent knocking at her front door. She'd slipped out when he was otherwise engaged. Six or seven minutes later she'd presented herself at Maidstone Police Station and asked to speak with the officer in charge of the murder of Marlene Johnson. A rather flustered DC Stanbridge had arrived first and shown her to the waiting room. He'd explained that his DCI was on way, travelling from Deal and would be with her in about an hour. She'd pursed her lips and he'd offered her tea. Then she'd waited. Fifty five minutes of staring at blank walls had almost driven her insane and just as she was about to give up he'd arrived.

"Hello, I'm DCI Matt Sanderson. Thank you for coming into the Police Station to talk to me. I'm sorry you've had to wait so long. I hope that DC Stanbridge has been looking after you properly."

Margaret regretted hiding from the police now that she was finally confronted by DCI Matt Sanderson. Failing to take their calls or answer her door seemed so ridiculous. He appeared to be a very nice fellow doing a very difficult job and she'd made it even harder for him.

"He has," she said. Ron was relieved by that response. Margaret Delaney was a formidable looking woman. She wasn't the sort he'd want to fall out with. Matt noticed that she had an interesting face, square with a mop of unruly auburn hair, parted in the centre and cascading over a prominent forehead. Her eyes were shaped like tadpoles, just as dark, under bushy eyebrows. The bridge of her nose was curved, the end upturned into a snout. Prominent cheeks complemented the piggy look. A square mouth with an unusual smile, raised on the left; falling to the right above a strong jaw. White teeth with prominent incisors. She was wearing a long sleeved grey body under a darker grey short sleeved knitted jacket. She had large breasts, went in at the waist and flared at the hips with large thighs. Her grey trousers were tucked into short black leather boots. He would have described her as a sumo save for the feminine touches, manicured fingernails with bright red polish, matching lipstick, a colourful scarf wrapped around her substantial neck and white diamond dangly earrings.

"Let's adjourn to a more comfortable room?" he said.

"That's better. Shall we get started?" Matt said. Margaret nodded. "Okay. Well before we go any further I must tell you that I'm investigating the murder of Marlene Johnson and you are not a suspect." Margaret nodded. "Furthermore you are not under arrest. That means you are free to leave the police station at any time. Do you understand?"

"I do."

"Right then, I'm going to ask you some questions and Ron is going to record what you have to say. Then we're going to give him some time to format his notes into your statement. Any questions?"

"Not at the moment."

"Well if you think of any, just speak up."

"I will."

"Okay, I'd like to start by recording your family's composition."

"Fine."

"Now I'd like to ask you some specific questions about your relationship with Patraicc." Matt said. "Would you like to take a break before we get going?"

"I'm alright at the moment."

"Can you tell me how you and Patraicc met?"

"We knew each other when we were growing up. Patraicc was three years older than me. I was an ugly duckling. My parents owned a small corner shop. I was lucky to always have money, unlike the other girls. Consequently I became a target for the bullies. They were always beating me up and stealing my pocket money. On more than one occasion Patraicc came to my rescue. He was like a big brother to me then."

"How old were you?"

"I was a teenager, about thirteen years old. Patraicc was sixteen. He was a little like me; ugly with very few friends. He had bright ginger hair that made him stand out in a crowd. He'd been bullied when he was younger so we had that in common but he'd grown, sorted the bullies out and climbed to the top of the pyramid. He was a lion of a man."

"Who were his friends?"

"Derek Stevens was his best mate. He was a year younger than Patraicc. They joined the Merchant Navy together in 1957."

"When did you get married?"

"He asked me after his first spell at sea; said he'd been thinking about it for a while. He was twenty-one by then and quite grown up. Derek was his best man. We got married in December fifty-seven."

"What was your marriage like?"

"It was strong and healthy. I'd always fancied him even though he was an ugly bugger. We'd dated a few times before he went away. I liked his parents and he liked mine. Both got on well. Mine were pleased I'd found someone with a job and they were impressed by his persistence. I was saving myself for the right man."

"What do you mean?"

"I kept my knickers on. That put my other suitors off."

"What happened after you married?"

"We were very happy and tried for a baby. I didn't fall pregnant straight away. We had to wait two years for that to happen and then I had Robin in September 1960. He was a beautiful baby; had a full head of black hair and olive skin, took after my father in looks. Patraicc was delighted. I overheard him several times, boasting to Marlene and Tommy about being married and respectable."

"How did you know Marlene and Tommy?"

"Patraicc met Tommy when he joined their ship, The Lady Irene. He was younger than Patraicc and Derek and the junior rating. Even though we'd grown up in the same neighbourhood our paths had never crossed, due to the age difference I suppose; four years is big gap when you're a child. Anyway Marlene was nothing like me. She was lean, pretty and popular with the boys; not so much with the girls. They probably saw her as a threat. She was very free with her sexual favours and carrying someone else's child when Tommy came home."

"Do you know who the father was?"

"Trevor Hazelwood. He didn't want to get married so Tommy stepped in.

Shouldn't have bothered. The baby was stillborn but they made a good go of it and she was always loyal, when Tommy was at home." Matt noticed that Margaret coloured a little after making that remark.

"What do you mean, 'she was always loyal when Tommy was at home?'"

… "Well I heard rumours about her carrying on when he was away."

"When was that?"

"When he was in the navy," Margaret replied, rather too hastily.

"Anyone in particular?"

"No just rumours. I don't even know if they were true."

Margaret sat down opposite the desk when she was returned and watched Ron as he carefully scribed her statement from the notes he'd made earlier.

"Feeling better?" he said.

"Much. There's nothing like fresh air to clear the head."

"The DCI should be back in a jiffy. He's just getting the teas sorted." Margaret smiled and looked around the office. She noticed a sign on the open door showing that the office belonged to Detective Inspector Fox. There was a photograph of the Queen hanging on the wall, in a silver frame, a bookcase filled with law books, several framed commendations with the Kent Police logo and a photograph of a young woman with a handsome young man, two children and a golden retriever." She wondered if the latter was Fox and his family.

"Do you know Detective Inspector Fox," she said.

"Who?" Ron said, looking up from his work in confusion.

"The man who owns this office."

"The DCI does. That's why we've got somewhere comfortable." Ron returned to his work and Margaret wondered why it was taking Matt so long to make three cups of tea.

*

"Hello Charlie. How are you getting on with the Deal and Walmer enquiries?" Matt said, into his mobile.

"The whole team's out taking statements, with the exception of Audrey who's still interviewing Patraicc's victims."

"Good and how are the plans for tomorrow morning's activities coming on?"

"I'm dealing with those personally; should be finished in an hour or two. What time do you want me to brief the troops?"

"6am… Send everyone home as you debrief them. I'd like to see a few fresh faces in the morning and ring me when you've finished."

"Hello Rose… I'm at Maidstone at the moment… I'm going to be very late again and I'll probably be out before you get up… You'll have to do the dog in the morning… I will… Sleep well… I love you too."

"Here you go. Three cups of tea and I managed to rustle up some biscuits," Matt said.

"Custard creams, my favourite," Ron said.

"Ladies first… Margaret?" She took a ginger nut and smiled.

"Okay. You were telling me that Patraicc was made redundant in 1972."

"That's right. After fifteen years of dedicated service he was, as he saw it, unceremoniously thrown onto the scrapheap."

"Why was that?"

"They said The Lady wasn't commercially viable, in other words too small. He'd noticed that the other ships in port were getting bigger all the time but he'd never dreamed of being made redundant. He loved the freedom of being at sea and said there weren't many ships with crews like his."

"What did he mean by that?"

"I don't know. He never did explain. I just assumed he was referring to the camaraderie."

"Why did they make him redundant?"

"Don't know. Most of the crew was offered jobs elsewhere but he, Derek and Tommy were paid off."

"How did he feel about that?"

"He was very resentful."

"What did he do after he was made redundant?"

"He bought one of those Ford Transit vans, brand new, just of the production line. Thought he was the business. Had it painted navy blue; just to be different."

"What did he do with his van?"

"He delivered furniture for a warehouse based in Dover."

"Did he have any other interests?"

"Apart from going out drinking with Tommy and Derek?" Matt nodded. "He liked to draw; could've been a professional, if he'd put his mind to it."

"What did he like to draw?"

"Chi… People," Margaret said, colouring once again.

"Pardon?"

"People."

"What about children?" Margaret felt uncomfortable under Matt's gaze.

"He drew portraits of Robin and Michael quite a few times."

"Any others?"

"No, just Robin and Michael."

"Were they any good?"

"They were portraits, much better than school photographs."

"What was your relationship with Patraicc like after he left the Navy?"

"He was often late on Friday's. Sometimes he didn't come home at the weekends."

"Why was that?"

"Delayed at work but he always stank of booze whenever he was late."

"How did that affect your relationship?"

"Robin and I'd wait anxiously for his return. If Patraicc's dinner wasn't on the table at six precisely and he did come home I'd be in trouble. Robin would always be hungry. His bedroom would be spotlessly clean and tidy. He'd read so there wouldn't be any mess and no excuse for an unwarranted beating."

"Why did you put up with him behaving like that?"

"I was bewildered. I couldn't believe that things could have changed so much. When Patraicc was at sea we were always happy. Mind you he only came home for two weeks in the spring, two weeks in the summer and two weeks at Christmas. I suppose it was easy to be happy when you only spent six weeks together. Every day was a party, especially with our friends living nearby."

"Who were your friends?"

"Tommy, Derek, Marlene and Patricia."

CHAPTER 37

"I understand that you and Patraicc eventually separated," Matt said.

"That's right," Margaret said, "in seventy-three, nearly two years after he was made redundant."

"What made you part company?"

"Apart from the drinking and bullying?"

"Yes."

"He was constantly pestering me for sex - unconventional sex. Up the bum no babies, was one of his most distasteful ideas."

"Anything else?"

"Oral sex; I gave him a blow-job once, just to please him. He promised to tell me when he was going to come so that I could withdraw but he grabbed my hair and sprayed his salty semen into my mouth. I retched and puked all over his chest. He gave me a black eye for that one and told me I was supposed to swallow."

"Go on."

"I screamed and the neighbours called the police. They listened sympathetically but said they couldn't arrest him unless he was breaching the Queen's Peace. 'What about my bloody peace,' I said. 'No prosecutions are permitted between husband and wife,' they said... They offered to take me to the hospital. 'And after I'm discharged,' I said. They suggested staying with a friend or relative until things calmed down or obtaining an injunction through a solicitor."

"What happened after that?"

"It was strictly straight sex; not Patraicc's cup of tea."

"Do you recall Patraicc having an accident in his van?" Matt said, just as his mobile rang. "Excuse me. I have to take this."

Margaret hadn't been surprised when Patraicc didn't show at 6pm. She'd been relieved. At seven she'd sat down with Robin and they'd tucked into the spaghetti bolognaise she'd made earlier. "It doesn't look like your father's coming home," she'd said. "I hope he stays out all night then we can sit up and watch television like we used to."… "Do you think we'll still be able to go Broadstairs tomorrow?" Robin said, as he changed into his pyjamas a little later. "I'm sure your father will take us in his van when he comes home and if not we'll take the train," she'd replied. "Oh, that will be exciting. I hope he stays out all weekend then we won't have to go out in that smelly old van of his." She smiled with the recollection. Her son was a good looking lad, slim and athletic with a shock of jet black straight hair, fine features and a cheeky grin. He'd obviously inherited his good looks from her side of the family as he was nothing like his father. "Off to bed now and don't forget to clean your teeth," she'd said. She'd heard the light switch click on in the bathroom, the sound of urine draining into the toilet, the flush and a few seconds later the light switch click off. "Back in the bathroom," she'd said, "wash your face and hands and clean your teeth properly, you can read me a chapter of your book before lights out." Later, as she'd settled into her empty bed she'd felt happy, another weekend without Patraicc was in prospect, a weekend of normality, a weekend without having to resist his strange sexual fantasies. She'd wished everyday could be that way, just her and Robin living in peace and tranquility, doing what they wanted to do when they wanted to do it.

"Sorry about that," Matt said.

"Now, where were we?

"Do you recall Patraicc having an accident in his van?" Ron said.

"I know that he had an accident… In the summer of seventy-two but I wasn't with him when it happened," Margaret said.

"When did you first become aware of the accident?"

"When Marlene telephoned."

"Do you remember the date?"

"No but I believe it was a Sunday."

"What did Marlene tell you?"

"That Patraicc had pitched up on Friday and fallen into her arms when she'd opened the front door. He'd been covered in blood from a cut on his forehead."

"Why did she wait until Sunday to tell you?"

"She said that Tommy and Derek wouldn't let her ring me before then."

"Why not?"

"They all seemed to know that Patraicc and I weren't getting on and they thought Patraicc had been misbehaving."

"What had he done?"

"I don't know… 'If Patraicc had wanted the world to know that he was injured he would have made it to the hospital on his own,' they said."

"Didn't he go to the hospital?"

"No, Derek treated him at Tommy's house."

"What injuries did he have?"

"He had nasty cut on his forehead, that's where the crescent shaped scar came from, a broken nose and a cracked rib."

"When did you go to see him?"

"On Sunday, Marlene showed me to the spare room at the front of her house. Patraicc opened his eyes and I asked him how he was feeling. He didn't appear to recognize me and closed them again."

"Then what happened?"

"Robin was in his room when he came round. He bleated, 'Mum, mum, he's awake,' as he bounded down the stairs. I went up and spoke to him again but he just closed his eyes. He started talking to Tommy on the Monday but he had no idea who he was, where he was or how he'd got there."

"How long did the amnesia last?"

"He knew who we all were by the end of the first week but couldn't remember the accident or the events leading up to it. Derek insisted he stay indoors until he could   remember what had happened or at least until his injuries had healed. He said there was no   point advertising the fact that he'd been in a fight or an accident."

"And you were willing to go along with that?"

"What choice did I have? I didn't press him to come home and would've been quite happy if he'd stayed there, except for the money. I couldn't manage the house without his help. I had considered reporting him to the police but decided against that idea as it would've resulted in the loss of my best friends. Derek made that very clear from the outset. I didn't want to see any of them getting into trouble for one of Patraicc's misdemeanours besides the police could've traced Patraicc's van no trouble. It was probably the only Transit painted navy blue. All the others were white. That's where the expression white van man comes from."

"How did you manage financially without Patraicc?"

It had become blindingly obvious to Margaret that Patraicc was not going to make a rapid recovery and that she needed to get a job. She'd never bothered to check the state of the family finances before the accident. Patraicc might have many faults but putting bread on the table had never been one of them. He'd never enquired about the family allowance so she'd always treated that as her own, but it didn't go far and certainly wouldn't pay the rent and the other household bills due at the end of the month. She'd no idea they were living from hand to mouth until that conversation with the bank manager. He'd been a thoroughly unpleasant little man and had they had any money to withdraw she would have closed the account.

As she'd scanned the jobs page of the local newspaper she'd regretted the extravagant outing she'd had with Robin on Saturday, two train tickets; two deckchairs - they could've managed with one, ice-creams, fish and chips and a visit to the Palace Cinema. They'd not felt that free since Patraicc had been made redundant and she'd gone mad. She should've held a little back like she usually did, for a rainy day; God knows it looked like there were going to be plenty of those from now on. On the last page she'd found something that she thought she could do that required no qualifications. The work would be hard, the hours antisocial and the wages meagre but she had to start somewhere; she'd not worked for twelve years. Shelf-stackers were required to fill immediate vacancies in a newly opened supermarket. She'd known exactly where the supermarket was; it was a first for Dover. They'd been opening up all over the country but up until now the closest was in Folkestone.

The interview had gone well. She'd been offered a position at nine pounds a week, fifty pence an hour in new money, ten shillings in old. Of course it wouldn't go as far as ten bob used to but they'd all known the pound would be devalued with decimalization. The only drawback was she'd have to work nights, Thursdays, Fridays and Saturdays. The Manager thought she should be at home on Sundays to give her husband lunch and on Mondays to see her son off to school. The cheek of it, telling her how to run her life; it was still very much a man's world, you could vote and you could have a job but in the end you were still expected to obey your husband. Things hadn't changed that much since the war. Marlene was impressed when she'd told her about the job and even offered to look after Robin whilst she was at work that first week.

"How did you manage financially without Patraicc?" Matt repeated. Margaret focused on him.

"I got a job," she replied.

She'd been excited about her first shift and arrived at Tommy's early. "Look at you, all dressed up in your smart uniform," Marlene said. She'd invited them in. They'd dined together, her, Tommy, Marlene and Robin. It was a jolly affair, just like old times only spoilt by Patraicc's brief appearance. She'd prepared to leave at 7:45. It was only a short walk. She'd kissed Robin and said, "Make sure you behave for Tommy and Marlene. I'll see you after school tomorrow." Robin had nodded unhappily. "Don't worry; I'll look after him," Marlene had said. "He can sleep with me tonight."

"Doing?" Matt said.

"Stacking shelves, in a supermarket."

"Nights or days?"

"Nights."

"Who looked after Robin when you were at work?"

"His father. Marlene when he was away."

That was when it had started, the abuse of her beautiful child. It was more than a year before she'd found out. Things had changed. She'd settled into her new job and couldn't be persuaded to give it up. Robin was nearing the end of his second year at secondary school and doing well. He'd regularly spent weekends with Marlene when Patraicc, Derek and Tommy were working away and then she'd come home early. A migraine was all it had taken. She'd found Robin cowering under the bedclothes in his bedroom. He was bruised, terrified and unable to speak at first. Then it had all spilled out. His affair with Marlene and… Margaret didn't want to think about the other things with Patraicc, Derek and Tommy. She'd packed her bags that very night, run away to her parents who'd moved to Maidstone and threatened to tell the police if any of them every crossed her path again.

"Did anything untoward happen between Marlene and Robin," Matt said.

"Nothing," Margaret said, shaking her head.

"What about Patraicc and Robin?" Matt said.

"Nothing… Why do you ask?"

"Because Robin was physically sick when we questioned him about his father."

"I know. He'd been feeling ill all day. It was just a coincidence."

"So you've spoken with him since Tuesday."

"I ring him most days."

"I don't believe in coincidences," Matt said.

"Why's that?"

"Because we know that both Tommy and Patraicc were paedophiles."

"WELL THEY WEREN'T WITH MY SON," Margaret said.

CHAPTER 38

"How did you get on with Margaret?" Charlie said.

"I don't think she knows what's happened to Patraicc and Derek but she's definitely covering for them and Marlene. I suspect that Robin was sexually abused by all of them, including Tommy. She said a couple of things that alerted me."

"Such as?"

"She heard Patraicc boasting about being married and respectable after Robin was born."

"What's wrong with that?"

"Well, when I was a child people that went around boasting about being married and respectable were either,"

"Married and respectable?"

"Or they had something to hide. In this case I think the latter applies. We know that Patraicc was a paedophile and believe that Tommy was as well. Can you think of a better way to avoid suspicion than having a wife and kids at home?"

"You don't think you're reading too much into this do you?"

"No. We know that Tommy was bi-sexual but his sexual preference was young men and boys, yet he married Marlene when she was carrying Trevor's child. Why would he do that?"

"Because he wanted to appear married and respectable?"

"Precisely."

"Did Margaret say anything else that aroused your suspicions?" Charlie said.

"In an unguarded moment she mentioned Marlene carrying on when Tommy was away. She went very red. When pressed she quickly back-pedaled and said they were just rumours. She didn't even know if they were true."

"Do you think she was referring to Robin and Michael's sleepovers when their fathers were away?"

"I do. Then later she slipped up again. She mentioned that Patraicc liked to draw and could've been a professional. I'm sure she started to say that he liked to draw children but quickly corrected herself to say people. I queried that response. She confirmed people and when I specifically asked about children she said that Patraicc only drew Robin and Michael. Well, we know that's untrue from the ship's master. Didn't he tell Roger that Patraicc, Tommy and Derek shared a cabin and their walls were covered with sketches of young men and boys?"

"He did. So that was another lie."

"I think Margaret suspects, as we do, that Robin and Michael are responsible for Derek and Patraicc's disappearance and Marlene's murder... Did you read the e-mail I forwarded about the number of homicides in England and Wales?"

"The one that said police recorded five hundred and fifty in 2011-2012?" Charlie said.

"Officials said the number of homicides in England and Wales increased from about three hundred a year in the sixties to about a thousand ten years ago. Last year was the lowest figure since 1983."

"The fall was not unique and there had been reductions elsewhere since the mid-nineteen-nineties," Charlie continued. "They believe that efforts to bear-down on domestic and family-related violence are a major contributor."

"Well, don't you think this is a case where officials failed to bear-down on domestic and family related violence?"

*

Michael felt uncomfortable, both physically and emotionally. The police had descended upon his home just after seven. It had been low key and typically British. He'd found three plain clothes officers, including DS Audrey McCullock, at his front door. They'd asked to be admitted and he'd invited them in. They'd failed to close the front door after them and their numbers had quickly swelled to six. Audrey had explained that she'd returned to arrest him for the murders of Marlene Johnson, Patraicc Delaney and his father Derek Stevens. She'd cautioned him and he'd denied involvement in all of the murders.

He'd been handcuffed; front stack and double locked according to the note taker. The cuffs chafed a little but not as much as his emotions. When he'd been escorted to their car he'd been unable to look any of his neighbours in the eye. He'd felt so ashamed. He'd been squeezed between two heavies in the back seat on the journey to Dover Police Station. There'd been no conversation amongst his guards. They'd only spoken to him in response to his questions and then only to say that his questions would be answered when he arrived.

The police station was a brick built edifice, Victorian by the look of it, with high sash windows and a blue front door. Michael noted they weren't going in that way as the black iron gates at the side of the building opened and they glided into the car park. They were obviously going to use the tradesman's entrance.

"Okay Michael, time to jump out," Audrey said. The two heavies grabbed him when he emerged and walked him through some iron gates leading to a ramp and the back door. The custody suite was empty save for two uniformed officers, both doing paperwork.

"Morning Sarge," Audrey said, "this is Michael Stevens. I believe you're expecting him."

"Matt Sanderson rang me earlier," Sergeant Armstrong said. "You'd better tell me why he's here."

"He's been arrested for the murders of Marlene Johnson on Monday 4 June 2012, Derek Stevens on Saturday 21 July 2001 and Patraicc Delaney on 23 December 2001."

Armstrong started typing. "Sounds like he's been busy boy," he said, smiling at Audrey. "Did he have anything to say when you cautioned him?"

"He said, 'I haven't murdered anyone,'" Audrey said.

"Has he had an opportunity to read your note of that reply?"

"Yes Sarge."

"Has he signed it to say that he agrees with your record of what was said?"

"He has Sarge."

"Good." Armstrong looked directly at Michael. "So you know why you're here then?"

"I do but I've got some questions."

"All in good time son: all in good time. I've got to book you in first."

"Okay, now that I've recorded your personal details I'm going to tell you what your rights are. You have the right to have someone informed that you are here. You have the right to legal advice and to consult with a solicitor privately. If you don't have one of your own we can call someone for you. You also have the right to consult the codes of practice governing police rules and procedures; that is this book here. They are continuing rights so if you don't want to exercise them at the moment you can do so later. Okay?" Michael nodded. "Sign here to say that I've explained your rights to you and given you a printed copy… Thank you… Right then; do you want someone informed that you are here?"

"My girlfriend, Denise Summers."

"Do you want a solicitor?"

"Yes."

"Do you have one of your own?"

"No."

"Would you like me to call the Duty Solicitor for you?"

"Yes please."

"Would you like a copy of the codes of practice?"

"I'd prefer a newspaper."

"Okay, sign here to show that I've recorded your wishes correctly… Thank you… As you've been arrested for a recordable offence police have powers to take your fingerprints, photograph and DNA." Armstrong looked at Audrey.

"Mark's going to do that."

"What about his clothing?"

"I'd like to bag that up for Forensics."

"Okay, put him in a baby-gro. We'll sort out some proper clothing for him later." Armstrong looked at Michael. "Any questions young man?"

"Any chance of a cup of tea and some breakfast?"

"In an hour or so," Armstrong said.

"Thank you."

"You've got a polite one there," Armstrong said, "doesn't look like a serial killer; mind you, they never do… I remember when I was a young copper. I ripped a young man from a motorcycle when he was trying to get away from me. He squealed like a frightened pig when he hit the ground. He was a proper little weed but he had a conviction for murder."

"Thanks Sarge. Let me know when the Duty Solicitor gets here."

*

"Hello Charlie, how are you getting on?"

"I'm knackered."

"Located Robin?"

"Yes, he's at work. How are you getting on with Michael?"

"He's in the cells. We're just waiting for the duty solicitor to arrive then we can get started. Let me know if anything interesting happens your end."

*

Michael really hated his father. Six years of torment and torture before he'd managed to escape into the marines. That had made him really hard. None of the other recruits could touch him emotionally. The Sergeant Major soon picked him out for special measures but he just got on with it. Nothing was as bad as the scars he carried from his childhood. Now he was back in Dover, his home town, waiting for his father. "Not long now," he thought, as he watched the first punters leave The Admiral. It was closing time on Friday night. Most of the customers were like his father, older men. He recognized Patraicc from his sleepovers but he wasn't interested in him tonight. He was there for his Dad.

He'd retired from the marines on a Sergeant Major's pension, bought a small house in Westgate-on-Sea and found a job as a butcher. He really enjoyed the work and was singled out for promotion. Now he was the manager in their largest branch. He'd rented a disused abattoir near Preston for his own work. He'd been there earlier. Everything was prepared. The stainless steel sink and draining board was gleaming. The butcher's block cleaned and oiled. The band saw and mincing machines were spotless. Even the floor had been sealed with the latest resin technology, to make it easier to clean.

The lights in the Admiral Harvey dimmed as the landlady agreed to a lock-in for her best customer. Michael settled onto the bench in the back of his van. It would probably be another hour before she threw him out. It was cold. He wrapped his thick green army surplus jacket around him and watched through the slit in the panel separating the front from the rear of the van. He mustn't nod off or his mother would be tormented once again.

The street was quiet, very quiet. Michael's eyes were sore. The oxblood walls of the pub beneath the portrait of the admiral and his name were imprinted on Michael's brain. No cars or pedestrians had passed for some time. He'd started counting to stay awake and thought he was hallucinating when he finally saw his father emerge from the darkened interior. Derek appeared pissed but happy. It had obviously been a good night. Drinks all-round and a quick fumble with the landlady. Now he was in a hurry to get home and give Patricia a good seeing to. She knew what she was there for, his most loyal receptacle. As he staggered off he didn't notice that he was being followed.

Michael overtook him in the van and pulled up on the right, just inside the mouth of the next junction. He parked opposite the gable ends of the houses so that he wasn't overlooked. He walked purposefully to the junction and listened to his father's approach. He could hear every footfall and his father's blasphemy as he bounced off the stone wall of the corner house. When he appeared in the open space in front of him Michael chopped violently at his father's throat, then caught him as he fell. Derek's feet skittered on the road as he dragged him to the open doors of his van. Duct tape covered his father's mouth, a cable tie bound his wrists, his hands brought together in prayer; a large strap secured his thighs, a second his ankles; a black sack covered his head. Derek wet his pants as the doors closed on well-oiled hinges. Then Michael drove away.

*

The wicket of the cell door dropped open with a metallic clang.

"Breakfast is served," Armstrong said, "and your solicitors here." Michael looked at him blankly, shook his head then re-called his predicament. "Shall I send him away for twenty minutes; give you a chance to wake up?"

"That would be good," Michael said, taking the polystyrene plates.

"Bacon, sausages, scrambled eggs, baked beans and sauté potatoes," Armstrong said, "delicious. The guy in number two didn't want his." Armstrong winked and after a moment's hesitation closed the wicket with another loud clang. "No breakfast for you today Nicholas, perhaps number two won't want his lunch."

CHAPTER 39

Denise was at home when the phone trilled. She ran downstairs and picked it up. It was 9am; the time Michael usually rang, when she was taking the day off. She was looking forward to speaking with him. They'd been engaged, unofficially, for three days.

"Hello Michael," she said breathlessly.

"This is Sergeant Armstrong from Dover Police Station. Can I speak to Denise Summers please?" Her heart skipped a beat.

"Speaking," she said meekly.

"I'm just ringing to let you know that Michael Stevens has been arrested and he's at Dover Police Station."

"What's he been arrested for?" Denise said.

"Please speak up. I can hardly hear you."

Yvonne appeared at her side. Denise felt uncomfortable and coloured.

"What's he been arrested for?" she repeated.

"I'm not at liberty to say but it's serious and he might be here for some time," Armstrong said.

Denise felt her head swimming. Yvonne noticed the colour draining from her daughter's face and took the handset from her.

"Sit down dear… This is Yvonne Summers, Denise's mother. To whom am I speaking?"

"Sergeant Armstrong, Dover Police. I was just calling to let your daughter know that Michael Stevens is in custody at this police station. Can you confirm that she's got the message?"

"She has. Can she have a word with him?"

"I'm afraid not."

"What's he been arrested for?"

"I'm not at liberty to say but it's serious and he could be here for some time."

"Thanks for ringing," Yvonne said. She replaced the handset; took her daughter's head in her hands and gently stroked her hair. "I'm sure it's all a big mistake. I can't imagine Michael hurting anyone. How about a nice cup of tea?"

*

"Who's the brief?" Matt said, when Audrey returned.

"Mister Davis; from Davis and Way."

"That's a bit of luck," Matt said. "Useless?"

"No, quite the contrary."

"There's a beautiful young woman at the front counter asking for you sir," Mark said.

"Really? I haven't had one of those for a long time."

"Says her name's Denise Summers; wants to talk to you about Michael Stevens."

"That's the girlfriend," Audrey said.

"Let's have a chat with her. I'm sure Mister Davis will be more than an hour with Michael."

Matt was surprised to find that Denise really was beautiful.

"Hello, I'm Chief Inspector Matt Sanderson," he said, "and this is Detective Sergeant Audrey McCullock. You must be?"

"Denise Summers, Michael's fiancé."

"How can I help you?"

"I understand that you've got Michael locked up in the police station."

"That's right. Why don't we step into the interview room," Matt said, opening the door. "Give us a bit more privacy... Please take a seat." Denise was surprised to find herself thinking that Matt had very nice manners. "That's better. Now how can I help you?"

"Can you tell me why he's here?"

"Of course, he's been arrested for the murders of Marlene Johnson, Patraicc Delaney and his father, Derek Stevens."

Denise was quiet for a long time as she digested the information.

"I presume you have some evidence," she said, fighting back the tears.

"Of course," Matt said. He proffered an opened packet of tissues as tears started to flow down her cheeks.

"Are you going to charge him?" Denise said.

"We've got to interview him first; see what he has to say. He's with a solicitor at the moment."

"I see."

"We would like to ask you some questions though."

"Why's that?"

"Because you're his fiancé and should know him better than anyone else." Denise nodded her assent. "Audrey will write down what you have to say then produce a statement and invite you to sign it when we've finished. Is that okay?" Denise nodded again. "How long have you known Michael?"

"About ten years."

"How did you meet?"

"He interviewed me for a job at Brooks the butchers."

"Is that where you work?"

"Yes, I'm his assistant manager."

"When did you become engaged?"

"Three days ago, on Sunday after a romantic meal in The Sportsman."

"How long have you been dating?"

"Since the twenty-fourth of June."

"So about three and a half weeks?"

"That's right."

"When do you plan to get married?"

"We haven't set a date."

"Why's that?"

"My mother was very upset about Michael's father being," Denise dabbed the corners of her eyes with the tissue, "wanted for that horrific murder," she sobbed.

"Do you know what Michael was doing over the Diamond Jubilee weekend?"

"We all finished work a little early on the Saturday and had Sunday, Monday and Tuesday off. I know that Michael went to Dover Castle on the Monday because he told me all about it on the Wednesday."

"What did he say about that day?"

"That he went to a World War two event; watched some actors demonstrating a skirmish, some children playing at soldiers and a fashion show with some ladies calling themselves the Spitfires. He even had a photograph of them in his mobile. Then he spent the evening watching the Diamond Jubilee Concert."

"Where did he do that?"

"At home, in his house, said he had a quiet night in."

"Did you watch the concert?"

"With my mother."

"Did you discuss it with Michael afterwards?"

"Yes, we both thought it was an amazing spectacle, something that the nation could be proud of."

"Did you discuss any of the highlights?"

"We did."

"And did you like the same things?"

"Pretty much."

"Were there any discrepancies in your recollections?"

"No. No, I don't think so."

"What was your favourite bit?"

"The performance of 'Sing' by the Military Wives Choir."

"And Michael's?"

"He really liked the projections onto Buckingham Palace and the band playing on the rooftop."

"Does Michael ever talk about his father?" Matt said.

"No, not really, though we have spoken about him recently?"

"When was that?"

"After you searched his house and told him Derek was wanted for Marlene's murder."

"I see, and before that?"

"No, he never really spoke about him."

"Didn't you think that a bit strange?"

"No, not really, you see my father left my mother and me when I was only nine. I've not seen him since so I rarely speak about him."

"What did Michael tell you about his father?"

"That he wasn't a very nice man. That he was always beating his mother up."

"What did you think about that?"

"I don't like to think about it. Michael isn't his father. He's very kind and caring. He looks after his staff, organizes the Christmas party every year, takes his mother out, helps his neighbours with their gardens and calls in on them when they are ill. He doesn't behave like a serial killer at all."

*

"Hello Tony," Matt said, shaking the solicitor's hand. "How did you get on with young Michael Stevens?"

"He's not having it," Tony Davis replied. "He can account for his movements on Sunday 3 June and Monday 4 June this year, less so for the 21 July 2001 and the twenty-third of December 2001."

"Is he going to offer any alibi witnesses?"

"No, he doesn't have any. As far as he's concerned he hasn't done anything wrong so he doesn't have to prove anything."

"What do you make of him?"

"He seems like a nice hard working young man."

"A serial killer?"

"I'm not going to answer that one, not with your track record."
Matt smiled to acknowledge the compliment.

"Thanks Tony… See you in about fifteen minutes?"

"How did it go?" Audrey asked when Matt returned.

"He's not going to put his hands up."

"That's nice to know. Does he think Michael's guilty?"

"He wouldn't comment on that one."

"How did you persuade Mister Davis to talk to you, off the record 1 mean?"

"He's like everyone else, doesn't want to see a killer go free. He's got a wife and kids at home just like you and me. If Michael had confided in him we wouldn't be able to use that as evidence but we'd know we had the right man."

"Do you think we've got the right man sir?"

"One of them, that's for sure and Charlie's got his eye on the other one."

*

"Hello Charlie."

"Hello Matt. How's it going?"

"We've got Michael's first account."

"What did he have to say?"

"Same as his witness statement; hasn't seen his father since he left home on the third of January seventy-nine. Went into detail about the domestic violence, lack of police intervention and his father going missing in 2001."

"Were there any variations to his original account?"

"None. He was consistent during the second interview as well. Confirmed his father was a chef and first aider on The Lady Irene. Described his relationships with Patraicc, Tommy, Marlene, Robin and Margaret's break-up with Patraicc etcetera... How are you getting on with Robin?"

"He's still at work, behaving normally as far as I can tell."

"Okay, I'll ring you later. Let me know if anything significant happens.

*

After lunch, Michael slept like he didn't have a care in the world. He didn't mind being locked up. All the time he was in the cell the clock was ticking. He'd already had his first review, after six hours in custody. The Duty Officer had authorized his further detention and another wasn't due until 10pm. He knew they could only hold him for ninety-six hours; after that they'd have to charge or release him. His cell was comfortable, he'd slept in worse places and he was getting three square meals a day. His only concern was Denise. He wondered how she was coping.

The alarm on the twin recorder wined as the machine prepared to record. This was the third interview Michael thought. The first two had been pretty straight forward. Sixty minutes a piece with a tea-break in between. Chief

Inspector Matt Sanderson had obviously been following the same script as Audrey had when she'd attended his house on Monday 16 July. Now he was going through the same pre-amble for the next interview.

"Would you state your name for the tape?" Sanderson said.

"Michael Stevens."

"And confirm that you are still under caution?"

"I am."

"Tell me about your training in the Royal Marines."

"What do you want to know?"

"What did they teach you?"

"About life and death."

"What did they teach you about death Michael?"

"How to die honourably."

"How to kill people?"

"That as well."

"How many people have you killed Michael?"

"I wouldn't know."

"Oh come on, you must have some idea."

Michael could re-call them all, each and every one; the ones from close quarters and the ones from more than a quarter of a mile away.

"Half a dozen, more maybe. You can't always be sure in combat."

"What did they teach you about life?"

"That it was worth living."

"Wasn't it worth living before you joined?"

"Didn't seem like it."

"Why was that?"

"Because my home life was miserable, with my father beating my mother all the time."

"When did the abuse start Michael?"

"I already told you."

"When did your father start abusing you Michael?"

"What do you mean?"

"When did he start to sexually abuse you?"

Michael felt the first globule of perspiration burst on his temple and dribble down the side of his face.

"He never abused me."

"That was why your home life was miserable and not worth living; wasn't it?"

Michael resisted the urge to wipe the sweat away. He watched Sanderson's eyes tracing it down the side of his face.

"I already told you. He never abused me sexually."

"When did it start Michael?"

"I already told you he never abused,"

"Officer, he's already answered that question twice. I really must protest," Tony Davis said. Sanderson didn't even acknowledge the protest.

"Was it when you hit puberty?" Michael stared at Sanderson but couldn't read the face confronting him. He'd made an error of judgement. Sanderson might look like Officer Crabtree but he was no fool.

"He never abused me sexually," he repeated.

"Officer, I think we should take a break so that I can take further instructions from my client," Davis said.

CHAPTER 40

Michael hated the consulting room. It was the one room within the custody suite with no window. It appeared to be at the epicentre of the building. It was barren. No pictures or notices adorned the walls. It contained a single long table and two chairs. Pale blue lino covered the floors. The ceiling, which was suspended, seemed oppressive as if the whole building was pressing down onto that one structure and in turn onto him. The consultation was a waste of time. He wasn't going to give Tony Davis anything. He didn't trust him and continued to deny that his father had ever abused him sexually. The interview resumed some thirty minutes later.

"Tell me how you did it Michael," Sanderson said.

"Did what?"

"Murdered your father?"

"I didn't murder him."

"Of course you did; picked him up when he was leaving The Admiral Harvey, about one on Saturday 21 July 2001."

Michael wanted to ask Sanderson how he knew that.

"I don't know what you're talking about."

"You watched him for a couple of weeks, like the professional sniper that you are, established his routine and planned it with precision. Didn't you?"

"No I didn't."

"Worked out when he was most vulnerable?"

"I don't know what you're talking about."

"And pounced on him when he was pissed?"

Michael was beginning to think that Sanderson was a mind reader.

"No I didn't."

"Took him away in a little white van?"

Michael was incredulous but shook his head negatively. That could be a lucky guess.

"Killed him, slowly, to punish him for the years of sexual abuse, cut him up into little pieces and scattered him across the county?"

Scattered him across the county; wasn't that what he'd told Robin?

"Was that a question officer," Davis said.

"It was."

Michael looked at Sanderson trying to read his mind. How had he come to such an accurate conclusion? He wanted to confess, to tell all. How his father had abused him and his mother, how he'd learned to kill like a machine whilst he was in the marines, how every mannequin dressed in the enemy's clothing was his father, how every victim of his bullet was the same but he wasn't going to let Derek ruin his life again. He'd been careful, very careful. Derek had been gone for eleven years. They hadn't found his body. How could they? He'd probably been ingested by hundreds of animals and thousands of flies.

"I won't dignify that question with an answer," he replied.

"Can I consult privately with my client?" Davis said.

"Well, what do you think?" Matt said.

"I think you're right," Audrey said. "Do you think he'll crack?"

"Would you if your father had sexually abused you for years?"

"I might if I wanted to show how clever I'd been."

"Then your father would have won. You would not have survived."

"Is that what you think Michael is: a survivor?"

"In his own way: not in the conventional sense of the word."

"I think I'm going to take up smoking."

"Shall we pop out for one then?" Matt said.

"Where were we?" Matt said.

"Killed him, slowly, to punish him for the years of sexual abuse, cut him up into little pieces and scattered him across the county?" Audrey said.

"I've no idea what you're talking about," Michael said. "Sounds like total fantasy to me. For the record, I wasn't sexually abused by my father, I didn't kidnap him and I didn't murder him."

Michael didn't sleep so well after the third interview. He was too busy worrying about Robin. He knew they'd interviewed him, as a witness, more than a week ago. Had they arrested him since? He hadn't heard from Sabrina but that didn't mean anything. Perhaps he'd been grilled and spilled the beans about Derek's murder. Maybe he wasn't in custody and that clever bastard had worked it out for himself. Perhaps he was a mind reader after all. Michael tried to think about something else. He focused on the good times he'd had with Denise and eventually nodded off.

*

Matt spoke to the lead officer from the forensics team upon arrival at Michael's house. He was pleased to be informed that Michael's car had already been lifted, that all of his clothing had been seized and that both were being examined as a matter of urgency. There had been no pressing need for him to attend St. Mildred's Road but he'd fancied a drive and a breath of fresh air. He noticed that the sea wasn't far from Michael's house and decided to go for a walk. Audrey fell in step beside him. She was a good girl, didn't chatter unnecessarily and listened when she was spoken to. Matt noticed there weren't any parking restrictions in Sea Road. It was on the edge of town and there were quite a few vans parked there. Audrey was fascinated when he started taking an interest in them.

"Penny for your thoughts," she said.

"Ring the office, Audrey. Get someone down here. I want all these vans checked out. See if any of them were on the move on Monday the fourth of June and establish ownership. I want to know about any that remain unclaimed. Also get someone to ring Thanet Council and find out if they've removed any abandoned or untaxed vehicles from Westgate since that date. If they have I want them seized."

*

"Hello Charlie," Matt said, when his call was answered. "I think it's time we brought Robin in for questioning. Is he still at work?"

"It looks like they're packing up for the day. The gates are closed and the staff have been leaving for the last ten or fifteen minutes."

"Good, apprehend Robin at the gates, secure the site, search his office and locker and any vehicles you find. Think forensics and call out a scene examiner."

"Anything else?"

"Take Robin to Maidstone, as planned. Seize his clothing; put him in a baby-gro and transfer him to Dover. Make sure he sees Michael's name on the custody officer's board then have a conversation with him outside Michael's cell before putting him to bed. I'll speak to him in the morning, after his rest period."

"Right you are, sir."

"And send a couple of trustworthy officers to keep an eye on his home address. They can secure it until the search teams catch up."

"Do you want me to treat the home address as a priority?"

"No, sort the business premises out first. I don't want to cause them too much disruption and have them claiming thousands of pounds in compensation for lost business. We need to keep them on side. They'll all need to be interviewed in the morning."

*

"DCI Matt Sanderson."

"What the fuck is going on?" Baxter said, when Matt answered his mobile.

"Good day to you sir; I was wondering when you'd call."

"What the fuck is going on?" Baxter said.

"I'm investigating a number of murders sir. There's no need to shout."

"Who the fuck do you think you're speaking to?"

"Detective Chief Superintendent Stanley Baxter, soon to be retired, disgraced ordinary Stanley Baxter." Matt could picture his face, red and bloated with rage. He held his mobile away from his ear as a litany of obscenities exploded from the speaker. When Baxter ran out of steam he quietly said, "I'd advise you to submit your papers as soon as possible," and terminated the call.

*

Robin was shaken. It had been a relief to discover that the heavies surrounding him were police officers. He was locking up when they'd arrived and he thought they were there to rob the premises. There'd been a spate of armed robberies at scrap metal merchants recently and the local police had been around to warn the dealers. They were a good target as they nearly always paid in cash. Some of the robberies had turned violent and one of his peers had been tortured by having a JCB driven over his legs when he

228

failed to give up the combination for the safe. They'd found him alive but he'd never walk again.

He was shocked when he was told he was under arrest for the murders of Derek Stevens and his father, Patraicc Delaney. He'd protested his innocence but that had made no difference. They'd searched his office and locker, and seized his clothing. The site had been sealed by the Detectives and he'd been carted off to Maidstone Police Station. He and the arresting officer, Detective Inspector Charlie Speck, had been confronted in the station yard by a fat detective who appeared to be Speck's senior. He'd not been able to understand what was being said until Speck said,

"If you don't fuck off, sir, I'll arrest you for obstructing police."

The check-in procedure had been a whirlwind. He'd asked them to inform his wife of his arrest and asked to speak with a solicitor. Speck had told him that officers were already searching his home and his wife was already aware of his arrest. He'd been stripped of his clothing, given some second hand gear to wear and had his DNA, fingerprints and photograph taken. Then he'd been bundled back into the police car and driven to Dover. The hastiness of the officer's departure appeared to have something to do with the fat detective he'd seen earlier.

He'd noticed Michael's name on the custody officer's whiteboard, as soon as he entered the cell block, next to his custody number and reason for arrest. Murder x 3. He was surprised when they'd asked if they could get him anything en-route to the adjoining cell but he'd since had plenty of time to consider those actions. They wanted him to talk; talk to Michael through the cell door. He was sure someone was sitting with his back to the wall between the two cells. Well he wasn't going to help them with their enquiries. He laid back, looked at the ceiling and went to sleep.

He woke to some yobbos shouting and screaming. It was dark outside. It was 10pm. He pressed the button on the wall and enquired about his solicitor. He was expected about midnight, was dealing with another job in Maidstone. The screaming subsided and was replaced by a monotonous banging. Someone was kicking the cell door next to his. He laid awake for what seemed like hours. Midnight came and went as did the banging. He heard the yobbos apologizing at 6am as they were being released. His tea arrived at seven together with his solicitor. He was already exhausted and the day had only just begun.

Michael heard Robin's voice as he was led away for his consultation. His night hadn't been any better. He'd resolved to stick to his story. He was confident that Robin wouldn't dobb-him-in. He'd suffered, just as Michael had and he had a lot more to lose. Michael felt sad when he thought of Sabrina, Rachel and Maxwell waiting anxiously for his return. Then he thought of Denise and wondered what she was doing. She wasn't very far away, sleeping in the seat of her little Citroen.

CHAPTER 41

The first interview had, as expected, dealt with the preliminaries. Robin's solicitor, Amanda Pocket, had said that's where they'd start. They'd want to go through his witness statement and get him to confirm the contents under caution. "You do not have to say anything," Pocket had said, "but it may harm your defence if you do not mention when questioned something which you later rely on in court. Anything you do say may be given in evidence. Do you understand that Robin?" He'd confirmed his understanding. Then she'd said that it was in his best interests to answer the detective's questions otherwise the court could draw an inference from his silence. He'd questioned that. She'd explained that the inference was likely to be unfavourable as the law and the public would expect an innocent man to protest his innocence at each stage of the investigation process. In other words, upon arrest, during interview and upon charge but she hoped it wouldn't come to that. Then she'd confirmed with him once again that he knew nothing of the murders.

"How old were you when your mother went to work?" Charlie said.

"Twelve."

"How old was Marlene?"

"Thirty."

"Attractive?"

"I suppose so."

"Someone you could trust?"

"I suppose so."

"Someone you could trust to break you in?"

"Pardon me," Robin said.

"Someone you could experiment with sexually?" Robin coloured. "Tell me," Speck said, "when did the sexual abuse begin?"

"What sexual abuse?" Robin said, as he recovered.

"The sexual abuse that started with Marlene?"

"She didn't abuse me."

"During your sleepovers?"

"She didn't abuse me," Robin said.

"Whilst your mother was out, at night, stacking shelves?"

"She didn't abuse me."

The buzzer on the tape recorder sounded to alert the interviewer that the tape was about to end. Robin almost sighed with relief. He'd get a few minutes to think as the tapes were changed over.

"When did you start having sex with Marlene?" Speck said.

"We never had sex," Robin lied.

"I'm not suggesting that you did anything wrong," Speck said.

Robin made no reply. His mother's voice was in his head; tell the truth but leave out the sticky bits. Robin watched Speck switch off the tape recorder. He signed the seal like an automaton and watched silently as Speck wrapped the seal around the master tape.

"Time for a break," Speck said. "Mark, put him back in his cell."

Robin saw Matt Sanderson as he was led from the interview room and heard Speck say, "Time for another chat with Michael?"

Was it only an hour since he'd sat in the same chair; in the same interview room; with the same officers, Speck and Goddard, and the same solicitor, Amanda Pocket? Robin asked himself. The interval had seemed much longer. His initial relief at being spared further questioning about his relationship with Marlene had worn off quickly. He thought he'd dealt with the humiliation superbly and was ready to bat off anything else they threw at him. That was before they'd taken Michael away. Now his nerves were getting the better of him. What had Michael said?

"Had time to think about the last interview?" Speck said.

"In what respect?" Robin said.

"I'm not suggesting that you did anything wrong."

"I didn't have a sexual relationship with Marlene, experimental or otherwise."

"And what about Michael, did he have a sexual relationship with Marlene?"

"Not that I'm aware of." Robin lied. He felt uncomfortable under Speck's glare and coloured once again.

"Exactly why did you leave Dover in 1973?"

"Because my mother and Patraicc didn't get on."

"Didn't you feel guilty, leaving your best friend, Michael, to his fate?"

Robin shifted in his seat. His left leg started to tremble and his foot twitched involuntarily.

"What do you mean?"

"Leaving him to Marlene, Tommy, Derek and Patraicc?"

"I didn't leave him to his fate," Robin said.

"What did you do then?" Speck said.

"My mother took me to live with my grandparents because she and Patraicc didn't get on."

"Just like that?"

"Yes."

"Without giving any notice to her employer?"

"Yes."

"Without giving any notice to your school?"

"Yes."

"Without giving you a chance to say goodbye to your best friend?"

"Yes."

"Why would she do that?"

"I don't know," Robin whispered.

"Pardon?"

"I DON'T KNOW."

"Was it because she found out that you'd been sexually abused?"

"NO."

"Come on Robin, start telling the truth."

"I AM TELLING THE TRUTH."

"Why did your mother warn Patraicc off when he contacted her?"

"BECAUSE SHE HATED HIM."

"Because he'd been abusing you and Michael?"

"THAT ISN'T TRUE."

"It is true, Robin."

"IT ISN'T TRUE."

Robin banged his fists on the table and stood abruptly. The officers remained seated.

"Why are you shouting at me?" Speck said quietly.

Robin wanted to run. He looked at Amanda Pocket, appeal in his eyes.

"That's quite enough, officer," she said. "I think it's time my client and I had another consultation."

The power supply drained from Robin's legs. He started to topple. Goddard was on his feet. He guided him to his chair. Speck offered water. Robin drank. The colour returned to his face. Then it was back to the routine of sealing the tapes.

*

"Do you think you can break him?" Matt said.

"I don't know." Charlie said. "There's telepathy between these two."

"There certainly is a strong sense of trust. Ask Robin if Michael's ever been to his workplace. I'll see what Michael has to say and we'll convene afterwards, compare notes."

*

"How many times has Michael been to your workplace?" Charlie said.

Robin smiled as he watched the lapwings wobble their legs in the mud to disturb the invertebrates and preen themselves on the grass verges. He didn't notice the pleasure boats swinging on their moorings to his left but his binoculars captured a marsh harrier flying low over the reed beds of Sheppey as she hunted for voles to pluck and pull to pieces. Then he returned to the foreshore and watched the teals, upended as they searched for food.

"Once," Robin replied.

"When was that?"

"In November 2001."

"Why did he come?"

"Out of curiosity; he'd heard a lot about my workplace and I'd been to his on many occasions."

"What did you do there?"

"We had a nice chat on the approach road then I showed him around."

"Was anyone else on site?"

"Everyone was on site. Michael wanted to see the site in action and came in on a visitors permit. You can check the visitor's book in the office. I introduced him to the manager. We had coffee and then I showed him around."

"Where did you go?"

"Into the office, to the weighbridge, the sorting area and the yard where I worked. Michael was very interested in the machinery."

"What did you talk about?"

"Old times."

"Anything in particular?"

"Our youth before I went to live in Maidstone. The good times we'd had, the trips to the seaside,"

"How you were going to murder your father and dispose of his body?"

"No, nothing like that."

"But Michael did return to the site with your father on 23 December 2001, didn't he?"

"I don't know what you're talking about."

"In a battered Ford Mondeo?"

"I still don't know what you're talking about."

"The previous owner came forward to complain, said he'd sold the car to Michael, said it had been dumped in Canterbury and towed, then the bailiffs chased him for the money. He was well pissed off."

"I still don't know what you're talking about," Robin said.

*

"How many times have you been to Robin's workplace? Matt said.

Michael spotted Robin in his silver Skoda Fabia as soon as he passed under the Sheppey Way. He'd never been able to understand his fascination with birds but wasn't surprised that he didn't notice him until he knocked on the passenger window with the knuckle of his right forefinger. Robin's smile was radiant, he really was a handsome devil, he still retained his thick black hair; not like Michael who had lost his, and had a swarthy complexion from spending so much time in the open air. No wonder, first Marlene, then Tommy, Patraicc and Derek had been attracted to him.

"Once," Michael replied.

"When was that?"

"In November 2001."

"Did he invite you?"

"I invited myself, out of curiosity. Robin had seen me at work on several occasions. I'd heard a lot about his workplace and it sounded fascinating."

"Was anyone else on site?"

"Yes. I wanted to see the site in full swing."

"Did you have to sign in?"

"Yes I did. Then I was introduced to the manager. After coffee he left Robin to show me around. I visited the office, the weighbridge, the sorting area and the yard where Robin worked."

"What did you talk about?"

As Robin climbed out of the car to shake Michael's hand an enormous grin lit up his dark features. "How are you Michael?" Robin said. "Good. And you?" Michael said. "Very well, what brings you all this way?" Robin said. "Do you remember when we were young?" Robin looked crestfallen. "When we used to talk about what we'd like to do to Tommy, Patraicc and Derek?" Robin nodded. Tears pricked the corners of his eyes. "Well, Derek won't be bothering us anymore," Michael said. "Has Derek died?" Robin said. "You could say that."

" What have you done Michael?" Robin said. "Cut him up into prime joints of meat." Robin's head swam as he imagined Michael working away with his boning tools and saw. "What have you done with his body?" Robin said. "Minced the flesh and fed it to the foxes." "What about the bones," Robin said. "Cut up into small cubes, discarded all over the county. You'd be amazed how efficient modern band-saws are." Robin was silent… "Why don't you show me the machinery in the recycling centre?" Michael said.

"Old times," Michael replied.

"Anything in particular?"

"Our childhood, before Robin went to live in Maidstone. The good times that we'd had."

"How you were going to murder Patraicc and dispose of his body?"

"No."

"You did return with Patraicc on 23 December 2001, didn't you? In a tatty Ford Mondeo?"

"I don't know what you're talking about."

"The previous owner came forward to complain about you, Michael. Said he'd sold the car to you, said you dumped it in Canterbury; that it got towed and the bailiffs chased him for the money. In his own words, he was well pissed off."

"I still don't know what you're talking about," Michael said.

"So you'll consent to an Identity Parade?"

"Of course," Michael said, without a moment's hesitation.

CHAPTER 42

"How did you get on with Robin," Matt said, lighting one of Charlie's Craven A's.

"He admitted showing Michael around his workplace in November 2001. Said he came in on a visitor's permit when everyone was there, visited the office, weighbridge, sorting area and the yard. Apparently, Michael was very interested in the machinery," Charlie said.

"What about 23 December 2001?"

"He didn't know what I was talking about; at least that's what he said… How did you get on with Michael?"

"Much the same, h e admitted visiting the premises in November 2001 but denied re-attending with Patraicc on 23 December."

"What did he say about the witness who sold him the Mondeo?"

"He didn't know what I was talking about; all hinges on the ID Parade now."

"When's that going to take place?"

"Tomorrow morning. That's when the witnesses and the ID suite are available."

"Who's the identification officer?"

"Crosby, the stickler; not a bad habit when you're the identification officer, makes a positive ID more credible."

"What are you going to do with Robin whilst we're waiting for that?"

"Put up with Amanda Pocket's representations about bail for her client and crack on with Michael."

"Have we got time for lunch?"

*

Robin recognized his father's sour body odour as soon as Michael opened the boot. When Michael unzipped the top of the body bag, Patraicc's cold dark eyes drilled into him. Robin was surprised that his father still had a full head of hair; his beard was greying but his copper top was still as thick as ever, like a cap perched on top of his head. The crescent shaped scar, that he knew so well, was still visible above his right eye and the twisted nose hadn't been reset. He really was an ugly bastard.

Robin had been having misgivings about their plan but now that he was confronted with the beast they all evaporated. "Have you prepared the car?" Michael said. "It's over there by the compaction unit." "Lead the way," Michael said as he closed the boot of the battered Ford Mondeo.

All that remained of the coffin was the outer shell; the engine, gearbox, wheels, glazing and electrical components had all been removed. The roof had already caved–in. "Does the boot open?" Michael said. "Of course," Robin said, as he eased it up with a crowbar. "And the CCTV's out of action?" "That's why I'm still on-site, being paid overtime," Robin said. "Let's get on with it then," Michael said as he returned to the Mondeo.

A few minutes later Michael cut the knotted gag from Patraicc's mouth. Patraicc appeared mute with terror; his eyes flicked back and forth between Michael and Robin. "Any last words?" Michael said. "No… I didn't think so. Not even an apology?" Michael dragged Patraicc out of the Mondeo. "We're going to put you in the boot of this wreck," Michael said. "Then things are going to get a little uncomfortable; claustrophobic in fact. Then you're going to be shipped off to be melted down with all the other rubbish… Do you want to say goodbye to your father Robin?" Robin shook his head.

The diesel engine roared as the coffin was dropped into the compactor. A few minutes later it was removed. Michael hosed the diminished wreck down with the fire hydrant before it was dumped with all the others into one of the ribbed containers… "Are you going to be alright when I leave you here alone?" Michael said. Robin nodded demurely. It was quiet save for the falling rain splattering the concrete. "Thank you," Robin said, as he shook Michael's hand. "I think I might do a spot of bird watching before it gets dark."

*

Michael parked the Mondeo in a resident's bay in St Edmunds Road, Canterbury, about forty minutes later. Parking was at a premium within the city. He knew that someone would complain about it being illegally parked in no time; probably a resident who couldn't park outside their house. Then the council would take it away to a car pound; contact the registered keeper who'd say it no longer belonged to him and that he'd given the log book to the new owner. A dispute would arise, the vehicle excise licence would expire within a few days and the car would be scrapped, all neat and tidy; achieved with minimal effort as far as Michael was concerned. The only thing left to do now was pop the car's keys into one of the city's many rubbish bins and make his way home.

*

"Hello Tony. Had a nice lunch?"

"Yes thank you Chief inspector. What's on this afternoon's menu?"

"A nice long chat with Michael about Marlene's demise."

"I see, should I phone the missus?"

"Tell Cynthia you'll be home in time for the opening ceremony."

"Midnight?"

"That should do it. I wouldn't want to be accused of dragging my feet."

"When's the ID Parade?"

"Tomorrow morning at ten."

Michael's ego received a boost when he realized that the big guns had been brought out. Not only was he being interviewed by the officer in charge but now his deputy, Charlie Spec, had been brought in to support him.

"We'd like to talk to you about the Diamond Jubilee weekend," Matt said. Michael looked to Tony Davis who nodded.

"What would you like to know?"

"What you did after you knocked off early on Saturday 2 June."

"I went home and read the paper."

"What were the headlines?"

"Britain honouring The Queen's Diamond Jubilee with four days of celebrations starting with the armada sailing along the Thames."

"We're you going to take part in the celebrations?"

"No but I found it all very interesting… I'd planned a very different weekend. I wasn't going anywhere near London. I planned to watch some of the celebrations on TV though; better than being there, amongst all those people and much more comprehensive. You'd have to be very lucky to see the Queen from the river bank."

Michael liked the Queen and admired her stamina; sixty years on the throne; he hadn't been alive that long. He was just fifty two and always tired at the end of the week. She was eighty six, remarkable, quite remarkable; mind you hauling meat around a butcher's shop and supervising staff was no easy number. Perhaps he'd be remarkable if he'd come from a privileged background.

"What else did you do?"

"I read the magazines."

"What did you do after that?"

"Had dinner then settled into my armchair and read the business headlines."

"What did they say?"

"That the markets had plunged again amid fears of a fresh global downturn. Then I must've drifted off; woke up about nine with a stiff neck and switched the TV on. "

"What did you watch?"

"A talent show."

"And after that?"

"I switched off; went to bed and listened to the heavy rain, whilst reading about The Duke of Wellington's campaign against the Mahrattas in India in 1803."

"What did you do after that?"

"Fell asleep."

"When did you wake up?"

"The following morning, pulled back the curtains; the skies were a light grey and the air was clear."

"Was that important?"

"Not really."

"What did you do after that?"

"I visited Deal Castle."

It was very windy when he arrived in Deal; the Union Jacks, of which there were many, stood out from their flag staffs like paper flags on children's sandcastles. When he parked the car in the field next to the castle fine raindrops peppered his windscreen. As he crossed the drawbridge to enter the castle he noticed the murder holes above the main entrance, the slot for the portcullis and the metal studs driven into the heavy oak doors. He admired the design of the entrance hall; a gun embrasure for a Cannon opposite the main door, to kill any successful invaders and a second set of re-enforced doors offset from the first.

"Did you meet anyone there?"

"After paying in the shop I began my tour of the inner courtyard between the six outer and six inner bastions which are shaped like the red and white roses of the Tudors. I noticed an elderly couple struggling to move a picnic table into the shelter of the archway of the offset doors and offered to help."

"Did they accept your offer?"

"Yes and when I'd finished the old girl asked me to join them for coffee."

"Did you join them?"

"I said I'd love to if they were still there when I'd finished my tour."

"And were they still there?"

"They were. I asked if they'd had a nice lunch. The old girl said that it was wonderful and the old boy commented that the weather could have been better. He offered me coffee. I sat and we chatted for a while and then I helped them put the table back where it belonged."

"What happened after that?"

"They said goodbye."

"Where did you go after you helped them move the picnic table the first time?" Charlie said.

"To the south east bastion; I looked for France but couldn't see it through the low cloud hanging over the channel."

"Did you meet anyone there?"

"I watched a young couple holding each other while their children climbed over a Cannon and thought how lucky they were."

"Did you converse?"

"No."

"What did you do after that?"

"I ducked through the doorway into the Keep,"

"What did you do there?"

"Noticed the walls were about ten feet thick and imagined the troops warming their hands in front of a large open fireplace in the soldiers' hall. Viewed a number of gun embrasures for cannon and muskets, the forge where they used to heat shot and listened to the audio tour."

"What did you do after that?"

"After climbing the double spiral staircase to the first floor I visited the Battery Office and the Officers Mess."

"What did you do there?"

"I looked at the coats of arms and portraits of The Captains of Deal Castle, including Thomas Wingfield, The Paymaster for the Kings works. He'd been responsible for building the castle in 1539 and was the first Captain from 1540 to 1551. Another portrait that caught my eye was of William Wellesley Pole who was the Captain of Deal Castle between 1838 and 1845 and the brother of The Duke of Wellington."

"That's the second time you've mentioned Wellington. Are you a fan?"

"I am. I think he's the greatest military commander this country's ever had."

CHAPTER 43

Matt and Charlie were seated in the TV room next to the canteen when the jingle for the local news was broadcast. It was 6.30pm. Their day was far from over.

"Welcome to the south east news. I'm Marc Evans...Tonight's top story. Kent Police have arrested a man for the murder of Marlene Johnson. Once again they are appealing for any witnesses who saw the victim on the seafront footpath between Deal Castle and Walmer Bandstand on Sunday 3 June to come forward."

"That's it Charlie; our last gasp before the Olympic fever takes over," Matt said.

"Anything from the incident room?"

"No, looks like our only witness is James Selbourne."

"A lonely old drunk, who the defence will tear to shreds."

"A veteran and people watcher, who the defence will have a job to discredit."

*

"What did you do after your visit to the Officers Mess?" Matt said.

"I visited a series of musket embrasures facing into the dry moat, linked by tunnels at the very bottom of the castle; weaved half-way around, splashing in puddles in the damp gloom and imagined the musketeers passing ammunition, firing their weapons and choking on the smoke, before it was drawn up through vents in the ceiling. What you might call real fighting. When I arrived at the powder magazine I was surprised that it was so small and wondered how long the powder would have lasted during a sustained battle."

"Go on."

"I climbed a steep flight of stairs from the Keep's central well after that and returned to the inner courtyard; then made my way up to the north east bastion. It was still dull and wet."

"Go on."

"I learnt that the Castle had been quiet for most of the eighteenth century but had been updated during the Napoleonic Wars, when fleets of merchantmen used to anchor in The Downs before putting to sea with a Royal Navy escort." Matt nodded. "And that the Castle hadn't been used as a defence since the end of those wars but the German Luftwaffe still bombed it destroying the Captain's House during the Second World War."

"Go on."

"Then I saw the elderly couple who we talked about earlier."

"What did you do after saying goodbye to them?" Matt said.

"I made my way to Walmer Castle."

"How did you get there?"

"I walked along the seafront."

"Did you meet anyone between Deal and Walmer Castles?"

"No."

"Are you sure?"

"Positive."

"Wasn't that where you met Marlene Johnson?"

"No."

"Between the paddling pool and Clan William House?"

"No… Where's Clan William House?"

"It's the smart bungalow on the footpath between Deal Castle and the paddling pool."

"I see."

"Does that make a difference to your answer?" Charlie said.

"No. I didn't meet anyone on my walk between Deal and Walmer Castles."

"We have a witness who was having a conversation with Marlene about the time you left Deal Castle," Matt said.

"He says that he saw her conversing with a man, matching your description, between the paddling pool and Clan William House a few minutes after they parted company. What do you have to say about that?" Charlie said.

"It wasn't me. I didn't speak to anyone."

"He described the man's clothing; a black pullover fleece, pale blue jeans and black Gore-Tex walking boots," Matt said.

"Can you describe what you were wearing?" Charlie said.

"I can't remember but I do own a black fleece, pale blue jeans and black Gore-Tex walking boots."

"We've checked the CCTV at both castles and that's what you were wearing," Matt said.

"I wouldn't be surprised."

"So why won't you admit that you spoke to Marlene?" Charlie said.

"Because I didn't speak to anyone between Deal and Walmer Castles."

"The same witness saw the man, who matches your description, embrace Marlene, kiss her on the cheek and pat her bottom."

"That wasn't me."

"He saw the same man a few minutes later scrubbing his face and hands in the public toilet."

"That wasn't me."

"I presume that was to remove all traces of her from your body?"

"That wasn't me."

"Because you were disgusted by the memories she brought forth?"

"Why don't you put me in front of your witness?"

"That's what we intend to do," Matt said.

*

Denise had eventually been persuaded to abandon her vigil by the arrival of the press. She'd driven home in tears narrowly avoiding a number of collisions. Yvonne was pleased to see her but disturbed by her disheveled appearance.

"Are you okay?" She said.

Denise collapsed onto the sofa. "Not really?"

Yvonne joined her. "What's happening?"

"They're still holding Michael and the press have arrived."

"The south east news said they had a man in custody for Marlene's murder and made a further appeal for witnesses but there was no media circus."

"It was just one press reporter, that chap, Dylan Barry who's been following the case right from the start. He was with a photographer."

"Did they speak to you?"

"Not when they arrived at the station but I noticed the photographer taking an interest in me and decided to leave."

"Have you had any sleep?"

"I slept in the car last night."

"What about food?"

"Nothing much."

"Well, I think you should eat something; then have an early night."

*

Sabrina had been glad to see the back of the police officers searching her house. They'd been there until the small hours seizing and packaging Robin's clothing. Rachel and Maxwell had gone next door to stay with Herbert and Carol and she'd spent the night on her own crying. The following morning she'd contacted Dover Police Station who'd confirmed that Robin was still there. Subsequently she'd received a phone call from Amanda Pocket, Robin's solicitor, who'd advised that Robin wouldn't be home before midday on Saturday. She'd asked about Sabrina's plans for the day and when she'd learnt they didn't involve Robin suggested that she carry on for the sake of the two children.

She'd tidied the house. The half empty wardrobe in their bedroom had brought the tears on. Then she'd collected the children. She'd explained what was happening as best she could then asked what they'd like to do. Both had run off to their bedrooms. She'd found them crying separately, done her best to console them, fed them then collapsed on the sofa and held them tight. Margaret had telephoned. She'd had lots of questions for her. They'd had a long conversation but she'd not learnt anything. Margaret had been as slippery as an eel and gone down in her estimations. They'd had a slanging match towards the end and Sabrina had put the phone down. She'd put the TV on, seen the news and switched to another channel. The whole nation appeared to be excited about the Olympics. She decided to stay up with the children and watch the opening ceremony; better to go to bed exhausted than have another sleepless night.

*

Patricia was completely oblivious to the unfolding drama. She was next door with her best friends Bobby and Cherry Brandy.

*

After the interviews Robin had been told that the officers were still questioning Michael. They weren't prepared to release him on bail in case he needed to be re-interviewed. He'd accepted that and listened to Amanda Pocket making strong representations on his behalf. He'd been able to tell, from the start, that the Duty Officer wasn't going to grant bail and switched off. He'd been glad to return to the solitude of his cell. The custody area had been quiet and he'd been able to sleep, the only interruption being his evening meal. He was worried about Sabrina and the kids but glad he couldn't speak to them. He'd answered enough questions for one day.

*

Michael had lost count of the number of times he'd been interviewed. Was it five or six times? He really couldn't remember. The interview room hadn't changed and neither had those present. He was sick of the inquisition, looking at the same faces and the same four walls.

"How long did it take to walk to Walmer Castle?" Matt said.

"About fifteen to twenty minutes."

As he'd approached the Castle he'd noticed that the design was similar to Deal; the battlements were low and squat to make it a hard target from the sea. There were a large number of canons on the seaward side but in all other respects it was quite different in appearance. A small stately home had been built on the top. He'd read that it had been added to accommodate Queen Victoria, Prince Albert and their family during a holiday in the autumn of 1842.

"What did you do when you got there?"

"I found the entrance to the rear and walked straight into a pleasant little shop selling snacks, souvenirs, books and plants."

"Go on."

"The ladies working there were very attentive and made sure that I had everything I needed to enjoy my visit."

"Go on."

"I found the cafeteria just inside the inner courtyard. I was tired and hungry after the walk and bought coffee and carrot cake. I was planning to have a proper meal when I got home."

"Go on."

"I read that the castle was the official residence of the Lord Warden of the Cinque Ports; former wardens had included Sir Winston Churchill, Britain's Wartime Prime Minister and Sir Arthur Wellesly, The Duke of Wellington. He'd resided there every autumn from 1829 until his death in the castle, which was in 1852."

"So your main interest was with the latter?"

"Yes."

"What did you do after that?"

"I visited the museum on the next floor which contained displays of the Iron Duke, including his death mask and a pair of his Wellington boots." Michael noticed that Matt appeared as jaded as he felt.

"Go on."

"I was impressed with the Duke's study. It was furnished almost exactly as I'd imagined it; a mahogany desk, which he stood at to write, and a Spartan camp bed that accompanied him on several campaigns."

"What did you do after that?" Charlie said.

"The gardens were a treat, despite the weather."

"Go on," Charlie said.

"I returned to the shop after that. One of the ladies asked me if I'd enjoyed my visit and asked if I would be interested in joining English Heritage. I was about to remind her when she blushed and said, 'I asked you earlier, didn't I, and you're already a member, silly me.'" Michael smiled with the recollection.

"What did you do after that?" Matt said.

"I walked back to Deal Castle, collected my car and drove home."

"What time did you leave Walmer Castle?"

"About four-twenty."

"What time did you get to Deal Castle?"

"Fiveish."

"So it took you forty minutes on the return?"

"Roughly."

"Ten minutes longer than the outward journey?"

"That's right."

"Why was that?" Matt said.

"Because I was in no hurry," Michael said.

"Was that when you telephoned Marlene?"

"I didn't telephone Marlene."

"From the red telephone box on the Dover Road near Walmer Green?"

"I didn't telephone Marlene,"

"To make a date with her on Monday 4 June at 7.30pm."

"FROM THAT CALL BOX OR MY MOBILE PHONE BECAUSE I DON'T HAVE HER NUMBER," Michael said.

Matt wanted to say, "Marlene's number's in your mobile and we found your fingerprints in the phone box," to test Michael's resolve but that wasn't the case and wasn't permitted under PACE.

"What time did you get home?" Charlie said.

"About six."

"What did you do after that?"

"I had a quiet night in and went to bed early."

"Okay, I think it's time for a break," Matt said.

"What else do you want to talk to me about?" Michael said.

"Bank holiday Monday, the day that Marlene was murdered," Charlie said.

CHAPTER 44

When Michael woke on Bank Holiday Monday the sky was dark and rain was beating against his windows. He listened to the radio as he breakfasted on cereal and toast. The rain was forecast to clear then sunshine and showers were expected. 'Typical bank holiday weather,' he thought.

He arrived at Dover Castle a few hours later and parked his car in a very muddy field. The skies were clearing as he trudged through the car park. He was impressed by the building which completely dominated the skyline; grey stone walls soared high above a flat plateau and loomed over ancient woodland. It was time to experience the atmosphere of the Castle during WWII.

Soldiers of the 2nd Battalion 56th Independent Infantry Brigade were camped outside the Inner Bailey walls, overlooking Castle Green. Their khaki uniforms looked smart but uncomfortable. Their display included an American Jeep and a variety of tents including one set up as Headquarters, with field telephone and first aid post.

"The battalion withdrew from Dunkirk in 1940 with only two losses and then trained for two years for the D-Day Landings," one of the Infantrymen explained to a group of spectators. A loudspeaker announced the Das Heer firepower display and people started to melt away to the taped barrier overlooking the green. Michael joined them, sat on the damp grass and waited for the commentary to begin.

"In 1939, the Germans introduced a new form of warfare known as Blitzkrieg. They concentrated their divisions into Panzer Units supported by the infantry and trained their Air Force to bomb a few hundred yards in front of their tanks. On 10 May 1940 they invaded Holland, Belgium, Luxemburg and France. The Allies were not so well organized; their senior officers were often miles away in Chateaus whereas the German High Command was regularly deployed with their troops. The Germans broke through the Ardennes Forest and made for the Channel in the hope of cutting off the British Expeditionary Force but they managed to retreat to Dunkirk and were evacuated to England as a result of Operation Dynamo. Dynamo was run from this very castle. Three hundred and eighty thousand troops were rescued, after the British Government called on the small ships to intervene." Michael clapped enthusiastically as the audience erupted.

"The German Luftwaffe was ordered to destroy the RAF for Operation Sea Lion, the planned invasion of Britain, but they couldn't defeat the British and so looked east towards Russia. Ninety per cent of Germany's forces were the Wehrmacht Infantry who were equipped with the best weapons of the time. Today we are going to see re-enactors from the German Infantry, who fought in Poland in 1939, France in 1940 and Russia in 1941." A group of soldiers marched onto the green. "This is a typical machine gun team from 1939 to 1940. We are now going to look at them individually, starting with the riflemen. Their role was to protect the machine gunners. They were equipped with the Mouser rifle, M35 or M40 helmet, ammunition pouches, bayonet, trenching tool, gas mask, stick grenades and Jack Boots. The Squad Leader was an NCO, who directed the team. He was armed with an MP38 machine pistol, a 19 milimetre P38 pistol, binoculars, map, case and compass. The Machine Gunner carried a MG34 light machine gun. It could fire single shots through use of the top trigger or nine-hundred rounds per minute by use of the bottom trigger. It had an effective hand held range of six to eight hundred metres or up to two miles when mounted on a heavy tripod. This man also carried tools for maintaining this weapon and a pistol. His number two carried the ammunition. We are now going to see a demonstration of this weapon in use, firing blanks of course."

"Now that we've demonstrated each of the weapons it's time to show you how the team worked together." The troops assembled in a line across the green. Stick grenades were thrown. The machine gunners fired and ran forward, the riflemen supported them, more grenades were thrown and the process repeated as they advanced. A loud blast on a whistle called an end to the attack and the audience showed its appreciation. "The Machine Gun team would attack weaknesses in the enemy lines. Junior Commanders were authorized to make decisions, unlike the Allies, and this gave them a great advantage in the early stages of the war. That concludes this demonstration. I hope that you will join us again at 3pm when we recreate a skirmish in Normandy in 1945. In the meantime Sergeant Bannon will be drilling the children and the ladies from The Spitfires will be holding a 1940's fashion show in the Band Marquee."

Michael drifted off to an old fashioned NAAFI van where he purchased a mug of tea and a piece of homemade bread pudding. He noticed a lady, dressed in white with wide brimmed hat arrive in a car with swept back wheel arches. It was escorted by two men on foot wearing trilby hats and grey suits. As she stepped out of the car he realized the lady was purporting to be the Queen Mother and that the young woman accompanying her, in a khaki uniform, was pretending to be the Princess Elizabeth. He watched them quietly inspect the British Troops and the RAF, paraded in front of a Spitfire.

When he'd finished his tea, Michael was drawn back to Castle Green where Sergeant Bannon was asking for some volunteers. A line of enthusiastic youngsters formed; thirteen were counted in and issued with rifles.

"Why are we here?" Bannon shouted.

"To shoot people," a young man responded.

"You're a genius, *but first we much teach you discipline. Have you ever heard the word discipline?* No? Pick up your weapons. Put your butts on the ground." Several children sat down on the grass. The audience rippled with laughter. Bannon picked up a rifle and pointed to the bottom of it. *"This is a butt;* place the butts by your right foot... YOUR RIGHT FOOT! COPY ME... Good... At ease, is with your feet apart and your weapon like this... *What are you doing boy?"* A child walked away sulkily. *"That's it; run away to mummy.* Some people don't like it when I shout at them; anyone like it when I do?"

"Me."

"What's your name boy?"

"Samuel."

"Samuel, stick your chest out; have you got a chest? Slope arms; put your hand under your butt, like this." A participant laughed. "I don't like people laughing at me, sonny." Bannon threw himself face-down onto the grass and kicked his legs vigorously in an outburst of bad temper. Michael laughed when he recognized the mockery in this display.

"Now, this is how to salute arms... SALUTE ARMS. Well done; now the last thing we need to learn is how to present arms. He held the rifle out in front of him. Got it?" His recruits nodded. "Let's try that then; PRESENT ARMS... Now from the beginning; at ease; legs apart; rifle butts on the right. ATTENTION. Legs together, rifles in. SALUTE ARMS; rifles on shoulders. PRESENT ARMS... Excellent; give them a round of applause everyone...Now if you see anyone with a camera, blow them away. Place your rifle on your shoulder so that it doesn't go backwards with the recoil and fire by shouting BANG." Bannon walked down the line of recruits.

"BAng."

"LOUder."

"BANg."

"LOUDer."

"BANG; he's dead."

"IT'S A MIRACLE...Altogether now; take aim, BANG - BAANG...Now we're going to march you out of here; left turn. Get away from me; you all smell horrible; left, right, left, right. Get off my field; left, right, left, right. Go and join the Navy." Michael laughed; the spectacle reminded him of his early days in the Royal Marines, when he was just a boy soldier.

At 2pm Michael was seated at the back of the band marquee. He'd chatted to the people representing the RAF during the interval and been into the shopping marquee. Children jostled for position in the seats in front of him while their parents lined the sides of the tent and stood behind him. Michael felt surprisingly comfortable in their company, as if he belonged, even though he was unmarried and had no children of his own.

A well-dressed lady appeared on stage. "Good afternoon everyone, my name's Penny and I am here to guide you through this afternoon's 1940's Fashion Show." Michael joined the welcoming applause... "Our first model is Helena. She is dressed for work. Under her coat she is wearing a crepe day dress made in one of five hundred sewing classes created in Britain since the beginning of the war. She's added a new collar and cuffs to make it more interesting. Where did the material for the collar and cuffs come from Helena?" The model looked sheepish.

"My mother's tablecloth."

"That's right ladies. We had to improvise during the war. Our second model is Sarah. Doesn't she look nice; washed your hair this morning?"

"Yes, I used a little sugar in water."

"Wasps a problem?"

"Only in summer."

"Sarah's wearing a deep blue hat with a little veil at the back and a royal navy wool suit; you can tell it's a wartime suit, there are only three buttons down the front and the pockets are false. Her blouse is made of parachute silk. Thank you, Sarah... Our third model is Helena. This time she's wearing a Khaki jacket from the American Airbase. She made the trousers. No gas mask though; John Lewis and the cinema won't let you in without a gas mask. Helena's got a new job working in the munitions factory. You can tell she hasn't been there long because her skin hasn't gone yellow. The bright red lipstick is from Max Factor. They go into the factories to encourage the use of make-up, to keep up the men's morale. Beauty before duty - that's what they say. Thank you Helena... Our fourth model is Sarah. She's wearing one of Helena's road kills over her shoulder, possibly fox and her black dress is new and American. Been down to the US Airbase again have we?" Sarah nodded. "The dress has short sleeves; we can't waste fabric. What's that hanging from your handbag?"

"It's that new-fangled stuff, plastic."

"And where are you off to?" Penny said.

"I'm going out for lunch; we're having spam fritters."

"Okay folks, this is the part of the fashion show that the men really enjoy. First up we have Helena wearing a bedroom jacket. Take the jacket off dear; underneath she is wearing a nightdress made from a new fabric called nylon, which stands for New York and London as it was invented between those two cities. Doesn't she look nice?" The men in the audience whistled to show their approval. Michael took a closer look at Helena, she was very attractive, more than six feet tall with very long legs... "The next model, Sarah, is wearing a cross your heart bra. Her slip's made from the rest of the parachute." Michael admired her sleek figure and found himself whistling with the rest of the crowd... "Our next model is Helena. I'm sorry that we have to whip through this part of the show but it's not very warm for our models today. Helena is wearing a liberty bodice which is fleece lined; it has rubber buttons on the bottom half; a girdle and silk stockings." A young man whooped and clapped louder than anyone else in the audience. "The next model is Sarah; she's wearing a slip made from nylon underneath taxi teasers; they're also known as passion killers." Michael laughed and applauded... "And now we're back to Helena, this time fully clothed wearing a cony or rabbit skin jacket with a deep purple crepe evening dress, which she made from a Vogue pattern. She's going to a ball at The American Airbase. She's had to pumice her legs to remove the hairs and used the grease-proof paper from the margarine to moisturize her skin. What are you going to eat?"

"Exotic fruit, pineapple and bananas."

"And finally we have Sarah as the blushing bride. The wedding dress has been borrowed and has already been worn seven times. The food for the wedding? Victoria sponge without cream or jam?" Sarah nodded, "So just sponge then. Sarah needs a husband. Yesterday she married a German. Can I have a man from the audience? Please make sure he's one of ours." A young man made his way up to the stage... "What's your name? A round of applause everyone for John, our lucky groom for today." Michael watched the audience take photographs of the happy couple and when they finally drifted away he approached the stage.

"Did you enjoy the show?" Penny said.

"Very much, I hadn't realized fashion could be so interesting. You presented it in a very amusing way and I had no idea that plastic and nylon were invented during the war years."

"Would you like a photograph with our models?"

"Why not, can you take it with my mobile?"

"Of course, as long as you promise to come back and see us at three-thirty when we'll be singing songs from the forties."

It had been a great day out. The weather had been fine, the firepower display, children's drill, 1940s fashion show, the battle and the sounds of the 40's had all been excellent. Michael felt a little sad when it was over but he still had another day off to look forward to.

CHAPTER 45

Michael noticed it was 8:30 when the gaoler brought a cup of tea to his cell.

"Time to wake up... The DCI will be down in about ten minutes."

"Can I speak to my solicitor?"

"Of course, I'll bring him through. The consulting room's empty."

Robin recognized the strain in Michael's voice and wondered if they'd finally broken him. He'd heard Michael being shuffled back and forth throughout the day. He'd counted four intervals of over an hour's duration when Michael was absent from his cell and wondered what they could be talking about. "It must be Marlene," he thought remembering that Michael had been arrested for murder times three.

Matt was feeling tired and impatient.

"This consultation's taking a long time. I wonder what they're discussing."

"Perhaps Michael's decided to confess," Charlie said.

"I don't think he's going to," Matt said. "He's going to make us do all the work. He'll plead not guilty in court, if we get that far, and protest his innocence, right to the bitter end. If he's convicted he'll appeal. He won't put his hands up, leaving doubt in the minds of the public."

"Do you want me to conduct the next interview?" Charlie said.

"You feeling positive?"

"I am, didn't hold the same conviction as you when we started but the more I see of him the more convinced I am of his guilt." Matt nodded. Charlie's mobile rang. "We'll be right down."

It was 22:30 when the second interview about Bank Holiday Monday began. In the first Michael had recounted his day out at Dover Castle.

"What time did you get home?" Matt said.

"About 6pm."

"Did anyone see you?"

"Kathy and Bridget next door; we chatted after I parked my car on the drive."

"What did you talk about?"

"Their garden and my day out at Dover Castle."

"Anything else?"

"Not that I can recall."

"What did you do after that?"

"Went indoors and prepared dinner."

"What did you have to eat?"

"Prawn cocktail, seafood risotto and champagne to toast the Queen."

"What did you do after that?"

"Watched the Diamond Jubilee concert."

"What can you remember about the concert?"

"Singing along to 'Let Me Entertain You' and watching the Bearskins outside Buckingham Palace."

"Anything else?"

"The duet of 'Need You Now,' 'We Don't Talk Anymore,' by Cliff Richard and 'Mama Told Me Not To Come' by Tom Jones."

Matt could feel his temperature rising. He was sure Michael was playing mind games with him. He checked his response and said, "Go on."

"'Mack the knife,' after the Queen was welcomed to the concert."

"Was that when you murdered Marlene?" Charlie said.

"I don't know what you're talking about," Michael said. "I was at home enjoying the concert and toasting the Queen with a bottle of champers." Michael's eyes creased. Charlie would kill him if he smiled.

"What happened after 'Mack The Knife?'" Matt said breaking the spell.

"I really enjoyed watching The Military Wives Choir and the African Children's Choir performing 'Sing' for Her Majesty's Diamond Jubilee."

"Go on."

"'Mystery Tour,' and the nation welcoming the Queen and the Duke and Duchess of Cornwall to the podium, the speech by Charles, the lighting of the National Beacon and the firework display. I felt really proud to be British and sang along to 'Land of Hope and Glory.'"

"What did you do after that?"

"Went to bed."

*

"He's a slippery bastard," Charlie said, lighting up in smoker's corner. "I wanted to kill him. I'm sure he selected those songs deliberately."

"'Let Me Entertain You,' 'Need You Now,' 'We Don't Talk Anymore,' 'Mama Told Me Not To Come,' 'Mack The Knife,'" Matt said.

"Do you think Michael's trying to tell us something?"

"At a sub-conscious level, yes."

*

"How did you get to Sandwich on Monday 4 June?" Matt said.
"I didn't go to Sandwich that day."

"Did you borrow a van from someone?"

"I didn't go to Sandwich that day."

"From Mister Moynihan?"

"No."

"Without his permission?"

"No."

"Take it from Sea Road for a few hours, go into Sandwich, return it when you'd finished and park it in the same spot."

"I didn't go to Sandwich."

"Moynihan's van was caught on the automatic number plate reader that night and in the early hours of the following morning."

"So, what's that got to do with me?"

"He was at home watching the concert with his wife and kids."

"I didn't borrow it."

"Have you got a set of keys for his van?"

"No I haven't."

"What were you wearing when you went to Sandwich that day?" Matt said.

"I didn't go to Sandwich."

"Your father's flat cap, tweed jacket, green trousers and brown shoes?"

"I keep telling you; I didn't go to Sandwich that day."

"The clothing he was last seen in before you murdered him in 2001?"

"I didn't go to Sandwich that day."

"It was a good plan Michael; fool Marlene into believing you were Derek, invite yourself over for dinner, dress in your father's clothing and murder her in her bed."

"I didn't murder anyone."

"Make it look like it had happened a lot earlier by releasing the bluebottle maggots and flies?"

"I didn't murder anyone."

"Tidy up, remove her diaries, address book and calendar?" Matt looked at Michael. He appeared as cool as a conman. "Leave in the small-wee hours, return Moynihan's van to Sea Road and go home?"

"I don't know what you're talking about."

"We do have a witness who saw a man, matching your description, walking in Potter Street towards the CCTV in Market Street. The CCTV shows the same man walking towards Marlene's front door."

"Let me confront him. That should clear this mess up."

"Is it true that you were trained in unarmed combat when you were in the marines?" Charlie said.

"Yes, everyone is."

"And you also trained as a battlefield paramedic?"

"Yes, I did."

"Your instructor described you as being exceptional in both practices."

"Did he? I'll take that as a compliment."

"So you would know how to disable a person by crushing their windpipe?"

"Yes, it's not difficult."

"And how to save that person by performing a tracheotomy?"

"Yes. Why would you want to perform both on the same person?"

"To make it impossible for them to scream or shout." Michael shook his head. "To incapacitate them and enable you to enjoy their discomfort."

"I think you've had too much caffeine Inspector," Michael said.

"What did you do with your father's clothing?" Matt said.

"I've never had any of his clothing."

"What did you do with the Natural Green hessian bag from Tesco?"

"I've never owned one of those."

"What did you do with the knives and sharpening steel, Michael?"

"The only knives I own are at home. I never take them out with me."

"What did you do with the overalls?"

"The only overalls I own are at home."

"And the latex gloves?"

"Same, they're at home. I use them when I'm painting or working on my car."

"What did you do with the bonds and tracheotomy tube?"

"I don't know what you're talking about."

"The ones you used on Marlene?"

"I still don't know what you're talking about."

"We're you trying to tell us something earlier with your choice of songs from the Diamond Jubilee concert?" Charlie said.

"No!"

"'Let Me Entertain You.'" Michael stared defiantly.

"'Need You Now.'"

"'We Don't Talk Anymore.'"

"'Mama Told Me Not To Come.'"

"'Mack The Knife.'"

"Is that you Michael?" Matt said.

"No," Michael said.

"A vain attempt at irony?

*

"Know anywhere we can get a drink at this time of night?" Charlie said.

"Lots of places in Deal, all unsuitable whilst this enquiry continues… Go home Charlie. Get some sleep. I need you sharp in the morning."

"I think I might watch the opening ceremony in the canteen first. I need some time to calm down."

*

"Hi Rose," Matt said. "Any good?"

"Excellent. You've missed most of it but I've recorded it for you. Finished?"

"For today but I've got to get up early."

"Oh."

"We can have a lie-in on Sunday."

"Promise?"

"We'll have to charge Robin and Michael tomorrow or release them on bail."

"Come here. You look done in."

"I am. Would you mind if I went to bed."

"Of course not, I'll switch this off. We can watch it together, another time."

CHAPTER 46

Inspector Crosby was in his element. He loved being the identification officer. In that role he was God. Everyone had to do as they were told once he'd started running the parade. The prisoner was already in his cell and the stooges in the waiting area when the first witness arrived.

Barry Cox was the disgruntled owner of the Mondeo that Michael had allegedly bought in 2001. He'd been brought to the ID suite by one of Crosby's staff and shown straight to the witness room. No one involved in the investigation was allowed to communicate with him until after the parade. Matt and Charlie had been admitted to the control room. They were allowed to watch but unable to take part.

"Right then," Crosby said. "This is the witness who allegedly sold the Ford Mondeo to Michael Stevens on 13 December 2001."

"That's right," Charlie said. Crosby disappeared. They watched him busying himself on the CCTV. The stooges were invited in and sat on a bench opposite one-way glazing.

"What do you think?" Charlie said.

"Crosby's done well. There's at least two that are dead ringers for Michael." They watched Michael enter the same room, with his solicitor Tony Davis, and listen to what Crosby had to say. Michael then chose position 5 of 10. Crosby and the solicitor left the room. They went to the corridor on other side of the glass.

"Settle down please," Crosby said, into a microphone. Michael and the others sat still facing the front. Crosby switched the floodlights on. Davis stood making notes. He nodded when Crosby addressed him. Crosby opened a door. Cox entered the corridor. Crosby stood facing him; he was a small man and had to look up.

"Barry Cox?"

"Yes."

"I must warn you that the man you sold your Ford Mondeo to may or may not be on the parade. Do you understand?"

"I do."

"Okay, I'd now like you to walk down the whole length of the corridor, take a careful look at each of the men on the parade, then come back to me." Cox nodded. "When you arrive I will ask you if," Crosby looked at his clipboard, "the man you sold your Mondeo to on 13 December 2001 is present. Do you understand?"

"I do."

"If he is present I will ask you for his number. Do you understand?"

"I do."

Matt and Charlie watched Cox slowly walk the line.

"He's certainly having a good look," Charlie said. They watched him return, ever so slowly, studying each of the faces before him. He stopped in front of numbers 5 and 3 then carried on. The control room was silent save for the whirring of the digital recorders.

"Is the man you sold your Mondeo to on 13 December 2001 present?" Crosby said. Cox nodded. "Can you speak for the microphones?"

"Yes he is."

"Can you tell me which number he is?"

"Number three."

Matt shook his head.

"Bollocks," Crosby noted the number in the log. "I thought he was going to do it," Charlie said.

"He took too long," Matt said. "It was eleven years ago."

*

"Okay gentlemen," Crosby said. "One of you can go and speak with the witnesses."

"I'll do that," Matt said.

"Charlie, come with me. I'll give you the exhibits."

Barry Cox smiled when Matt opened the door to the first witness room. "How did I do?"

"Very well," Matt said, "unfortunately the man we have in custody wasn't the man you picked. I'm very sorry."

Cox looked at Matt in disbelief. "But I'm sure I picked the right man."

"He was one of our stooges I'm afraid."

"But I'm sure it was him."

"I'm sorry Barry. The man you picked was a volunteer."

"Oh. I'm so sorry. I haven't been much help have I?"

"You've been very helpful. Now if you'd like to come with me I have someone waiting to take you home."

*

Michael was gutted when his solicitor told him that two of the witnesses had picked him out. He'd hoped there wouldn't be any.

"What happens now?" He said.

"The police will have some more questions for you?"

"Like what?"

"Why you lied about meeting Marlene in Deal on Sunday 3 June and going to Sandwich on Monday 4 June."

"Well?" Matt said when Tony Davis joined them in smoker's corner.

"Still not having it, I'm afraid."

"Told you," Matt said. "That's a fiver you owe me." Davis smiled. "We had a little wager earlier. I said he wouldn't have it even if we did get a positive ID. Shall we crack on?"

*

"The witness who saw a man, matching your description, meet Marlene Johnson on the footpath between Clan William House and the paddling pool has positively identified you as being that man," Matt said.

"He's mistaken. It wasn't me. He probably saw me in that area on Sunday 15 July when I attended the Royal Marines concert. The one held in memory of the eleven marines who were killed by the IRA in 1989."

"The witness who saw a man, matching your description, walking in Potter Street towards the CCTV in Market Street has also positively identified you as being that man," Matt said.

265

"I'm not surprised," Michael said. "I look like my father and you've been circulating his photo in the press for weeks."

"That was the same man the CCTV shows walking towards Marlene's front door on the day that she was murdered."

"That wasn't me. I was at home watching TV."

"I put it to you that you were the man that Marlene met in Deal on Sunday the third of June and that you murdered her on Monday 4 June 2012."

"It wasn't me; both of your witnesses are mistaken."

"Why don't you stop telling lies and tell us the truth?" Charlie said.

"I AM TELLING THE TRUTH."

Spittle peppered Charlie's face. "NO YOU'RE NOT; YOU'RE LYING."

Michael wiped his face. He looked at Charlie. Hatred burned in his eyes.

"I've told you a hundred times I didn't kill anyone."

*

"Hello… Roger?"

"Hello Boss."

"Anything from Forensics?"

"Nothing?"

"Okay, put the answerphone on and send your team home. Thank them for their efforts."

"What's happened?"

"We're not able to charge them. There isn't enough evidence. We've got strong circumstantial that Michael murdered Marlene but nothing else. The CPS agrees. The whole case hinges on forensics now."

*

Michael found Robin waiting in reception. Ladywell Road looked fantastic in the early afternoon sunshine until he realized they were being photographed.

"Run," he shouted as a press reporter approached with a microphone. They were playing tag now. Michael gave Robin a head start as they ran over Priory Road into Effingham Crescent. After forty paces he slapped Robin on the back.

"You're it," he shouted, then ran with his best friend upon his heels.

Neither tired quickly; they were fit and before he knew it they were on Effingham Street. Michael slowed to let Robin catch him. They metamorphosed into Cowboys and Indians as they ran along the Folkestone Road and Great Train Robbers as they entered Dover Priory Station. It was time to go home.

CHAPTER 47

The smell of damp glutinous mud stained the air when the workmen arrived to take possession of the Dutch barge, a corroding steel hulk riding high above the salt water on a cracked mud bank between a waste paper merchants and a fuel storage site. She was tucked into a cutting linking the River Stour to the estuary. Sluice gates prevented the river from emptying into the estuary at low tide but they could be operated remotely in the case of flood.

The wheelhouse had the appearance of a cell; a squat black box with barred windows. Varnish peeled from the door and a redundant chimney poked through the roof. The main superstructure above the rusting deck was covered with canvas awnings that flapped like tattered entrails in the onshore breeze, their remnants attached to the barge with ropes tied to handrails. Her hull was a dull black above the water line and contrasted with the bright green seaweed that clung to her bottom. Chains, rusted red, secured her to two capstans on the untidy quay.

Loose corrugated steel panels flapped on the roof of the waste paper merchants. Pigeons and seagulls made their nests in the rafters. Yellow and white dumper trucks stared at wet bales of rotting cardboard, stacked against the boundary fence, a new bright green mesh. Cyclists passed by uninspired by the landscape, after the beauty of Sandwich Town and Pegwell Bay.

Motorists hurried. Telegraph cables zigzagged across the Ramsgate Road. The gutted turbine hall of Richborough Power Station loomed nearby. This was no-man's-land, a site for regeneration, flat and uninspiring.

Phil Onslow, an enforcement officer from the Environment Agency, noticed it was low water. The Stour was just a trickle as he climbed onto Betsy. As expected there was no one in residence. After three years of trying he'd finally got a re-possession order for the site and was looking forward to Betsy's demise. The salvage men would arrive tomorrow and start cutting her up.

"Okay lads let's get the door to the wheelhouse open," Onslow said. A stocky workman holding long bolt cutters in his right hand with the blades resting on the deck sprang into action. Moments later two severed padlocks fell to the floor. The door refused to budge. It disintegrated when the same man kicked it.

Onslow illuminated the lamp and returned the hard hat to his head. When he peered in, the light snagged the cobwebs lining the doorway. He snatched a stick and wound them like candy floss onto its end. He rubbed his hand over the dusty wheel then explored the chart table's interior. He found an artist's sketch pad. He handed it to the stocky workman, standing at the door. Then found a number of wallets. It was his duty to seize any personal possessions before Betsy's destruction.

"That's disgusting," the workman said. "Fucking disgusting, whoever, drew those pictures was a fucking pervert and should be hung from the nearest tree." There was a murmur of general agreement from his workmates before Onslow retrieved the sketchbook and retired into the wheelhouse. He was revolted by what he saw; the terrified faces of young men, boys, detailed, in colour, almost photographic, and the spectres of the rapists' naked bodies outlined in black ink.

Onslow closed the sketchbook. He felt giddy and his head was spinning; suddenly he felt like a prisoner within the close confines of the wheelhouse. He had to escape. He threw the sketchpad onto the chart table and made for the open door. It seemed smaller somehow. Invisible hands held him back. Heavenly searchlights filtered through the thinning grey sky. They illuminated the scene as he tripped through the doorway. The stocky workman caught him in a bear-like hug as the colour faded from his face and he passed out. He was in another place; the photographs in the wallets swum about his subconscious and found their mates within the sketchbook.

A loud crash brought Onslow back to reality. The decayed timber covering the hold collapsed under the weight of a large torch. The flashlight illuminated the muddy interior. There, in a jumbled pile, the white bones of a skeleton were revealed. The owner of the torch yelled and stepped back. His colleagues stepped forward, out of curiosity, and gazed into the cavernous interior.

"EVERYONE OFF THE BOAT," Onslow shouted. He was surprised how calm and detached he sounded. "Everyone off the boat, come on, chop, chop." The workmen gaped at him quizzically, as if he was speaking a foreign language. "Come on, move, our work is finished here. This is a job for the police."

CHAPTER 48

Matt Sanderson felt nauseous as he reviewed the scenes of crime photographs taken on Betsy. Thirteen bodies had been removed from the deep stinking mud within her hold during a painstaking forensic operation spanning two weeks. The forensic teams had done a wonderful job, working 24/7 in very difficult circumstances.

There had been a press-frenzy when the story broke just after the closing of the London 2012 Olympics. Part of the Ramsgate Road had been cordoned off for the world's journalists such were the international dimensions of the enquiry. They were much more interested in this story than the murder of Marlene Johnson a few months earlier.

As Matt looked through the photocopied sketch books for the umpteenth time he noticed several things. The images of the victims were in colour, very detailed, almost photographic. Their outlines had been drawn in pencil and the colour added later. Seven of the victims had been matched with photo booth pictures found in the wallets under the chart table. The remaining six had been found within dog-eared family photographs from happier times.

His initial question, who were they, had been answered. They were all youngsters fleeing Pakistan and Afghanistan, looking for a better life in the west. They'd entered Britain illegally. Their families had been too afraid to report them missing. Matt had a team of family liaison officers working in Pakistan and Afghanistan chasing down the details. The victims had been traced via their photos and in several cases DNA samples had confirmed their identities.

He noted that in every sketch the rapists were drawn in black ink outline only; no colour had been added but they were very detailed. He thought that each could have been a work of art but for the subject matter. He was sure they were finished to the artist's satisfaction, as all were signed with a flourish. Minds even sharper than his had examined the signature and all agreed that it was Patraicc Delaney.

The last drawing in the final sketch pad confirmed this. There on the paper were coloured depictions of the paedophiles; Patraicc Delaney, Derek Stevens and Tommy Johnson, and in between in black ink outline, two detailed images of the woman he knew to be Marlene Johnson, full on and in profile.

He'd visited Marlene's grave. The missing headstone had been replaced and showed a simple epitaph. Tommy Johnson 1940 – 1998. Loving Husband of Marlene Johnson 1942 – 2012. May God Forgive Us. For the moment they rested in peace. Privately he hoped they were burning in hell but he doubted things would remain that way once the inquests linked them to the murders in Betsy.

Derek remained wanted for the murder of Marlene. He and Patraicc had been circulated on the UK's Most Wanted for the murders of the young men found on the barge. It had been a press sensation all over the world. Their images had been front page news. Some poor unfortunate fellows who resembled Derek had been dragged into police stations by angry mobs but to date they'd not been found. Matt wasn't surprised. He was still convinced they'd been murdered by Michael Stevens and Robin Delaney in 2001. Privately he thought that was what they deserved.

EPILOGUE

Matt Sanderson never did solve the murder of Marlene Johnson. That was the only blot on his unblemished record. With thirty-one years of distinguished service he retired after repatriating the thirteen victims to their families in Pakistan and Afghanistan. He attended each of the funerals with the male members of their families while his wife, Rose, prayed with the women in their homes. A month before his retirement he handed the case over to his successor, who eventually passed the enquiry to the cold case review team.

His retirement bash was held in The Chequers Restaurant, on the ancient highway between Deal and Sandwich. There were sixty guests, a fine meal, plenty of drink, a dreadful speech from his Superintendent who'd examined his personal file to extract every embarrassing detail, followed by a late evening dancing to disco, Motown and reggae.

He, Rose (and Mutley) continue to enjoy the beauty of Sandwich Bay and the surrounding area. They rarely speak of the terrible events of 2012 but on the twenty-fifth day of August each year they walk to the headstone which marks the spot where Mary Bax, a young girl, was assaulted and murdered on the same day in 1782 by Martin Lash; a Lascar and deserter. There they lay flowers and pray for Mary and the victims found in Betsy's hold.

*

Michael married Denise on New Year's Day. It was a small ceremony attended only by immediate family and close friends. She moved into Michael's house in Westgate-on-Sea. Their only child, Hope, was born a few months later, a miracle baby. Denise was 42 and Michael nearly 53.

Michael is happier than he's ever been. Patricia's forgotten Derek, through the joy of being a grandparent. Michael's childhood friendship with Robin continues. He frequently visits his family in Sittingbourne with his own and they reciprocate by visiting Michael's seaside home. Most of their neighbours and friends believe in their innocence.

THE END

Printed in Great Britain
by Amazon